Davus

The Black Squire; Or, a Lady's Four Wishes

A Novel: Vol. I.

Davus

The Black Squire; Or, a Lady's Four Wishes
A Novel: Vol. I.

ISBN/EAN: 9783337067069

Printed in Europe, USA, Canada, Australia, Japan

Cover: Foto ©Andreas Hilbeck / pixelio.de

More available books at **www.hansebooks.com**

THE BLACK SQUIRE;

OR,

A LADY'S FOUR WISHES.

A Novel.

By DAVUS.

"A document in madness ; thoughts and remembrance fitted."
HAMLET.

IN THREE VOLUMES.

VOL. I.

London:

SAMUEL TINSLEY & CO.,

10. SOUTHAMPTON STREET, STRAND.

1879.

THE BLACK SQUIRE;

OR,

A LADY'S FOUR WISHES.

CHAPTER I.

GOLD IN THE ORE.

'You are welcome to your country, dear Antonio :
You have been long in France, and you return
A very formal Frenchman in your habit.'
              WEBSTER—*Duchess of Malfi.*

AN old stone house, moderately ornamented, and in
tolerable repair, relic of a dismantled abbey; a
meadow, long and wide, with large ponds at the
end of it; near the house a few old trees; within a
sunk fence, a small pleasure-ground and a large
walled garden; at a little distance, spacious yards
and plenty of farm-buildings. Picture to yourself
these, and you have the outer aspect of Fulmere
Grange, with its stone-mullioned windows. All
within is drab and brown, and substantial. Brown-
and-drab paper and paint, drab curtains, sofa, and
chair-covers, drab-and-brown carpet, brown-and-

drab table-cloth, drabby-brownish prints, brownish-drabby paintings, decorated the drawing-room.

The dining-room was furnished with solid mahogany tables, side-board, and chairs with rusty horse-hair bottoms, drab curtains, drab-and-brown carpet again; drab-and-brown everywhere. And, for all its drab-and-brown, the house was a cheerful, even a jovial, place. The host and his hospitality would make any house look inviting, while he said, upon one fine forenoon:

'Then, parson, you will dine with us to-day at six o'clock, to meet Dick, my son, just come home from college. He has not been home but for a day or two this long while. He was at school in France, you know. But what are you going for in such a hurry? My lord will be here directly. I want to introduce you to him.'

'What's the good?'

'Where's the harm? You will, maybe, want to write to him some day about parish matters, or subscriptions, or such like; and it will be better to know him. And mayhap he'll take a fancy to you —who knows?—and give you a living.'

'No doubt.'

'Don't go, though. I hear the bell; that's him.'

Lord Mercia is announced.

'How do, Gryffyn?' said my lord, entering.

'My lord, let me introduce to you Mr. Martel, our curate.'

The earl bows and puts out his hand, speaking quickly.

'You have not been here long, Mr. Martel? How

do you like Fulmere ? I hope you'll take care of the foxes. Do you shoot ?'

' No, my lord.'

Here the door opened again, and there entered a stout, bluff figure in black.

' This is Mr. Pettifor, my lord,' said the host, after greeting the visitor, who without preface began :

' My lord, I want some money of you.'

' I believe most people do that come to me,' replied the assaulted nobleman.

But Mr. Gryffyn came to his rescue ; and, stepping between him and the enemy, cut the matter short, saying :

' Mr. Pettifor, I transact Lord Mercia's business. We will talk of this another time. I did not understand what you wanted to see my lord for.'

And without giving the sturdy applicant time to renew his attack, he asked Lord Mercia whether Mr. Meylor were coming this year, as usual, to shoot with him. My lord said, ' No.'

' We hear he is going to be married,' said the agent.

' Oh no, he is not going to be married. He can't afford to be married.'

' I have always understood, my lord, that he has twelve thousand a year.'

' Very true, I believe, Gryffyn, very true ; but he spends it all on himself, you know. And what is he to do when he is married ? Eh! Gryffyn ? No, Meylor is not a marrying man. He is going to India, I believe, to shoot tigers. Much better have come here to shoot partridges and hunt foxes.

4 THE BLACK SQUIRE.

Better shoot tigers than be married, though. Eh! Gryffyn?'

The agent laughed a hearty 'Ho! ho!' The curate bowed a kind of side assent to the logic; and the baffled Mr. Pettifor, who was as good-natured as he was blunt, grinned and chuckled. Tickled by this practical view of finance in high quarters, and, as a man of inquisitive mind, glad that he had stayed to hear it, the curate, accompanied by the defeated applicant, made his bow to the grandee and his worthy agent, and left them to talk business, if they pleased, or gossip, as was more likely.

'You see,' said the curate to his fellow-clerk, as they went off together, 'you see, riches are relative things. There is a man who cannot afford to marry on twelve thousand a year!'

'That's nonsense,' said the other.

'So would a labouring man say, if he were told that a clergyman could not afford to marry on two hundred a year. And yet it is too true, as those who do it find out. Civilised wants are artificial, but they are pressing. The man who has fewest wants is the least civilised, and the nearest the gods.'

'I,' replied the other, 'am highly civilised; I have a great many wants; I want some of that man's money.'

'So you said, very plainly.'

'He is the lay impropriator of my parish, and I am the vicar, with £94 6s. 3½d. a year, to teach, and preach to, and look after, thirteen hundred people.'

'I wish you may get what you want, but you

would be happier to get rid of your wants,' said his friend, with a parting preachment.

And now these are gone, we may return to the two they left at the Grange. Would the reader know who is this great lay impropriator, with such sound notions of domestic finance? He has been announced as Lord Mercia, a great earl, who is one of the finest specimens of the grand seigneur to be found in Europe; and as such he is known in every capital and court, from the Pope's at Rome, where he kept a pack of hounds and hunted the Campagna, to the Emperor's at Vienna and Louis Philippe's at Paris, where he introduced steeplechases. Full-fleshed and middle-sized, fair-skinned, flaxen-haired, red-whiskered and blue-eyed, like an old Saxon prince of the Heptarchy, the earl was stout and erect, and his port full of fire and nervous energy. Some great men, since trade has ruled our land, go through the world with downward looks and chilling, churlish brow, as though in fear that the commonalty would press on them and tread upon their toes. Our earl is a man of other metal. He walks his way with his head up, a smile upon his cheek, and a sparkle in his eye, as though the idea that any one would wish to trespass upon him could never enter his brain. His speech has something of a hasty stutter, and his voice, though not loud, strikes the ear sharp, and not much modulated. His garb is gallant, glittering with pins and jewels and chains, radiant with bright colours, and flowing in easy folds. Easiness and a generous, frank good-nature suffuse his whole bearing. He is known by the initiated for the only man of his day who has spent a life about town with a heart unhardened. And yet what has his life been but one long, lamentable mistake ?

By way of contrast, look at his agent, in his way and kind and degree a notable man too. His industrious and useful life is as admirable in its fruitfulness as his brilliant and kind-hearted employer's is pitiable in its barren waste. But David Gryffyn, in his threefold quality of farmer, grazier, and landagent to the Earl of Mercia, is an original in his generation. He resembles more, in their better features, the smaller squires of a generation or two back. He is six feet high in his stockings, bigboned and lean ; his rosy, flat-featured face is set in a framework of white hair, from the crown of his head to his double chin, and his small eyes twinkle in it with perpetual good-humour. Though he dresses in black, there is no starch about him, no official white tie, but a black silk rope, as it were, twisted round his throat. All his garments are loosely made and carelessly tossed on, and at least one leg of his trousers is sure to be caught up on the top of his boot. His dressing, indeed, is a rapid affair.

Such as the man is, such is his housekeeping, free and easy. Breakfast at seven a.m., dinner about one p.m., though he is not much more strict about time than he is about the niceties of the toilet. Only on company-days does he profess punctuality. But he is seldom without a stray guest : for his business is extensive, and he is so hospitable that none are sent empty away. Hungry callers of almost every degree are invited to sit down at his

well-filled board, and whoever is invited knows that
he is welcome. Three o'clock in the summer is Mr.
Gryffyn's hour of rising, and six in the winter, and
he is mostly on horseback as soon as he is dressed.
He seldom, indeed, goes afoot, holding walking to
be waste of time and strength. And often, on a
summer morning, he is heard in the village before
six, calling up Dick and Tom, Jack and Harry, and
the rest, to their work; for he employs most of the
men in the parish, and an easy master he is, though
so uncomfortably early in rising. Compliments upon
his early hours he always declines, saying, 'Nay,
nay; I get up because I can't sleep; there is no
merit in it. It is not when you get up that matters
so much, as what you do when you are up.' Like
all early risers who live much in the open air, he
falls fast asleep in his chair at every unoccupied
moment, but he wakes up again to business as
readily and as quickly. His directness, liberality,
and good-humour have done almost as much for him
in business as his sagacity and quickness. He says
little, but his word goes far. He knows too how to
keep his money with liberality, as well as how to
make it with honesty; and if he has become rich,
it is not by setting his heart upon riches, or any such
glittering toys; while yet, as his men will boast, he
breeds from a thousand ewes and milks a hundred
cows. In helping and giving and lending to poor
people he is most bountiful, even to carelessness;
and he is liberal—in the old-fashioned English sense
—of that which is his own. Riding far from home
one day, he stopped at a cottage to ask what had

become of a cow that he had lent, according to his
custom, to the cottager.   The man was not at home,
and the wife did not know him.

'Which d'yer me-an?' asked she; 'old Gruffun or
young Gruffun?'

The cow had calved and her calf had grown into
a cow since the loan was granted, and, in graceful
acknowledgment of the original ownership, the pair
were named after the lender in the way the good
wife indicated.

The truth is, Mr. Gryffyn had, as he often said,
no longer need to be over-careful.   He had got together a handsome fortune of some fifty thousand
pounds or more, as it was supposed, having begun
life as a boy with a borrowed capital, and a large
debt to work off.   'I never knew peace of mind till
I did it, nor trouble after it was done,' he would say.
Born of a respectable family of small proprietors, his
plain, and for a long time hard, and always laborious,
life did not prevent him from being a perfect gentleman at heart.   Of course, such a man knew the value
of money; but he did not value worth by money.
If he had never had leisure, or perhaps inclination,
to read books, he had read men from the peer to the
peasant; and his native shrewdness and large experience, his cheerfulness of spirit and liberality of
sentiment, made his conversation, uncultured and
blunt and bluff as it was, very agreeable to sensible
men of all ranks; so that, seeking none, he was
sought after by all.   Few men had more friends,
and no man was a faster friend, than David Gryffyn
of Fulmere Grange.

CHAPTER II.

A PERPLEXING QUESTION.

'I am not yet of Percy's mind, the Hotspur of the North ; he that kills me some six or seven dozen of Scots at a breakfast, washes his hands, and says to his wife, " Fye upon this quiet life ! I want work." "O my sweet Harry," says she, " how many hast thou killed to-day ?" "Give my roan horse a drench," says he, and answers, " Some fourteen," an hour after, " A trifle, a trifle." '— *1st part Henry IV.*

'WELL, parson,' said the host, in his drawing-room, as they awaited the announcement of dinner, soon after six o'clock on the same day, ' you have seen my lord—what do you think of him ?'

' It is not the first time I have seen him—I have known him by sight for years; nor was it much I saw. The little I did see was pleasant, of course ; all lords are pleasant fellows. However, to do him justice, I do not hear two opinions about your lord.'

' No, no; everybody loves him that comes near him ; I am sure I love him as my own son. He is one of the best men in the world—or best-natured, anyhow. But every good horse has some bad fault— that you know, parson ; and it is the same with men.

His fault is that he can't say 'no' to anybody or anything; he can't keep within bounds, and never could. It is not all his fault, either. What could you expect? When he was quite a boy, the old lord, who was otherwise a careful man enough, kept a drawer filled with bank-notes, and gave the young un a key to it. He was to take what he would, and when he would; only he must leave noted on a slip of paper the date and the sum he took each time. He never knew the value of money—how should he?—and he never will. Uncommonly quick, too, is my lord. I would as soon go to him as to any one for an opinion to be given off-hand; let him sleep upon it, and it is not worth a rush. Ay, he is a quick un, is my lord—has the quickest eye to a horse or a man of any one I ever saw. He soon took your measure, parson.'

'And what did he—umph! but I don't want to hear it; listeners seldom hear good of themselves.'

'Perhaps so. But my lord is not the man to say harm of any one; he is all good-nature—a deal too much so. I have known him do such things as no other man would do. He once made an allowance of some hundreds a year to a person in need, who, most folk would say, bore no relationship to him, nor had any other just claim upon him. When my lord got into trouble, I had to dock all our expenses right and left; and I thought it only right to tell him that his pensioner had lately come into a considerable fortune, and that my lord's allowance was no longer needed, and ought to be stopped. "No, no, Gryffyn," said my lord, in his quick way; " while

that person thinks it right to receive, I shall not
think it right to recall, it." That is the man all over.
The world has done what it could to spoil him, and
has not above half succeeded ; and that is a good
deal to say of any man,' quoth the agent. ' But here
comes Dick ; he wants to know you ;' and, turning
as he spoke, he remarked, with more parental than
personal pride, ' You don't see much likeness to me
in my son here, now, do you, parson ?'

Looking to the object of this remark, the parson
(who was, in fact, not a parson but a curate) saw a
young man of scarce the middle height, tightly built
and roundish-faced, and so fair as to be almost feminine in complexion but for the relief afforded by a
plentiful sprinkling of freckles. These brought the
fair skin into harmony with the amber eyes and
amber hair ; and though his features were not cast
in that monotonous and wooden mould libellously
termed ' Grecian ' by those who do not care to look
at the Grecian marbles, yet there was a certain Greek
vivacity and brightness about the youth's whole
appearance that was pleasant to eyes more impartial
than those of a parent. It was plain at a glance
that he had got his coat from a good tailor, and gave
some of his mind to his trousers, and was not in-
curious in waistcoats and boots, but was, in short,
something of a dandy. But there was not a bit of
buckram about him : his manner was simple and
cheery, and assured enough, as he glanced gaily over
his new acquaintance and pastor ; and the pair
seemed at once set upon such terms as a favourable
inspection after a friendly report might warrant.

The dinner was soon announced, and the company, to the number of eight, were told off into the dining-room. There was a young rector, Mr. Burgoyne, tall, florid and fat, clean-shaved and collarless, his ample jowl rolling over his snowy priest's stock. He was handsomely, even grandly, dressed in speckless and rather tight black, of the finest quality and of the latest and most effective ecclesiastical cut. The expression of his fat young face was severe; its lips, naturally full, were already pursed up by habit, and after each curt and consequential utterance they, as it were, snapped smartly together like a trap going off,—a fashion that seems to be most affected by high and mighty officials and horse-dealers, and other folk of an oracular turn. Altogether, an air of assumed importance pervaded this young clergyman. His grandfather had begun life as a framework knitter, under the name of Buggins. As he (being a clever, careful fellow) grew into a master hosier, he became Buggin, and then Burgin, by the will of his neighbours. His son increased the business, married a clergyman's daughter, and was Burgoin by his own (or his wife's) will. He was an old friend of our host, living at a neighbouring town. The influence of a legal brother with a ducal patron had procured a living for his son so soon as he was in priest's orders; and the father, dying suddenly, left him some fifteen thousand pounds, or, as another report said, twenty thousand. Then the son put a coat-of-arms upon his carriage, and finally adopted Burgoyne as the family designation. Next to this very prosperous young man sat a rich general dealer and speculator—he was white-waistcoated, of course; then a young, good-humoured, lisping land-agent, a Mr. Pocket; a broad-backed, brass-buttoned, blue-coated, top-booted farmer of the old sort, a Mr. Grains, worth his eighty thousand pounds; a solicitor, Mr. Troughton; and a sub-altern, Mr. Lionel Matchlock, who came together from the garrison-town. These, with the parish doctor, Mr. Whittle, made up the party invited to meet the heir of the house on his return from college for good. His sojourn had been but a brief matter of five terms. He passed his Little-go in the first class, and had then taken his name with honour off the boards.

At dinner nothing worth notice occurred, unless it were that Mr. Grains, who rarely condescended to dine abroad, and was most hostile to new fashions, having drunk off the contents of his finger-glass, stopped the servant who was refilling it with water, saying, in the most decided and even reproachful tones, 'Thank you; no more of *that!*'

'So Mr. Richard is not to be a clergyman?' said Mr. Whittle.

'No, Dick has chosen to be a farmer like me; and I cannot blame him. You may be sure, doctor, I feel glad enough to have him at home. But if he had chosen to be a parson I would have bought him a living, and a good one.'

'I am very glad you did not,' said the young rector, with severity. 'That buying and selling in the Temple is a terrible scandal—a profanation of holy things that will bring down a curse on this country.'

' Parson, I don't believe that the buying and selling of doves, sheep and oxen, and the money-chang-
ing in the Temple of Jerusalem, means the buying
and selling of glebelands and tithes in our parishes
in England.'

' As the immortal Squeers, of " Dotheboys Hall,"
puts it, " The fact is, it ain't a Hall. We call it a
Hall up in London, because it sounds better. A man
may call his house an island if he likes ; there's no
act of parliament against that, I believe." ' I take
this of Squeers to be the philosophy of calling
names in general, whether good or bad,' said the
curate.

' Now, parson, attend,' said Mr. Gryffyn to the
beneficed clergyman : ' answer me this :—if a man
gives or bequeathes lands or money for the maintenance of a parson in a parish on condition the
donor's family, or those to whom they may by the
law of the land transmit the right, shall have the
appointment of the parson, tell me this : have
churchmen a right to repudiate the conditions, and
keep the lands or money ? Is the dishonest and
discreditable part acted by the patron who sells
the living, or by the churchmen who try in the
name of piety to evade their engagement to the
donor ? If the conditions cannot be kept, should the
endowment be kept, or should the money go back
to the donor ? tell me that. Do the family who
sell the temporalities behave ill ? or do the churchmen who would keep the gift, and break the con-
tract ? Honesty, honesty, honesty, I say. There
are many ways of looking at the question : and that

is the way of a plain man of business like me. It wants no Latin, or Greek, or mathematics either, to see what is right there.'

The lawyer laughed. But Burgoyne replied evasively :

'You would not object to adjust more fairly parishes and incomes ?'

'I would respect all contracts. When I accepted gifts, I would be true to the terms, with lay-patrons no less than others.'

'You would not impose upon a parish a man whom they could not endure, or profit by ?'

'That's easily said, but not easily proved. You know, and I know, that a parish is not, like one man, all of one mind.'

'But,' persisted Mr. Burgoyne, who was saying his lesson, 'look at the men who hold family livings. Don't they hunt and shoot ?'

'Aye, some of them hunt and shoot too, when they know how. A healthy man can't be always at his books, can he ? He can't always sit in the house. Would you turn a strong man into an old woman because he is a parson ? Is that the way to gain respect in England ?'

'But is not all that hunting and shooting a scandal ?'

'It is not the question whether a man hunts or shoots : that depends partly upon another question, whether he makes it his relaxation or his occupation ; partly, too, whether he is able-bodied and hardy ; and partly, whether he was brought up to it. But the question is, does he teach, by precept and by example, his parishioners to live soberly and honestly, and to love God and their neighbours ?'

'But they won't listen to a man who hunts and shoots.'

'Don't tell me that ; I know better. I have not lived sixty-seven years in the country with my eyes shut.   There's a neighbour of mine—you all know him—Mr. Palmer, of Finchdale : I won't say he is the best and most useful clergyman within thirty miles round, but I will say there's not his better. And I have known this country, man and boy, as well as most folk.'

'But is he a magistrate !'

'To be sure he is, and heaps of good he does.   I don't know what we should do without him.'

'How can his parishioners bear to see a man in the pulpit, who punishes them on the bench ?'

'I doubt if he ever sat on the bench in a parishioner's case in his life.   There you show, parson, how much you know of the man you sit upon and condemn.   Such a gentlemen as Mr. Palmer would no more think of sitting on the bench when one of his own parishioners is brought up before it, than a squire, who is not a very bad un, would think of sitting on a game case which is brought up by his own keeper.   No, no; gentlemen like Mr. Palmer don't do business in that way.   I am surprised you don't know him better than that.'

'Then you would have those who hold college livings made magistrates, because they are good men ?'

'Not I.   I don't know much about their being

good men—I suppose you mean clever, in their way; but there are many ways of being clever; and I am not for having every clever clergyman made a magistrate. I am for those who hold family livings—whose fathers, or brothers, or cousins, or kin are neighbouring landed proprietors. They carry authority and local knowledge to the bench; they know the people: and, what's more, the people know them. But I would not have your fellows of colleges made magistrates. They may, or they mayn't, be clever; but whatever else they know, they don't know the country, its ways and customs: and the country don't know them. They are apt to be overstrict; and the people are sure to be jealous of them as strangers. I would as soon see a retired Indian colonel, or a retired sugar-baker made a magistrate as one of them. They are all three, no doubt, very worthy respectable men, but not fit for that job—in my opinion. Why, I have myself been asked over and over again to go on the bench. But, no thank you: as an agent and a farmer, I should be out of place; and so is your clergyman, when he is not connected with the landowners, who are the nat'ral heads of the district. But your black squires as I call 'em, like Mr. Palmer, are the very best of magistrates. They are invaluable on the bench as checks upon the lay squires, who will pay attention to them, but not to strangers.'

'But,' reasoned Mr. Burgoyne briskly, 'what with benching, and hunting, and shooting, Mr. Palmer cannot have much time left for his parish and his sermons.'

' Wrong again, parson. Your brother chip there can tell you better than that. I'll be bound for Mr. Palmer doing his duty by his parish. I know it as well as I know our own; for Lord Mercia owns half of it. And Mr. Martel can tell you what sort of a scholar the rector is. I only know he can make a good speech : though, to be sure, he'll never speak if he can help it:—he ain't of the windy sort. But no man knows him better than our curate does, nor is a better judge, I take it ; 'let our parson speak up for his friend.'

' I do not know that a man can do his friend a worse service than to speak up for him, without very great need,' said Martel.

' Nay, but there is need ; let him have his due, when it is questioned.'

' Well, as you say, I have the good fortune to count him friend, as did my father before me ; and if I am put to it, I must say that, in my poor judgment, there are few clergy in the diocese who preach so well as Mr. Palmer ; who take more pains, or who could pass so good an examination in the old English standard of divinity, that used to be thought so much of, and is still thought much of by me. Mr. Palmer has the best of it by frequent writing, so to speak, at his finger-ends ; and, if he approved the practice, he could preach it by the hour extempore : so steeped in it is he.'

' I did not know he set up for a theologian, beside all his other occupations,' snapped the controversial Burgoyne, somewhat contemptuous of a curate's interference, as beneficed sacerdotalists are apt to be.

'Nor does he: he has his own way of doing his work, and is not ashamed of it. I have often heard him say that when he was ordained, he took for his model the chaplain of Sir Roger de Coverley. I do not know that he adopted his list of divines exactly: but I know that he did so in part. And this too, I know—that he never allowed himself to be tempted into shirking the duty of compiling and writing sermons *for himself*. He was never tempted to steal the "Plain sermons" or the discourses of Drs. Newman and Manning, which offer eloquence, ease, and popularity, at the price of only sailing under false colours twice a week, and taking credit for work which has not been done, and of which the preacher is quite incapable.'

'I do not see,' said the young rector sharply; 'I do not see how the convictions of farmers and farm-labourers are to be aroused by a fine gentleman with a pleasant voice and handsome elocution, who has selected for his Sunday readings in the pulpit the antiquated sermons of old-fashioned and obsolete divines.'

'As to being antiquated and obsolete, I trust you are mistaken, as you are regarding my meaning,' spoke the curate, led by heat into longer discussion of his friend than his cool judgment would approve. 'What Mr. Palmer has done is this—he has with much pains worked up and digested out of those old divines, whom you despise, a regular series of simple short village addresses; and indeed he works away at them regularly week after week to this day: whereby, you see, he comes to know some-

thing of them ; and every new year's day he posts
upon the church-doors a list of the subjects upon
which, unless something special intervenes, he purposes to preach on each Sunday morning and evening throughout the year. I have more than once,
indeed several times, dropped into his church as a
chance hearer, and have never heard from him a
poor sermon, or any but a right good one well-
delivered, that is, so far as I may judge. He is,
to my mind, about as instructive and effective a
preacher, in a plain homely way, as it has ever
been my lot to hear ; and I have heard most of the
best known of my time in London and in Dublin.'

'But his church, eh ? what about that ? What
state is that in ?'

'Very good, very good indeed': you will be
happy to hear, and I am happy to tell you :—but
again, in his own way. The fact is, that before
one of the "Tracts for the Times" was issued,
and during the first year he was rector, he restored his church, and of necessity on his own
plan ; for church-architecture had not come into
fashion, and church-architects and their bills were
not. Mr. Palmer is by way of being himself something of an artist and architect ; and he had then
just returned from Italy, after spending a year
there, chiefly in visiting its churches and inspecting
its works of art, not in Rome only, but in many
of the provincial towns, and especially in those of
Lombardy. Taking his hint from what he there
saw, he banished from his chancel all seats but
chairs, carpeted it richly, and made everything

handsome, according to the fashion he had observed
abroad. He put up stained windows as good as
could then be got; and, being himself a dabbler
in sculpture, under the tuition of his friend, Mr. Lawrence, he cleaned and recut with his own hands a
good deal of the stonework that was fretted away and
worn flat, or defaced. Last of all, he re-seated, at his
own cost, and by the hands of village workmen
and carpenters, the whole church, copying the few
old oak benches that were left in it. However, I
have sung his praise too long; he is not the man to
thank me for blowing his trumpet: he is of the
old school before the days of puff and fuss and bustle,
pomp and vanity and advertisement. But many of
you know him, if not as well as I do.'

'I know him only by sight,' said the lawyer, Mr.
Troughton; 'but I have always admired his nice,
clean, gentlemanlike appearance.'

'Ay! he looks clean, wholesome and pleasant,
don't he?' said the host.

'And very courteous,' added the younger agent,
Mr. Pricket. 'Whenever we meet, we speak; and
very agreeable I always find him.'

'Yes, he knows about what to say, and how to
say it, to every one, wherever he is,' chimed in again
the elder agent.

'Are both those nice-looking young ladies that I
have seen riding with him his daughters?' asked
Mr. Troughton of Mr. Gryffyn.

'Mr. Palmer has but one daughter, one child; the
other young lady is a Miss Fisher, a relation of
theirs. I do not know in what way, but she stays

with them off and on a good deal, from time to
time.'

'They call the daughter the " Goldfinch," because
she is a "lass wi' a tocher," and lives at Finchdale,
don't they, Mr. Martel ?'

' I cannot say how other people call her ; for myself, I always call her " Miss Palmer." '

' Quite right too, sir. So do I,' said the lawyer ;
' but I may call her a very pretty girl. Don't you
agree with me ? or is Miss Fisher more to your
taste ? Some think her the better-looking of the
two ; do you ?'

' Is thy servant a dog that his mouth should water
for bones ?'

'Ah ! ha ! good ! the young lady is thin, to be
sure, though I should not have ventured to call her
" Bones,"' said the lawyer, professionally pleased at
having administered the retort courteous. ' But she
is *very* thin, Mr. Martel. So is not Miss Palmer thin,
and she will have a fat fortune, will she not ?' proceeded Mr. Troughton, with an eye to the main
chance, after his kind. I am told her father had
two thousand a year of his own, and got two more
with his wife, and that it all comes to the daughter
—to say nothing of his living, of about a thousand
a year, I suppose.'

'So does everybody suppose, no doubt. But, for
all that, begging your pardon, I can set you right
about the living,' replied Martel. 'I happen to know
that its net value, at the utmost, is £330 0s. 2½d. a
year.'

' That is it,' said the elder Gryffyn, ' to a ha'penny.'

'Ah, well, when we see a clergyman with good horses and carriages, and plenty of servants, we are apt to set him down as having a large living; you see, it seems to exonerate us laymen from doing anything for a church that is so rich,' replied Mr. Troughton reflectively; adding, 'I suppose it is a mistake in nine cases out of ten.'

'In ninety-nine out of a hundred,' said Gryffyn. 'Livings of eight hundred or a thousand a year are none so common, as I found when I was on the look-out for Dick, in case he turned parson. There are not over many at six hundred, I can tell you; no, nor at five hundred either; nor too many at four, when outgoings come to be looked at. Two hundred is about the mark, and rather over than under, I fancy, from what I see about us. But Mr. Palmer don't need any, if you come to that; not he. He is one of a good many that bring many times more than they take.'

'And the Goldfinch—I beg your pardon, Mr. Martel: excuse the joke; we will set it against your "Bones,"' said the lawyer pleasantly; 'the Gold-finch will be a fine catch for somebody's cage one of these days, I guess.'

'I guess it will be somebody who is not in want,' replied Mr. Gryffyn. 'Mr. Palmer is in many things a very liberal man, but he is uncommonly particular about some others. Quiet and easy-going as he looks, he is very high in his notions. It is not the first that comes he will take for a son-in-law, if I know him. He comes, as he thinks, of a family of crusaders, and it is true a good many Palmers lie cross-legged in his chancel; and, whether they be his folk or not, it is sure enough that a good many thousand acres lying up and down the conntry belong to his family. His wife, too, was a lady of an old titled family, and the niece to a duchess.'

'She was a sort of duchess herself, by all accounts,' rejoined Mr. Troughton, 'in the way of wasting money, anyhow.'

'Too true, I fear; and if she had lived long, I don't doubt she would have ruined him, for he never said her nay, and it was a regular love-match. A fine lot of money they spent between them in the ten years she was his wife! He's saving it back now, though not quite so fast as they spent it. But he likes to be quiet, and lives retired enough with his daughter. His wife and he were never out of great company. She could not be happy without it. They did not belong to the family of the Sponges, who visit everywhere, and ask no one home to their own houses. That's the cheap and nasty way. Mr. and Mrs. Palmer had a different way to that. They not only went to great folk's houses, but they entertained the great folk again. They were none of your second-rate, hanging-on sort of quality, that can't take too much or give too little. He was always a deal too proud to be one of your shabby "*fashionables*," as they call them. And you and I who have something to do with the management of estates, Troughton, know that four or five thousand a year does not go far in keeping open house for lords and ladies, and ladies'-maids, and gentlemen's gentlemen, and all the sort of them.'

'You surely do not think that is the best kind of man for a clergyman!' cut in Mr. Burgoyne, delighted.

'I don't know about the "best," that's a long word. I know he is, and always was, a very good un, though he is better now than he was then. You know we must all grow better as we grow older, parson; you and I, and all of us.'

'I would have no family livings, and have no sale of livings,' retorted Burgoyne, less pleased.

'What would you have then?' asked the host. 'Would you have parishes elect their own clergymen? Try parish elections, and see what you'll get by them: a crop of scandals the first six months such as the sale of livings would not produce in fifty years.'

'Certainly,' said Burgoyne, with honest effort, 'certainly, no word less strong than "scandal" will describe the scenes to which a few such elections have given rise.'

'Then what would you have?' asked Gryffyn.

'I would have promotion go *wholly* by *merit*.'

'Ugh! merit!! Parson, promotion never did go *wholly* by merit, and never will, in any profession or business under the sun, while this world lasts. Nobody goes wholly by merit, and why? Because nobody can do it. Man, you know, judges by the outward appearance, parson; and I defy you or any man to measure out exactly a clergyman's services, either in quantity or quality; and, more than that, no man tries to do it.'

'I should be sorry to think so.'

'No, parson; if it's the truth, you wouldn't be

sorry to think it, I hope—no need to be sorry ever about being true and right.'

' I take it,' said the lawyer, that the outcry about the sale of livings comes chiefly from dissenters who do not understand, and from dignitaries who do not wish it to be known, that so many of the clergy *live very much on their own resources.*'

' The bishop is the best judge and the proper person to appoint and to promote the clergy,' roundly asserted the rector ; ' he should be the patron always.'

' The bishop is the patron often ; and what does he more than another ?   He, just like any one else, " after anxious consideration," as he says, puts in the man he knows, or thinks he knows, best : that is, his friend, or his friend's friend ; or, maybe, some one that his chaplain, or his wife, or his wife's friends recommend, or, worse than all, whom his party (if he is a party man) recommends. I should like, then, to know why is their man likely to be a better man than the son upon whom his father has spent one fortune to give him a university education, and another in buying him a *living*, as they call it, that he may not be made all his life a journeyman to men no better than himself, who have friends at court, or in the bishop's palace, if you like that better—men whose livings have not been bought with hard cash, but mayhap with soft words or party services.'

' You know, Mr. Burgoyne,' said the lawyer, 'all canvassing of every sort, however adroitly done, comes under the head of what the law in its wisdom has called " simony," and might as well have called " sorcery." '

'Ah !' said the curate, 'just as money painfully extracted from the clergy is called "Queen Anne's Bounty !"'

'Well, well; but tell me this,' said the host, 'tell me, parson, why is the bishop's wife's or bishop's chaplain's pet, or some fighting-cock of a party that they call a "*saint*," likely to make a better rector than the man that the squire would choose ? Answer me that, parson. Nay, he is never a bit better, and most likely not half so good.'

'And pray why ?' asked Mr. Burgoyne.

'Because the choosing for this or that parish, unless when, as in the case of one of the squire's family, the man may have been familiar with it from his youth, is very much of a chance any way, do what you will. I have thought this question over and over for Dicky often and often. *Ordination* is the thing; and ordination lies wholly with the bishop, when the laity and clergy have furnished him with testimonials. THAT'S our security for getting the right clergy, and that's all we can have. We are to remember the Church is worked by means of men, and shares man's imperfection. As for the bishops being better patrons of livings than the laity, whether fathers or squires, why, I have heard of a bishop saying that "he, *as a father*, was the best judge of his son's fitness for a living ;" and I have myself heard one say in public—what many a bishop might say—that he owed all his success in life to a certain great family. Why, then, the bishop is as much their man as I am Lord Mercia's ; and he will be likely to promote the members and friends and dependents of that family over the heads of their betters, it may be, and pretty surely their elders, in the ministry. Beside that, isn't the prime minister a layman, and doesn't he represent the laymen of England? and doesn't he on that score appoint the bishops? Then tell me this, parson—why shouldn't a layman appoint the parish parsons? Didn't a layman make a very good choice when he chose you, Burgoyne, eh?'

At this good-natured home-thrust there was a cry of 'Hear, hear!' and the lawyer remarked:

'It is the old question, you see, of "*lay investure*"—Thomas à Becket and Henry the Second over again, in little, you know.'

But Mr. Gryffyn, regardless of historic illustration, followed up his own line of argument with modern instances.

'After all, the lay patron only picks the man for this or that particular place out of those whom the bishop has received with regulated, legal, and lay testimonials from their own parishes, and has examined and ordained to the general ministry of the Church. What more would you have?'

'We want the right man in the right place.'

'You want the right man in the right place, do you? Then the odds are twenty to one that the lay patron knows both the place and the man better than the bishop or the bishop's council (if he has one) does. It is ten to one that the bishop has never lived two years, or a year, or perhaps at all, in a country parish, and knows no more about the different sorts of country parishes than I know about

France—and that's not much, is it, Dick ? And, if I am not much misinformed, a usual question privately asked by bishops before promoting a man is, " Has he any private fortune or independent means ?" as a needful qualification—a part of his merit, in fact.'

' Then let the parish choose its own pastor !' cried Burgoyne, desperate.

' You have just declared against that, Mr. Burgoyne,' said the lawyer.

' Against election fights I did ; but take the unanimous voice of the parish.'

' Did you ever hear the unanimous voice of a parish that was not under one man's rule ?'

' I never did,' said the host. 'The scandal of the election itself is nothing to the division of a parish into organised electioneering parties, or religious parties, which are still worse. And what do you think would be the temper of the beaten minority towards their new pastor, whom they knew chiefly through misrepresentations, detraction, and calumny ?'

' Ah !' said the lawyer, ' I know something of electioneering ; and I tell you, I do not think a greater judgment could fall upon a parish than the spirit such an election would breed. The effects would be injurious to the last degree, not only to Christianity at large, but to the heart of every man and woman in the place—fatal to their morals and understandings both. And such evils are sure to be encouraged and dignified with the name of " holy " zeal by ambitious " potentates " who are " not strong

but by a faction." Elections for parliament are harm-
ful enough to morals. Political liberty is a fine
thing, but we pay a high price for it, and sometimes
lose personal liberty in the tussle; for party-spirit
is an arbitrary ruler. But, for Heaven's sake, let us
keep clear of electioneering in Church matters!' said
the lawyer, with a fervency that was quite impres-
sive.

'Yes, yes,' echoed Mr. Gryffyn; 'the people should
have, and they have if they please to use it, a voice
in all *ordinations.*'

'*That* is the *plebis suffragium,*' remarked the
lawyer.

But Mr. Gryffyn had not done with Burgoyne;
he took up his question again.

'What would I have, do you say? Why, I hold
that any man who is good enough to be a curate is
good enough to be a rector. A priest is a priest, as
you gentlemen say: if he is not priest good enough
to be a rector, he is not priest good enough to be
a curate, and do rector's work. "Cure of souls,"
d'ye say? Why, isn't a curacy a cure of souls?
And, for what you or I know, one cure of souls is
as important as another. What is the difference in
value between the souls of men in this or in that
parish? Who can tell me that? Spiritualities and
temporalities, do you say?' cried the host, who was
worked up into some warmth. 'Don't tell me about
spiritualities—stuff and nonsense! Why, a CURACY
represents the SPIRITUALITY; but, you see, it is
TEMPORALITIES you mean when you talk about
"*livings*"—what men "*live*" upon, eh?'

'Oh! Mr. Gryffyn,' said the rector, with unctuous
and patronising gentleness of rebuke: 'all that is
of the earth, earthy.'

'Why, so is the glebe-land; so are the tithes;
so is the bishop's palace and his income; so is your
body and mine, my friend,' retorted Mr. Gryffyn.

'But, surely,' shuffled the rector, changing ground,
'you want cleverer men in some places than in
others.'

'I know that, I know that. But your examina-
tions won't always tell you which is the cleverer
man. There are different sorts of cleverness, as well
as different parishes; and it is not every layman, or
every bishop either, that knows the right man when
he sees him. Listen to me: are not our M.P.s, in a
way, picked laymen? Now, if all the M.P.s were to
choose each one a parson for his own parish (as I
have been told they did once upon a time, about
two hundred years ago), do you think they wouldn't,
or do you think they didn't, choose each according
to his own private fancy for all sorts of reasons?
Choose! why a man is no more safe to choose a
good parson, than he is safe to choose a good wife.
Young ladies and curates are both on their preferment, you know. I beg your pardon, parson mine:
I know, if I had to choose, and so far, I wish I had,
I should choose you. And I have got you already,
you see; and the living is not worth your having:
rather less than you've got as curate, ain't it? But
I should choose you if the living were a living.
You read and preach in a way that I can listen to,
and you are good company for young and old; and

if I am not made better, it is not your fault, but mine!' shouted the hearty host, who having done a long day's work and eaten a good dinner and drunk his pint or so of wine, had now talked himself into a heat.

The belauded curate, who knew how much of this was due to his own merit, and how much to the after-dinner good-nature of his host, by way of stopping the terrific current of eulogy, broke in with a random apropos.

'That reminds me of a fable of Sadi's, an Eastern poet, you know. A man volunteered to read gratis in a mosque; but he had a voice that his hearers could not endure, even at that rate. The super-intendent, a considerate, kindly man, not willing to hurt the feelings of the gratuitous but inharmonious reader, said, "My friend, this mosque pays its regular readers a stipend of five dinas; now, I will give you ten to go to another place." The man of discords took the money, and took himself off. Pre-sently he came back with an injured air, and said, "Oh, sir, you have wronged me in sending me away from this station with ten dinas. The people I went to will give me twenty dinas to go away: and I have not yet consented. The emir laughed, and said, "Take care, and don't be in a hurry to accept their offer; for it is likely that, rather than you should remain, they will give you fifty to be quit of you." You see the choice of ministers is a universal difficulty, and the most voluntary prin-ciple, and even gratuitous services, will not meet it: our Church is not the only one that has trials in the matter.'

'Ho! ho! ho!' laughed the jolly host. 'To be sure, that's just what I say. Here is my other parson friend (who must excuse me, because I have nursed him on my knee as a little boy), he is always talking to me about "work, work," and "paying according to work." Why, all depends upon what sort of work it is. It's quality, not quantity, we want. There's a deal of unfinished work.'

'That's better than none,' said the parson.

'No, no; a deal worse than none, nine times out of ten; a deal o' work I'd have at no price. I'd sooner, like the Ameer, pay a man handsomely to leave it alone.'

'But you would call the reading of daily prayers good work, would you not?' snapped the young rector.

'Aye, aye; every man should offer his prayers twice a day in the family, and alone as often as you will. But for daily prayer in church, there's hardly one in five hundred in our day who could attend it, in this hard-worked, ill-fed, cold country, without neglecting his first duty as a man, the "six days labour" of the commandment, as I take it. And so you cannot have the COMMON Prayer, which the exhortation, you know as well as I do, points to and calls for. And for "work," to read the same prayer day after day, word for word, is neither good work nor bad work—it's no work at all; at least, if it be work, it's work that any one can do. It's wicked waste, to put a man to the cost of two or three thousand pounds, a sum that would make him independent, only to qualify him to do that which I, for twenty or thirty pounds, could get a parish boy with a good voice, taught by a music-master, to do in six or eight months. And talk of " good," he shall be a good boy, too. But I want a man for my pastor who, besides being able to read, is apt to teach and to preach.'

'Oh !' snorted Burgoyne, indignant ; 'any boy can preach !'

'Aye, another man's sermons; but it's not any man that can listen to him.'

'There are eight or ten volumes of excellent, plain sermons written to supply that want by very learned men,' said Mr. Burgoyne.

'But isn't that cribbing sermons, even if you buy them ? And then it's not everybody can preach them,' retorted his elder. 'I don't know much about books and learning, but I know something about men ; and I know that writing and preaching properly two fresh sermons every week, is a very different sort of work to reading the same prayers over and over again, day after day, for ever. In preaching and teaching, it's not only *what* you say, but *how* you say it, *when* you say it, and *where* you say it. You talk of your new sermons, let me tell you I have some first-rate *old* sermons, that I am very fond of reading at home. A young curate came here, who, it seems, had these same sermons, and preached 'em. Shall I tell you what it was like ? It was just the old song :

'" Jack stole his discourse from the famed Dr. Brown,
But by preaching it shockingly made it his own."

I couldn't listen to him, do what I would. And if

he had preached as well as he did ill, I should have found it hard to listen to one in the pulpit, who was like a child out of it. He was a good lad, and an earnest lad, very; but there was nothing in him, and nothing could come out of him. A man's work is not all done in the pulpit; and I doubt if any man can teach you well in the pulpit, for preaching is teaching, or it's nothing, to me at least; but I doubt if any man can help you in the pulpit, except on some special occasion, who does not know you out of it.'

'That is it,' said Mr. Burgoyne sharply; 'visiting is the thing we want. You will at least allow that to be a good work.'

'Oh! there you are again, are you? You go too fast, parson. There's preaching and preaching, and there's visiting and visiting. A poor old man (not in this parish, mind) said to me one day: "Our parson's a famous un to visit us; he comes to see un every week, he does. One day I told un I couldn't be good nohow." "Well, and what said he?" I asked. "Parson told me to read a psalm. To-day he ax un whether I'd dun' it, an' I sed yees; an' he ax un if it dun' ma good, an' I sed noa." "Then what did he say?" "He told un to read it agen an' agen, till I felt better." There's visiting for you! And here's some more. A tradesman tells me his parson is grand at visiting—"He just hops in one day and leaves a tract, and hops in the next day to ask if I have read it." Now,' said Mr. Gryffyn, 'I'll back the postman's work against such as that: he'll make a hundred visits to your one.'

'They are both men of letters,' lisped Mr. Pockett.

But Mr. Gryffyn, regardless of the wit, went on with his hobby.

'For work, let me tell you—good work—is not so common anywhere. Work, work! How much of the lawyer's work is good?—Mr. Troughton will tell you. Of the doctor's?—ask Mr. Whittle. Of the farmer's?—I could tell you, if I would. Of contractors'?—you may see that in custom-houses and bridges that have fallen down, in soldiers' shoes without soles, in ammunition carts without wheels. Of Parliamentary work?—how many acts are useful? how many are intelligible? how many can't you drive a coach-and-six through? how much of the law can you understand without your lawyer? how many speeches can you trust? Of railway kings and directors?—how do you like the financing? Have you any shares or debentures in Sir Hocus Pocus's line? if so, you'll have some work to come by your money, I doubt.'

'But,' persisted his rectorship, with the heedless enthusiasm of youth, 'you think the best man is the working man, do you not, Mr. Gryffyn?'

'I say, again, that depends on the sort of work he does. There's rare work, and there's sad work— eh? ain't there, now? It takes a clever man to do and say some things, that a wiser man would leave unsaid and undone. That leaving undone is not showy work, but it's often the best work a man can do; and the best work's the least talked about mostly. The knowing what to leave unsaid is about the best gift of a preacher: knowledge is not enough

—he should have discretion; and that comes of experience, mind you, and experience comes of time
and trouble; though, look you, a man who's not
sharp will never get experience so long as he lives.
Experience is a scarce article, and I say that is
what we ought to pay well for, because it has been
dearly bought. The work of experience is good
work; but it's not every man that knows good
work when he sees it, and so the best men are not
often put atop. Bustle and flash and talk and advertisement is what folk look to mostly in all trades,
and honesty's apt to go to the wall—eh, lawyer?
eh, doctor? And then, for the Church, why, she
doesn't pretend to pay men to a penny their price, as
some professions make believe to do; and I doubt
if she could, if she would. For, mind you, not one
in a hundred who really works hard ever boasts or
talks of what he is doing: the lad who talks about
hard work is the lad that means to ask you for beer:
—that's my experience. But this I must say for
the Church—that in it more men work for the
work's sake than in any other profession or calling,
except, perhaps, the army:—eh, Mr. Matchlock?
Why, he's asleep! and quite right too. But I was
going to say the Church does pay one here and there
well, and there is nothing she should pay for better
than for experience; men with experience have
a right, if any one has, to independent positions.
And look ye, besides, they are not very young: they
won't want the pay very long; they'll soon pass it
on, and let others have their turn, and keep the pot
boiling. There's no such block to promotion as put-

ting the young uns into the high places, and there
is no discouragement like placing a boy priest of
two years' standing over a number of able and devoted men who have for many a long year borne the
burden and heat of the day. You'll be told, no
doubt, of the young un who gets, maybe, two thousand a year for two years' work in the Church, that
he is giving his youth and his strength to its service. What then ? He is only doing what most
others have done, and have given their middle age
to boot. Then many talk of zeal. I'm for experience, not experiment ; experience keeps men out of
mischief, and does not meddle and muddle. It
mayn't be quick at work, but the work it does is
good, and will last, and is cheap in the end ; it will
" wash and wear," as they say. I am not a Latin
scholar, as you know ; but I was at school once, and
I think I remember that *senator* means a man of
age and experience, and that *senates* mean, properly,
councils of experienced men. You are a Latin
scholar, and should know that better than I do.
But you will know it better still, parson, if you go
with your eyes open and your mouth shut till you
get a grey poll like mine. And you mustn't mind
an old man telling you something beforehand ; your
father and I learnt a good deal together, and I have
only given you a bit of his mind about the new-
fangled notions of " *work.*" '

'Very fantastical notions they are—don't you
think so ?' said Mr. Pockett to Mr. Troughton, who
had been talking together aside during a good deal of
the discussion, and were now rising from the table.

'That is a fine word of yours, Pockett—"fantastical." Where did you get it?' asked Mr. Troughton, who laughed a little at his friend's finery.

'Oh! I got it from Mr. Martel,' lisped Mr. Pockett, laughing in turn.

'And I got the idea from you, Mr. Pockett; so you owe me nothing, and may go to bed easy,' retorted the other.

The ensign, who had sat up most of the night before playing 'blind-hookey,' had recruited his energies with a snooze, and now roused up his faculties again for another night's work; and Dicky, who had sat amused with the doctor, though not quite approving the baiting of the pretentious parson, rose too, with the gilt-buttoned farmer and white-waistcoated factor, who had done some strokes of business; and the party broke up betimes.

'Are you going?' asked the host. 'You are early.'

'It is time we were all in bed,' said the lawyer. 'You are a three-o'clock-in-the-morning man, and set us a good example.'

'Never mind me,' said the host; 'you have your ways, and I have mine. When a man can't sleep, it's time to get up—that's all I say about it.'

CHAPTER III.

THE MAN IN THE MANSE.

'Two houses in St. Ronan's —— were the clergyman's manse and the village inn. Of the former we need only say that it formed no exception to the general rule, by which the landed proprietors of Scotland seem to proceed in lodging their clergy, not only in the cheapest, but in the ugliest and most inconvenient house, which the genius of masonry can contrive. It had the usual number of chimneys—two, namely, rising like ape's ears at either end, which answered the purpose for which they were designed as ill as usual. And the disordered and squalid appearance of a low farm-house, occupied by a bankrupt tenant, dishonoured the dwelling of one who, besides his clerical character, was a scholar and a gentleman.'—SCOTT—*St. Ronan's Well.*

'For he hadde nought geten him yit a benefice
    o   o   o   o   o
But al that he might of his frendes tente
On bookes and his lernyng he it spente.'
              CHAUCER—*Canterbury Tales.*

THE departing guests had donned their wrappings, had lit their cigars and pipes, and were waiting the turns of their various vehicles. The curate was just starting to walk to his rooms in the village, a mile off, when the host interposed with :

'Mr. Burgoyne, your way is through our village. You'll take our parson ? You pass by his lodgings.

It is an over-wet night to walk, when one may ride.'

'Very well,' replied, gruffly, Mr. Burgoyne, who was a little put out.

The curate shrugged his shoulders, and muttered something about preferring to walk. But the host would not have it so.

'No! no! no! Mr. Burgoyne will take you, and drop you at your crib.'

The smart rector's pair of greys flashed up to the door; a blaze of light from his lamps displayed the showy equipage, with its many-coloured paints and pipings, and harness glaringly mounted. The unbeneficed senior was getting up in front, but was asked, for no obvious reason, to sit behind. It was again on his lips to say that he would walk; but he felt it beneath his dignity to notice the slight, and, beside, he did not like to cross his kind host. At the village the road forked off into two branches, which met again at what was called the town end. These two roads were alike in the rector's way home; but one would lead him past the curate's lodging, the other would not. Our clerical grandee took the latter, though his servant reminded him where the curate lived. So the unbeneficed elder brother was, after all, set down in the muddiest part of a very dirty street, to trudge home through the wet and the slush; and, having calculated upon being set down at his door, he had put his goloshes into his pocket.

'Drive on,' said the amiable junior, bespattering with mud from the wheels of his chariot his senior, who went off muttering pretty loudly, 'Dirty snob! what else could one expect?' And on he waded, ankle-deep in mire, while the polite proprietor of the pair of greys rolled homeward, leaving darkness and the fuming curate behind him. The angry Levite had not far to go; though, for the matter of dirt, he might as well have walked five miles. He felt his way past the dark church to the flickering lights of the low public-house, behind which stood the modest, not to say slovenly, cot wherein he rented two wee rooms, at the rate of eleven shillings a week, with attendance, if he could get it. Scraping the slush from his boots, and shaking the rain from his hat and coat, he let himself into the lower room, floored with damp brick, and lit his tallow candle at the handful of smouldering fire; for in those days free trade had not bloomed into monopoly, and the poorest could get a little coal.

It would seem to unaccustomed eyes but a cheer-less, comfortless home. Our friend apparently thought better of it. He first mended the fire, then changed his wet boots for dry, and his not new coat for one much older, seized a book, drew to the fire his hard, high-backed, wooden chair, set his candle at his back and a foot upon each hob, and, with a grunt of satisfaction, was soon immersed in one of his favourite Bishop Taylor's divine pastorals. Poverty, damp, discomfort, neglect, fled before the sacred magic of the poet-preacher's wand, and the enchanted reader was soon as one who, having nothing, yet possesseth all things. When this is said, need it be told that the edition of the 'Holy

Living and Dying,' which he was reading, was not that which Archdeacon William Hale Hale ' revised, abridged, and adapted for general reading.'

At length, rousing himself from his rapt abstraction, ' This will never do,' said he ; ' it is far too interesting ; I shall not get to sleep to-night. Lay him by,' said he, closing the volume, and rising to look for another. ' H'm !' he muttered, as he restored it to its place and scanned his pet shelf ;— ' H'm : South's "Sermons," Fuller's " Holy and Profane State," Barrow's " Sermons," Bishop Hall's "Contemplations," Robert Hall's " Sermons," Berkeley, Butler, Paley—— that shelf will not do, it would keep me wide awake. Ho !' turning to a lower and less honoured shelf ,' here we have him, the Bishop of St. Botolph's "Billingsgate Sermons,"very suggestive, very suggestive indeed—of sleep : now for the arms of Morpheus !' and he sat down to read. Then, as he traced each "winding bout of linked dulness long drawn out," downy slumber, with soft owl-like wings, began to hover o'er him, and swift descending pounced upon his eyes, and sealed his senses ; dreams came, and the preacher's work was done upon him. Then did the cold night air chill his marrow, and he awoke—to find the fire gone out ; and with the candle sputtering in socket, he shuffled off shivering about midnight to repose under the cold shelter of white-washed walls upon his curtain-less chaff bed. There for the present we will leave him. May ' pleasant dreams and slumbers light ' visit him, as he lies stretched on his uneasy pallet. Not that it was uneasy to him, any more than the scrag of mutton cooked on Sunday, and eaten cold each day after, until the bare bone was graciously given to his favourite fowls on Saturday, was to him hard fare. Being methodical up to a certain point, he had carefully taken his scale of diet from the rations allowed to Wellington's soldiers in Spain, and counted his cost at about ninepence halfpenny a day. You see he was not past sympathy with peasants through being overfed or lapped in luxury; and there was no need to him of many fasts or artificial mortifications of the flesh. Those some bishop might possibly require in the perfumed chambers of his lordship's palace; they might be wholesome for many men with four thousand, or seven or eight thousand a year's salary, and four months' holiday out of every year; or they might profit such dons as have taken priest's orders and plentiful pay with no priestly work; ordained to celibate and pensioned ease in luxurious rooms, and to high feeding in glorious halls, while waiting for the fat and dignified college living; meanwhile—— writing all the same their articles

'On music, poetry, the fictile vase
Found at Albano, chess, and Anacreon's Greek.'

To these and such as these, lay or clerical, plainer living might haply suggest higher thinking; and possibly even a more conscientious sense of duty towards those committed to their charge in Church, or State, or College. Have we not read records of 'Fellows' fasts and mortifications, that remind us

of Mr. Pembroke's laments over lukewarm dinners
and ill-made beds; while the Baron of Bradwar-
dine was pleased with a Scotch peasant's roughest
fare and a few bundles of straw stowed in the cleft
of a sand-rock.

CHAPTER IV.

THE MEET OF THE HOUNDS, AND THE MEETING OF FRIENDS.

'Rose could not go ahead across country as Froude had no scruples in doing.'—J. H. NEWMAN—*History of My Religious Opinions*, p. 38.

'Childe Harold wends through many a pleasant place,
Though sluggards deem it but a foolish chase,
And marvel men should quit their easy chair,
The toilsome way and long long league to trace.
Oh ! there is sweetness in the mountain air,
And life that bloated Ease can never hope to share.'
                                        BYRON.

OUR slumberer was roused before seven o'clock by the stamp of a horse, and a loud shouting under his window :

'Hulloa ! parson ; are you up ?   Not you.'

'Yes: here am I,' replied, from an upper window, the gentleman so called from sleep.

'Up, aye : but not dressed.   Well, you mu't put your boots on ; for you mu't ride a-hunting with Dick to-day.'

'Can't.'

'Why not ?'

'I've had my day this week.   Judy won't come out again on this side Sunday.'

'That don't matter; I'll lend you a nag; you shall have my new grey.'

'Couldn't.'

'But you must; you'll like her; she's as easy as an armchair, and can go as fast as you please, they tell me.'

'I don't suppose she can jump, though; and I should not like to lame her.'

'Never you mind the laming; I'll take my chance of that. If you do lame her, why I can afford to get another.'

'So could not I.'

'But my groom has ridden her over some little fences, and he says she won't refuse.'

'Your son will want her to-morrow.'

'Nay; Dick has one hunter, and I don't mean him to have more. Say you'll go.'

'I'll think of it, and send you word.'

'Nay, nay; say the word now—you can't refuse; it's Dick's first day.'

'Well, if I must, I must. Where do the hounds meet?'

'At Cranberry Hill; Dick will be with you about half-past nine, and I will send you the grey. Dick has forgotten the way, if he ever knew it; but you know all the bridle-roads, parson, you do.'

'My dear father, how you did talk last night,' said Dick, as they sat at breakfast together. 'I never heard you half so hard and sharp on any one, as you were upon Mr. Burgoyne.'

'Was I, Dick?'

'Didn't you "work" him? I was quite sorry.'

' Well, you know—hang the fellow!—I was put
out with him. He's hard enough upon other people.
He's for ever talking about his " work," and his nonsense. Those new-fashioned fellows are all alike;
they're just as full of tricks as a cage of monkeys.
I heard only yesterday morning how badly he had
behaved to the family of his uncle, Burgin, the
lawyer, who died suddenly a short time since. He
was clerk to the board of guardians, you know, and
when the duke used to attend the board at Bedwell,
Lawyer Burgin was always very attentive—used to
wait upon his Grace, and set a chair for him, and
dust it with his pocket-handkerchief, and all that
sort o' thing, which you would not catch Troughton
doing for duke or prince either. So when the living
of Lapsham fell vacant, having no more relations or
friends to give his good things to, the duke offered
the presentation of the living, which is worth about
three hundred and fifty a year, to Lawyer Burgin
for his son, if he wanted it. But his son was for the
law, you know, so he recommended his nephew;
and that's the way Jack Burgoyne got his living
within two years after his taking orders. Then his
father died and left him thirteen or fourteen or
fifteen thousand pounds, or very likely more; and
altogether, for a young man of seven-and-twenty, he
is uncommonly well off, and has no wife or child.
Well, you know, within this year the lawyer died,
and he had just been unlucky in some speculation,
so left his family, for the present, at any rate, in great
distress. They applied for some help to Jack Burgoyne; and what do you think he said, Dick? He

had his church to restore; and he must attend to the needs of the house of God before he could think of any man or woman, relation or not, who was not of the spiritual flock, over whom the church of God had made him overseer. Those are his very words, for his letter was given me to read.'

'A regular case of "corban"' interrupted Dicky.

'I don't know about that,' said his father, who did not quite catch the allusion; 'but I know I was very vexed with him; that's what made me so sharp on him last night. You know "if any man provide not for his own, and specially for those of his own house, he hath denied the faith, and is worse than an infidel." I don't say that quite applies to him, but I do say that he has behaved very badly, and very ungratefully. You cannot plead the service of God for neglecting your duty to man—which is the best service you can render to man's Maker. That's the way I read the Bible; and that's the way you will read it, Richard, I hope. Well, well, I dare say Burgoyne won't mind anything that I have said, or can say. But it's time for you to be off, Dick. How is it you don't sport your red coat? I know you have one, for I saw the price of it in the tailor's bill they sent from college—a stiff price too.'

'I thought perhaps you would not like me to wear it here, father.'

'Hum! Perhaps it's as well not. Some of the lords and squires might be jealous of it. Not that Lord Mercia is one of them; or that you or I need ask any one what we are to wear. But I dare say you are as well as you are. You look clean—and so

you should: for you use water enough of a morning
to rot an oak-post; though where's the harm, if you
like it? You look well on it. But I won't make
you vain,' he added, as Dick rose from the table and
displayed in full length, to the admiring gaze of the
paternal eye, his well-chosen and well-made hunt-
ing-dress, setting off, by its workman-like and easy
cut, his well-knit figure. Indeed Dick did look
very well, better probably than he would have
looked in scarlet. The dark chocolate-brown of his
coat and waistcoat showed off to advantage his
fair complexion, and harmonised with the creamy
leathers and well-cleaned tops that clad his well-
turned legs. Round his neck a dark-blue bird's-eye
waterfall was fixed by a huge onyx-headed breast-
pin big enough to fasten the thickest of shawls; and
a heavy-thonged, silver-mounted whip, and straight
and heavy silver spurs, completed a quiet sportsman-
like and gentleman-like equipment.

His companion joined him in a dark-grey tweed
suit, and, with trousers tucked into black boots, if
not quite the beau-ideal of the English hunting
parson, might very well pass for an Irish P.P.—the
'Father Fritz' of the hunting-song of old Ireland.

'Sir Pat bestrode a high-bred steed,
And the huntsman one that was broken-kneed,
And Father Fritz had a wiry weed.'

But no weed were you, gallant Sybil Grey, high-
born daughter of the homicide Mundig! Walking or
trotting, cantering or galloping, over the fields or on
the road, in saddle or in harness, how dainty and
airy was your stepping! your mouth how sensitive

to sympathising, gentle hands! how high your spirit! how docile and free your temper! May your manes, if anywhere they exist in space, accept this tribute to your virtues!

As the pair from Fulmere sped merrily through the mist that veiled the moist, spongy meadows, or plunged through the deep black slush of winding lanes, and threaded intricate bridle-gates, ever and anon, on the right hand and on the left, before and behind, they espied specks of scarlet flashing fiery through the haze, now singly, now in groups of two and three and four,—spotting the grey landscape with bright sparks,—all making for the one point.

The elder, whose vocation it was to hold forth, and who, in season or out of season, seldom missed his opportunity, gave vent to his feelings.

'You know I am no sportsman; going to cover in the best of countries on the best of hacks is good enough for me. But, half Frenchman and Celt as I am, I have the old Saxon love of the free country life, and I delight in the hounds and the horn, sailing, as we do now, over the springy undulations of green pasture, and scenting the dewy perfume of the earth as it steams up and is borne upon the morning breezes.'

'Dewy perfume, is it? Choking fog I should say, and very rank-smelling.'

'Well, then, see the variety of company opened to a poor hermit like me. I feel more amiable and charitable when I ride an occasional day in sport with all my neighbours of every degree.

4—2

' " The high, the low, in pleasure all uniting,
      Here I may feel that I too am a man ?"

Believe me, nothing so much as fox-hunting im-
proves the feeling of rural society, and puts rich
and poor into good humour one with another.
Business divides, their sports unite, them. Nothing,
I say again, so makes us know and like each other
as free and common recreation, and, above all, recreation in the open air. In this capitalist-ridden
land of ours these hunting holidays are the only
days on which the fields are free to the multitude.
The old Sir Rogers were patriarchal in their habits,
with open hands and gates and doors, and easy
about their grounds to all but poachers. The new
men are traders in land, and as tenacious of every
inch of their dirty acres as they are about their
formal gardens. When we are talking of free trade
and free schools, and free chapels and free churches,
and coal-pits free from monopoly, let us think what
free land and free range is here; air free from the
smoke of long chimneys, water free from manufacturing pollutions. What free fellowship too : squire
and yeoman cheek-by-jowl; tradesman, peer, and
parson riding shoulder to shoulder, like Canterbury
pilgrims. That is what I call society.'

'When the hounds are not running, you mean ?'

'Why, yes,' said the speaker, going on with his
theme. 'Man is made for recreation as well as
work; and if it does not come to him in good form,
he takes it in a worse—in dancing-saloons and
public-houses, in unwholesome, stuffy meetings, and
in more unwholesome claptrap speeches and late

hours. In old countries like ours, thickly populated, there is always a tendency to that sort of evil. The settlers in new countries have abundance of amusement in the open air—in free plains, in Nature's woods, by waters unpreserved and unpolluted ; their toil is pleasure, for it is in pursuit of game for the food's sake.'

' We can't help being civilised,' said the junior loftily.

' What a civilisation it is !' sighed the senior sadly. ' " I tell you what would do you a vast deal of good," said an Arkansas bishop to an English dean ; " and that is two thousand miles with me in my buggy. You here are too civilised by half. You want some good, honest barbarism put into you ; you would get along a vast deal better." It was true enough : Nature is the cure. Green pastures and clear streams and fresh air for ever, against clubs and scandal and meetings and committees, spouting, and tea-fights !'

' But fox-hunting is a luxury, you know,' put in the younger.

' You got that from the goodies,' said the elder ; ' I like to hear them talk of "luxury !" The funk and the falls, the fatigue and the soaked clothes, the lame horses and the long rides in the wet and in the dark, would open the minds of our sedentary preachers on the subject of luxury, and teach them the wholesome and homely truth that one man's meat is another man's poison.'

' There are other outdoor exercises beside fox-hunting,' said the little Gryffyn.

' Yes ; but they are most of them solitary, and apt

to be churlish. The beauty of fox-hunting is its
sociability. A philosophic historian tells us that—
"Tournaments had a value beyond the mere exhibi-
tion of a childish pageant; they brought together
all classes of society, and bound them for the time
at least in a connecting link of common tastes and
enjoyments. The king emerged from his palace, the
great baron left the dismal seclusion of his feudal
castle, the citizen quitted his workshop, the peasant
abandoned his plough, and all met together on the
same platform of a common enjoyment and a common
expectation." Now, we have heard of a "tournament of doves;" I call ours a tournament of foxes.
Talk of civilisation! Think of the manufacturer's
"hands," who pass the prime of their shortened span
of thirty-five or forty years in the crowded slums
and cellars of Manchester, Birmingham, and Shef-
field, of Glasgow, Leeds, and Bradford, Stockport,
and Rochdale! And all for what? That their em-
ployers may die worth a million of money! And
that is called national prosperity. Now tell me
whether emigration on the grand scale is not the
cure for them and for us of the minor gentry, or the
poorer educated class, if you like that better—men
whose incomes range from one hundred to six hundred a year? But don't let me talk any more of
these things now, or my holiday will be spoilt; I
shall have too much of them to-morrow—"carpe
diem, Juan."

'You talk of sedentary preachers, Mr. Martel. It
seems to me that you are by way of being a hunting
philosopher.'

'As much of that as I am of a sportsman, no doubt. The fact is I am a poor recluse, who breaks loose now and then into the hunting-field as his one chance of studying the varieties of the genus man, and getting a little wholesome change and stimulus. Now look about you; we are close to the meet. There is a mob coming to-day. Do you know any of these swells ? No ? Don't you see your own chief, Lord Mercia ? To his right, Lord Canobie ; to his left, Count Beaulieu—three of the greatest dandies in Christendom, and in all respects really very accomplished men. See what horsemen they are ! and what horses they ride ! With a fair start and good luck, no man can beat them : if any, that is the man—Lord Billingsgate ; and a shocking bad style of man he is. Just turn quietly, and look at that lady on the grey pony, with the flow of loose black hair, handsome as paint and sculpture to boot. You know who she is ? No ? Lady Parthenope Sanfoin, a daughter of the Duke of Bellisle. The family are all handsome in that style.'

'Nearly as handsome as gipsies, in fact,' suggested little Gryffyn.

'And who is that with her ? The Marquis of Banagher, the model of a high-bred Irishman, with a pedigree as long as his legs ; and perhaps, if there be a best here to-day, the best horseman out. I should like to see the man that can "beat Banagher" across a country. A courtier of many courts, he is just as much at home drinking whisky "phonch" with wild Irish squires in the wilds of Connemara. He'll break an arm out hunting in the morning, and make a capital speech in the House of Lords at night.'

'He is very hideous.'

'I believe no lady in his company ever thinks whether he is ugly or not, so polished and agreeable is he.'

'What a contrast is his death's head and skeleton figure to Lord Mercia's full, blue-eyed fairness!'

'Types of the Saxon and Celt; but I suppose they would rather consider themselves descended from some Norman sea-cook of the Tanner's grandson.'

'But, Martel, I say, look at that outrageous swell! Who is he?'

'Oh, that is old Bunkum and Co., hunting for fashion. At present he is like his calicoes, of rather a loud pattern. Maybe he'll live to be some day as well bred as his horses, which are of a particularly good stamp, and cost a mint of money. You see we have here aristocracy, plutocracy, and mobocracy, like ourselves. There is your lawyer, a busy man, yet seeming busier than he is, as Chaucer says; and here is your squirette or squireen, a rustic mixture of Epicurean and Stoic, holding that a good house, with plenty of good eating and drinking, tempered by an excessive indulgence in field sports, is perfect felicity. And look at that jovial English lot beyond him—a slashing tailor, a crashing glazier, a bruising miller, and those fair ladies who can cut down many a scarlet-coated, buckskin-breeched gentleman. Here is the country doctor, ready to bind up broken bones, and there is a flight of young farmers, ready to break their bones for

honour, or for customers; they want to sell their
horses. Here, a dealer of the older sort, rusty-
coated, rusty-booted, and of fresh, clean-shaven
face; there, his modern brother, sallow and dissipated to view, with Hyperion curls and hat of the
newest fashion, and coat and breeches of a cut that
lords might covet, as they do, to their cost, the
horses that he rides. Like Chaucer's friar—in
that, if in nothing else—he "somewhat lisps for
wantonness, to make his English sweet upon the
tongue," when he is asking an alarming price. And
last, if not least, we have the outer circle of grooms
of all degrees, bravely clad in blue and green and
brown, and belted; mostly well-mannered, now and
then saucy. And on the outskirts of all, perched
upon every place of vantage in the surrounding
fields, is the peasant, ploughman, herd, blacksmith,
or mechanic, from village and town, with many a
wife and many a maid, and many more children—
unsophisticated human nature all agog for the hunting of the beast of the field. Chaucer's picture is,
as some say, though I do not believe them, the
creation of the poet's brain, for that his age was one
of feudal stateliness and restrictive ceremonial. But
his immortal sketch the hunting-field always brings
to my mind; and whether it be realistic or ideal,
true or fanciful, it is certainly true that on five or
six days of the week, from the beginning of Novem-
ber to the end of March, men of all orders and occupations may be seen assembled at the several meets
in the favoured counties of England, riding, talking,
joking, laughing together, as they do not in other

places, with all the freedom that consists with good
manners.   If there is any undue reserve it is between members of the different sets of the same
order.   Between the different orders of the state a
hunting-day is a day of reasonable liberty, equality,
and fraternity : fox-hunting and good-fellowship
go hand in hand.'

The lecture was stopped by a sonorous ' How do
you do, sir ?   I am glad to see you,' addressed to
Martel, *ore rotundo*, by a grey, fresh-looking man,
mounted on a large horse all in the rough, that
might be a valuable hunter, or might fit a van. The
rider, for a sportsman, was very carelessly, not to
say ill-dressed in a rough pilot-jacket and baggy
cord breeches, with unclean top-boots and a shocking bad hat.   As our friends came up, he was
announcing to some listeners, with bell-mouthed
clearness, that men betted and gambled and specu-
lated only through cowardice.

' They are cowards, sir ; they are afraid of work.
They dare not set themselves down, sir, like men,
to win their bread in an honest way.'

' Who is he ?' asked young Gryffyn of his companion.

' The famous Joe Hobson, the most successful
horse-dealer, and one of the best 'sportsmen and
cleverest fellows in England.   He is a great man
in his vocation—the tip-top of his profession—and
talks more to lords than to us little folk.   But I
have the honour of knowing him well.   I was his
pastor once, and a very good Churchman I found
him ; he never missed church, never was late, and

never missed responding, and always knew what the sermon was about. Let us stop and hear him ; he is a professed wag, and now and then his jokes are good, especially when they are in the way of business.'

'Hobson,' said one of the group, pointing with his whip, 'your man forgot to clean your boots this morning.'

'Ah, lazy dog ! he did not bring the broom to besom me down and make me smart, as I bid him, before I started a-hunting.'

'That's a goodish-looking nag you are on,' said another.

'Ya-ars, sir ; I dare say he might suit you. I believe he is a good horse ; but you, sir, are a better judge than I am.'

The better judge, looking into the mouth, and observing strong symptoms of antiquity, said :

'Rather long in the tooth, Hobson.'

'You must have length somewhere, sir, if you want a hunter,' replied Mr. Hobson gravely.

While the circle laughed, there pushed into it hurriedly and bluntly a sporting farmer, who, having in vain offered his horse throughout the last season to Mr. Hobson for one hundred and fifty pounds, and having always received for reply a shake of the head and ' Thick shoulders, Mr. Pugson—he has thick shoulders,' had at last sold the thick-shouldered beast for eighty pounds to Mr. Hobson, who had just re-sold him for three hundred and fifty.

'So you have found out that my horse had not thick shoulders !' broke in the disgusted Mr. Pugson.

'Oh-h, Mr. Pugson! you know I always told you that he had thick shoulders: a horse of his size and make must have thick shoulders, if he is to be a hunter and carry weight. You know I said he had thick shoulders, Mr. Pugson.'

The conclave laughed again, and the ever-ready Hobson, turning to a baronet, who had bought from a friend for an old song a horse for which his friend had paid Mr. Hobson a great deal of money, said:

'I congratulate you, Sir Arthur, on having got for a mere nothing an excellent hunter.' Here, happening to turn his head, he caught lowering on him the angry eye of his late dissatisfied customer; but nothing disconcerted, our rural debater proceeded: 'And you, sir, I congratulate also, upon having got out of your stable a horse that you hated.'

'Oh, that cunning old man! he is as crafty as a committee of convocation!' muttered the gentleman, who was a keen Puritan, and hunted priests as eagerly as foxes; while, on the motion of the pack towards the covert, the group dispersed to seek at the covert-side favourable points for observation and starting.

Hark! that long-drawn frantic note, almost a scream, which the first scent of a fox forces from the excited hound. The challenge is taken up, now here, now there, and Gaylass opens her throat responsive to the note of Brilliant, and now from all parts of the covert bursts a chorus of canine melody such as he who has not heard it can never imagine, and he who has heard it can never forget.

Now, gentlemen, keep wide open your ears and your eyes, sit down in your saddles, gather up your reins, and fix on your hats firmly. Jealous first-flight men are pushing for a start.)

'Hold hard !' storms the master; 'pray, gentlemen, hold hard !—you, sir,' speaking to an unmistakably flying clergyman, 'you, sir, must think your horse very slow to be so desperately "edgy."'

While it is thus with emulous riders, less ambitious men and better sportsmen, who love hunting and not steeple-chasing, and wish only to see sport, keep cool and watch, and miss no chance of viewing what goes on in the covert.

'Tally-ho ! gone away !' screams one.

Toot ! toot ! sounds the horn.

'Now, gentlemen, ride as hard as you like !' cries the master cheerily, as the pack has cleared the covert and is streaming away in the open ; and he, horn still in hand, in high satisfaction, puts his horse at the first fence. Now, you with raw horses and wild colts, and you who are raw horsemen, summon up all your nerve to meet your difficulties, or to hide your fears; this is capital training in self-control.

As in war, so in hunting : the soldier engaged sees little of the battle, and the hard-riding fox-hunter sees little of the chase beyond that which happens close to himself. Of the three hundred or four hundred riders, he is alive only to the existence of some half-dozen, whom fortune has favoured with a place at that corner of the covert where the fox broke away, and who have thus got off with the hounds. In a fox-hunt, as in life, a good start is half the

race : those who get it are clear of the ruck, and
can go at their leisure, and see their way, and choose
their ground, and pick their places in every fence
free from pressure ; while the crowd in the rear are
jostling and hustling and crushing and crossing con-
fusedly, and each gets in the other's way.   And yet
no degree of hurry and racing will bring those who
have started badly into the front rank until there is
a check ; or if by any struggles they could catch the
first started, they could not long keep pace with
them, since the previous exertions have exhausted
their horses.   The wiser part play the waiting game ;
patience and steady watching for their chance may
and often does right them in the end.

But none of these eager ones are the men from
whom you could learn the varying fortunes of the
day—they are the performers ; the observers and re-
corders and critics are the skirters and shirkers, who
seldom jump, and do not much like hard galloping.
The lookers-on here, as elsewhere, see the most of
the sport—like great commanders, they take up
their positions on every rising ground ; and they
will tell you how the hounds ran, racing with
Stubbleford and Stacksby right before them ; how
they turned, and Leigh was passed, and the Wharple-
down brook was crossed, with its muddy waters and
rotten banks, brimful from the late rains; how Horsey
and Junker jumped in, got out again on the one
side, while their horses emerged on the other, and
how Junker, light and active, stood upon his head
on the bank to let the water run out of his boots ;
how, heedless of these mishaps and of many more,

the pack swept swiftly on by pleasant Pigwell, a
land blithe with green pastures, which the red oxen
graze that were bred far away in the narrow, un-
sunned valleys of beautiful Devon; how the chase
tracked more slowly the leas of Thorpe, untouched,
by plough or harrow, and skirted the ruinous ascents
of Burgh; then turned to pass under the spreading
beeches and larches of sandy Summerton, and over
Calderton's stone walls, and by many a bridle-lane,
and over many a tangled thorn and yawning ditch,
reached the sweet meadows and grass-grown streets
of Asham—ancient, castellated, classic town, whose
memories, fraught with youthful pleasures, rustic
joy, and healthful sports, more pleasant learning,
and kind companions, are treasured dreams to many
of years long flown, that grey hairs, and chilled
blood, and the thickening infirmities of age cannot
make them forget so long as memory will work at
all in the chambers of the brain.

Let us follow our friend on the borrowed grey as
he gets away from the covert. A young, quickset
hawthorn hedge, uncut, and tall, and dark, fronts
him; a man in pink, grandly mounted, rides at it,
and sailing aloft through the thinnest " growers,"
disappears behind it, leaving no trace of his passage
through. The gallant grey follows, without thought
of refusing, rises about three feet from the ground,
and drags her rider's head through the thick of the
branches, and, despite his covering arm, lays his
cheek open with a thorn.

'You've been among the lawyers,' remarks a hard-
riding farmer to the bleeding victim of Diana.

But what cares he! The rapturous coursing of the blood through the frame, the flow of the spirits in him, who, long-chained to the musty desk, is once more mounted on the fiery-footed steed, sweeping unchecked through glorious green landscapes, marked by many a grey church-tower and many a brown copse—these delights, animal and spiritual, give new zest to existence, and expel black Care from the seat of the horseman.

Swish! bang! There goes the binder of Farmer Crump's fence! What cares he! Martel's grey has just got over the back-rail with a scrape of the hind legs. What cares he! A young lady, with streaming habit, comes flying over the post.

'You are steering very straight, Miss Sitwell.'

'My horse is rather taking his own way, Mr. Martel.'

What cares she! The grey is going racing pace, without trouble to herself or rider. Another flight of low rails and a ditch.

'What's that I hear?' says an old sportsman, who had been eyeing Martel's nag. 'Does the grey rap timber?'

The rider has his private misgivings. He is safe as yet, and thanks his stars that the fields are large, the fences have their weak places, and the company is select; while, behind the goodly shoulders of the swift-going grey, he sits at ease, as between the springs of a well-hung carriage, and surveys the exploits of the field. Not far off is a strong fellow pulling and hawling at his horse with main force and the cruelest of bits. Our philosopher knows the nag, and that a lady could ride him with a silken thread. 'That,' said he to himself, ' is your governing with vigour; there will presently be a rebellion and downfall.'

What a contrast is yonder flaxen-curled schoolboy, about fifteen years of age, sitting so still on that flying colt, while the hot Belzoni blood, unchastened by experience, is inclined to over-jump every fence. There! he is down at last. No; the stout boy keeps his seat, unmoved as a centaur, and picks up his nag after a lengthened scramble.

' You ought to have been off, sir,' cries an admiring veteran, intent to teach the young idea how to ride to hounds. ' You would have relieved your horse, and he would have got up quicker.'

How gallantly they go, those two young ones, taking each fence, as the watchful father, at a little distance, directs the son, with whip upraised and waving, like the conductor's wand in an orchestra. But oh! crash! smash! thud! What is this? The colt, in the act of rising, has thrown himself down upon a flight of rails that crown a bank. What means that? It means that there is a deep gravel-pit on the other side, and that the colt saw it, and stopped in time. Clever colt! But will that spoil your jumping courage? Probably; I believe history records that it did.

' It wasn't the hoss's fault, 'twere mine,' sputtered a grizzled, middle-aged grazier, creeping out of a ditch, with his mouth full of mud. ' If I'd ha' let him alone, he'd none ha' fallen, not he. He never made a mistake in his loife,' jabbered, in apology, the dismounted horseman, rising with his head through the crown of his hat, in hot zeal for the honour of his Irish favourite, and remounting with the alacrity of a lad, to recover lost laurels.

'Quite a day of adventure!' chuckled Martel, pleased with himself because his horse was fast.

See that all-accomplished horseman, Lord Heaton! He is charging a fence; it is plain that he tumbles on the other side. The grey, away to the left, tips the hedge in a weaker place, and lands in time to let her rider see what had happened. Close under the narrow bank whereon my lord should have landed is a pond, happily shallow. The horse falls into the trap, jumps a little too far, overpasses the bank, and rolls through the mud and water, heels over head, to the pond's mouth. My lord, ever awake, sees the situation before it is too late, drops from his horse upon the narrow ledge between the hedge and the water; quick as light, runs round the pond; picks up the prostrate steed, when he has rolled through the utmost slush; remounts him, and continues the run without losing twenty yards by the mistake.

'A clever performance, and worth the seeing,' thinks our curate. 'On other days I ride a nag that can jump anything in reason, and cannot gallop much; to-day I ride one that can gallop any pace, and cannot jump much. I begin to fancy that I see more of the fun upon the galloper—more of these first-flight men, any way.' Then, as he rode, he sang a stave of old St. Hubert's hymn:

'" I'm a hunting physician, can cure every ill,
  If you'll cry tally-ho, without bolus or pill."

'But, h'm! hah! hoh! What have we here? A
very ugly fence indeed! And now I wish I were on
my "jumping Judy." Well, I'm married to Sybil,
for better, for worse; so here goes.'

She pricks her ears, sets her head, and right
through the thickest of the hedge crashes the galloping grey, headlong into a great gully beyond.

Now look out, Mr. Martel, for your pate is in
peril! Over it are suspended in thin air four iron-
shod hoofs.

'Ridden over, by all that is unsportsman-like!
Are you hurt?' is the question.

'Not a bit, thank you,' is the response.

A moment's delay at this one not very practicable
spot in a most obstructive fence. The rider is up in
the twinkling of an eye, and has the grey, happily,
out of the ditch; remounts in a trice, a little shaken,
but none the worse.

'Ah! is that you, my gay fellow?' cries a gentleman in scarlet, coming alongside and looking into
our friend's face. 'I little thought you were the
man I was trembling for, when that tailor rode over
you. No harm done, I hope, my dear fellow?' looking at the wound on the cheek.

'An old scratch; I am all right. But, my dear
Franklin, what a pleasure! what a go! Where
have you dropped from?'

'I followed that white-trousered tinker that rode
over you, with the intention of killing him if he
killed you.'

5—2

'This is the best of hunting,' said the grey-coat; 'at least, it is one of its many good things, that one can't get a spill but he falls into the arms of some old friend: all one's old cronies turn up in the hunting-field some time or other. I would have undertaken ten such tumbles for the joy of seeing you. I have, in fact, fallen into a prime thing; if that fence had not turned me over, we might not have forgathered to-day, for you fellows behind would hardly have caught us first-flight men, you know.'

'You are the old boy still—all chaff and jaw. But what an age since we met!' said the new-comer. 'The last time was with the Puckeridge, and I found you then in much the same plight as you were in just now. I remember your nag had fallen over a bank upon your leg, and had pulled off one of your tops; and when I got over, you were squatting on the ground, tugging yourself black in the face to get your boot on again. In those days you sported pink.'

'And do you remember how we went home and dined together, with Vivian and Lomax? and how we talked of literature and Byron? and how we sickened old Max, and sent him to sleep? and how he woke up singing out, like King Richard, "Catch my horse!"'

'But what are the hounds doing? We have been getting slower and slower, and are come to about a walk.'

'Why, they have lost their fox—that's what it is. It is about over with us for to-day. Where have you put up your horses?'

'At the old crib—Jack Straw's Castle, at Cogsford.'

'Then just send word by your man that you'll not be there to-night, and come home with me and dine and sleep.'

'How far?'

'Oh, close—only about five miles.'

'All right.'

'You shall have curate's fare for once in your life; it will do you good—cool your blood, and rest your digestive organs. You can set it down as a fast-day: and we'll talk of old times.'

And so it was arranged.

CHAPTER IV.

'Wherein I spake of most disastrous chances,
  Of moving accidents by blood and field.'
                                        Othello.

'What I like about fox-'untin', my lord, is, that it brings
people together, as wouldn't otherwise meet.'
                            LEECH'S *Hunting Sketches.*

WHILE the incidents related in the last chapter were
occurring towards the front, the field was tailed off
to the length of two miles or more, where, far in the
rear, rode Dicky Gryffyn. He had been unlucky:
was on the wrong side of the covert when the fox
went away, and, trying to make up lost ground by
a short cut through a rough and impracticable place,
he got a fall, and had a stirrup-leather pulled off,
which had to be recovered and replaced. These
delays put him wholly out of the run for this turn,
and ancient skirters and boys and second horsemen
were the only folk in sight. He had nothing to do
but to listen for the cry of the hounds and follow
upon the track of the horsemen; to keep a good
look-out ride slowly and feel his way; to have his nag

fresh, and trust to some check or favouring turn of
the chase. From the pitch of a rising-ground he
espied presently a group, as it seemed, gathered
round some accident that had occurred at a brooklet
not far off in the valley. Here was at least something to do. Dick was a quick lad and long-sighted,
and soon saw what had happened. A lady's horse
had made a mistake at the drain, and had fallen.
The skirt of her habit had in the struggle got en-
tangled among the horse's legs, and was almost torn
off by the animal in the act of rising. A grey-headed
respectable-looking pad-groom was holding the horse
and waving back with effective authority some
common-looking riders whose delicacy was not fine
enough to restrain them from gratifying their curiosity by intruding upon the young lady; who, under
the horrible fear of having to masquerade it in the
tight, tailless costume of a page, was nervously en-
deavouring, without proper appliances, to refit the
heavy skirt to the body of her habit. Part of the
rent she had adroitly managed to repair, but the
rest seemed past her skill. A habit-skirt is of great
weight, and no ordinary pins are strong enough to
bear it.

Dicky divined the dilemma in a trice, and, snatch-
ing from the bird's-eyed and purple glories of his
silken neckcloth its huge onyx-headed fastening, he
beckoned to the pad-groom, and, saying who he
was, gave it for the use of his mistress.

With its Brobdignag aid the habit was soon sufficiently pinned up to allow of the young lady's remounting her false steed, and, having learnt from

her groom her deliverer's name, she mastered her nerves by a valorous effort, and rode forward frankly to thank him. She knew his father well, and had seen Dicky as a boy; but he was now a smart young man, and in so far a stranger that the situation was, under the circumstances, embarrassing. However, she got through her task with apparent case and undoubted grace; said that they were old friends, expressed surprise to find Mr. Gryffyn returned home just in time to render her help in the first trouble she ever had of this sort, made kind inquiries after his father, and, again thanking him for his timely and complete assistance, begged him to resume his sport and lose no more time, but follow the hounds, which must now be ever so far off. Altogether, she seemed as little discomposed as a young lady, who had just passed through an ordeal so trying to the nervous system, could be.

But, despite her feminine powers of dissimulation, Dick could perceive that she was a good deal shaken, and that, for all her valiant efforts to hide agitation under a cheerful manner, her spirits were nearly upset. Altogether, he thought that she wanted 'looking after,' as he expressed it to himself; so, relinquishing all idea of farther hunting that day, he gallantly proposed to see the lady safe home. And she, after some show of reluctance, accepted his escort, conscious of an uncomfortable possibility that his services might yet, in some way or other, be needed again.

And so it fell out that, instead of following the foxhounds that day, Dicky Gryffyn was destined by his fate to a quiet ride beside a young lady, to whom he had by good fortune been enabled to render some assistance, and whom, even under these most adverse conditions, he could not but feel with conscious pleasure to be more than commonly attractive.

After the first greeting and expression of her thanks she seemed scarcely to look at him, but, from the top of his Lincoln-and-Bennet to the sole of his well-made boot, nothing had escaped her eye, and the verdict of her taste upon the survey was, 'Neat and nice.'

In order to effect a diversion, under cover of which her nerves might be composed and she forget her disaster, Dick, profiting by his French education, exerted himself to find small talk, and chattered away as well as he could about everything and nothing; told of his private tutor in England, of his subsequent schooling in France, of his terms at Trinity, Cambridge, and of his return home to settle down into a farmer, whose talk must be of beeves and of crops.

Though but a farmer's boy (as, it is too true, she called him in her heart), she allowed that he was agreeable, well-bred, and good-looking. Under the easy flow of his cheery chat her nerves recovered their tone, and dialogue took the place of monologue.

'Do you know, Mr. Gryffyn, that I have my doubts whether you know who it is to whom you have played the Good Samaritan, though I reminded you that we are old friends?'

H'm—haw! Mr. Gryffyn must confess his great

stupidity; he had a sort of recollection—er—that is, he had not quite the pleasure of remembering.

'Can I help you to call to mind Miss Palmer?'

To be sure! How could he be so dull? He felt all along that he ought to know, and in a way he did, only his memory was so treacherous.

The young man had good taste enough to restrain the commonplace compliment that rose to his lips, and which with some ladies he would have uttered glibly enough, about the impossibility of forgetting, and so forth; but for a youngster he was a fair judge of times and persons, so he turned the conversation with the indifferent and almost abrupt question:

'Do you hunt much, Miss Palmer?'

'I do not hunt at all, Mr. Gryffyn. I see you look at my poor habit in surprise; but it is true. I am never more than a distant and admiring spectator of the sport. I have the pleasure of a scamper over the fields, and sometimes, not often, the excitement of a mishap—not such as to-day's, though. I see a great deal that amuses me, from a safe and respectful distance. Good John Bromby here'— turning to her grey-headed groom—'good John Bromby has been at this sport so long that I believe he knows the mind of every fox in the county, and every bridle-road and gap; and he generally contrives to post me where I can overlook the hunting without getting in the way of the huntsmen. I should have seen it all very well to-day, had not this naughty Tom Thumb done what, I must say for him, he never did before.'

'My experience is small, to be sure,' said the gentleman, 'but I think that the meets of such first-class packs as this must be among the finest sights of Europe. I suppose, though you do not hunt, Miss Palmer, you go to the meet to see it.'

'I have been to the meet now and then, and, being a great lover of horses, I agree with you that the display is superb; but I never venture near the meet unless papa is with me, and seldom then.'

'Do you disapprove of it?'

'Well, I do not wish to be prudish, nor affect to be better than my neighbours; but it is my, perhaps foolish, idea that ladies are in the way at that sort of place. My way is to look on slily from a distance, like our dear old friend, Addison's Spectator. I see more, and am seen less, which is an advantage both ways in ladies' eyes, whatever gentlemen may be pleased to think of them.'

'I suppose Mr. Palmer is a great sportsman?'

'No, indeed; he would disclaim the fair honour of being a sportsman, as well as the doubtful honour of being a sporting man.'

'But he is very fond of hunting, is he not?'

'Indeed, I do not think he is. With him hunting is more of a mechanical habit than an active liking. He has been used to it ever since he was a child and could sit upon a Shetland pony. And I am sure he would miss it very much, and would perhaps suffer in his health from the want of it; but he says, and I think most justly, that he does not really hunt, either according to the ancient or the modern meaning of the word. He does not like clubs, and company in stuffy rooms, but he is sociable, and dearly loves to meet his friends in the green fields under the sky. He enjoys the air, and the ride, and the nice horses; but the great attraction for him is the meeting of people from all quarters twice a week, and hearing the first news of everything that is going on in the London world, and seeing often some of the celebrities of Europe. Papa calls our hunting-field the catholic meeting. He declares it is the best and the least exclusive club in England or in the world, and the only one where may meet together his royal highness the prince and his honour the sweep of the next town, and representatives of every grade between them. That is papa's view of the hunting-field; and that, Mr. Gryffyn, is one reason why I do not, unless very well protected, venture to the meet—an abstinence which papa quite approves. But, as I said before, I see a great deal that amuses me from afar, thanks to the admirable pilotage of good John Bromby here.'

'And now,' said Dick gaily, suppressing a sigh, 'we are close to Finchdale, and you are safe home. So I may leave you in better hands, and go to gladden the heart of my father, who is so irregular when I am away that he may be at dinner when I get back.'

'But, Mr. Gryffyn, you positively must take some luncheon with us. You surely will not have taken this long ride, and have given up your day to me, and sacrificed all your sport, and then refuse our hospitality! Papa would never forgive me for not bringing you in. It is the Bench day, but he has promised to be home early. Besides, you must come to recover your property that has been of such use to me,' she added, smiling.

There was for Dick no declining, if he had really wished it, which he did not. Only he thought it proper to make some affectation of excuse, per- haps, because he was anxious to accept the invita- tion.

'Oh, Barba, dear, how late you are! And, oh, what is the matter?' exclaimed a veiled lady, upon whom they came suddenly, as they emerged from a bridle-road into the village street.

'Ah, Kitty, you are very cunning! I believe you are a witch; but I cannot stop to tell you my adventures now. Let me introduce to you Mr. Gryffyn. My cousin, Miss Fisher; who is to thank you for taking care of me and so politely return- ing me safe.'

The veil bowed, and the hat came off to salute it; but the introduction put a stop to conversa- tion till the party arrived at the rectory.

They were not long seated at luncheon when a gentleman entered the room in haste, went up to Miss Palmer, and, taking both her hands in his, said hurriedly:

''I could not be so near you, Barbara, without coming to shake hands with you. Your father I left at Mudford. He desired me to tell you that he was detained on magistrate's business, and would not be home till evening.'

He who said this was a pale, bronzed man, seemingly about five-and-thirty years of age, in features no way noticeable, unless for a fine brow, swelling out upwards at the temples, and giving or enhancing a general air of refinement, which Gryffyn, young and raw as he was, felt at once; and felt jealous of it.

'And now I have said "How d'ye do?" I must say good-bye, or I shall miss my train.'

So saying, the new-comer made a sort of sweeping general reverence to the company, whom he had not before noticed, and left the room, accompanied by Miss Palmer, who, excusing herself to the others, went to see him off, and on her return, said:

'That is our cousin, Colonel Edward Denny, of the Guards. He has just returned from Egypt. He was in so great a hurry that I could not introduce him, but he is coming to us next week; and to tell us that seems to be all he came for now.'

'No, Barbara dear; he said particularly that he came to shake hands with you.'

'Did he, dear? I forgot it; and that, to be sure, was very wrong of me.'

'And he overlooked us altogether,' added Miss Fisher, looking towards Mr. Gryffyn.

'And that was very wrong of him. You shall tell him so, Kitty, when he comes to us next week.'

When Dicky Gryffyn had taken his leave, which he did soon after this interruption, Miss Fisher began at once.

'Now that he is gone, dear, do tell me who is that young man, and what is it all about? Eh, dear?'

'Dear, I told you his name is Gryffyn. You have seen his father.'

'He is very good-looking.'

'The father, dear, or the son ?'

'He looks very nice.'

'Indeed, he seems very nice, and pretty behaved, dear. Shall I tell him you think so ?'

'But what brought him here, Barbara ? And what was all that about his neck-scarf, and the onyx pin that you gave him ? Eh, dear ? I don't understand it at all.'

'You must know, then, that I got a tumble to-day. That naughty little Tom Thumb spilt me on a bank over a little brook, and then set his foot on my habit, and nearly tore off my skirt—almost made a page of me like Mysie Happer, you know, among all those horrid men, dear.'

'Among all the gentlemen !'

'Ah, no, Kitty dear, not so bad as that; but among the farmers and grooms, and that sort of thing. But they were not very near, you know. John Bromby—you can fancy John's dignity—made them keep a respectful distance, till young Gryffyn, who is but a boy, you know, dear, rode up just in time to help John Bromby and poor me, who were at our wits' end. We did not know what in the world to do. I got so hot ! Imagine the position, my dear ! I thought I should have fainted, or gone off into fits, or into hysterics, or something of that sort.'

'You are not very likely to give way to anything, my dear.'

'I hope not, I hope not, Kitty; but it was so horrid ! I had hard work to keep up, when that good little hippo-Griff was sent flying to my aid. My difficulty, you know, was to pin up, to " fix," as the Americans say, my habit-skirt.'

' Oh, how dreadful !' said the tragic little cousin ; and she put up her clasped hands, and turned up her eyes.

' And that, dear, is the history of the onyx pin, about which you are so inquisitive,' proceeded the other calmly. ' Whatever we should have done without it I am sure I do not know ! But it was large enough and strong enough to hold the main-sail of a man-of-war in a gale !'

And then she told all the story that we know.

' A very gallant cavalier, I protest !' said Tragedy ; ' and handsome too, and very well-mannered, dear, and speaks nicely.'

' Yes, indeed ; nicely enough to give orders to the farm-labourers about the pigs, dear.'

' Yes, dear, but he can talk to ladies too.'

' Indeed, dear, he seems to be too well brought up to spend his days in talking to clodpoles, as he is likely to do.'

' Is he indeed ? But I know, Barbara, you are only saying that to provoke ; for it is not at all your usual way of speaking. Will he call again, dear ?'

' Indeed, dear, I do not know.'

' No matter. Shall we walk into the village, and see your old people—your " clod-poles," you know —since you have changed your dress ?'

' Kitty dear, I am so glad you have found your tongue ; you know you let all the entertainment of this very polite young gentleman fall upon me, dear.'

This dialogue was followed by another in the course of the afternoon tea. The two ladies had long sat wrapt in reverie, when Miss Fisher broke silence.

'Now, dear, do tell me, what do you really think of him ?'

'Of Cousin Edward ?' asked Barbara, startled by the question.

'No, dear, I know what you think of him ; but I mean of your deliverer, Mr. Gryffyn.'

'I told you, dear, that I think him a nice boy—too nice for a farmer's boy, as he is, you know, Kitty.'

'Farmer's boy! Indeed, Barbara, I think you give him very little credit ; yet all his attention was directed to you.'

'To say the truth, dear, I did not mind him much.'

'I am sure he made himself very agreeable.'

'Did he, dear ? I was thinking of other things.'

'Other people, you mean ; but I doubt whether your thoughts were employed on any one nicer,' spoke Kitty, with shrewish intent.

'Those are your sentiments, are they, dear ?'

'I think his manners very gentle, and his dress and address equally in good taste, and that he is a nice little man altogether,' stoutly spoke up the fair advocate, piqued into warmth by the other's coldness.

'Yes, dear, I think he is very like other young men ; he seems a good kind of boy. And since you

will not have him a farmer, he may pass muster
very well among the crowd of country fox-hunters,
dear.'

'I think, dear, you are very provoking, and very
ungrateful to forget the help he gave you in that
horrid situation, and the nice way in which he did
it, as you yourself said.'

'There, dear, don't tell me any more; I know
all about it. See what it is to dispraise a gentleman
to a lady! I was only doing it to try you, dear.
Indeed, Kitty, I think it will do very nicely; you
have my vote and interest, dearest, I am sure. It is
well to have a perfect understanding, is it not, Kitty,
dear?'

You see, dear reader, that the hunting at Finchdale was anything but a '*fast*' affair; it was, as
Barbara told Dicky Gryffyn, a steady-going habit,
as humdrum and uneventful in its way as the daily
dinner. And so for Mistress Barbara to get a tumble,
and bring home to luncheon the unknown knight
who had rescued her, set the whole house agog.

'What was that young gent's name?' Mr. Trimmer
the butler, did not catch it, though he tried hard
and he wondered how Miss Barbara came to bring
home a strange gent to luncheon when master
was not at home. 'And Colonel Donny neither
didn't know him, for I took partic'lar notice,' said
Mr. Trimmer; 'nor Miss Barbara didn't introjuce
him neither,' added the aggrieved butler.

Then John Bromby came in and told his tale
and Miss Janet, the housemaid, said it would be a
match, she'd be bound for it; and James, the foot-

man, laughed and winked at Miss Janet; and Miss Janet, seeing Mr. Bromby, said:

'La, Mr. Bromby! is that you? How do you do? How funny you do walk, Mr. Bromby!'

'Well, then, it's ridin' as does it,' says Mr. Bromby.

'It looks as though it was so funny like. But, Mr. Bromby, do you think that nice young Mr. Gryffyn will marry our young missus? He has such be-au-tiful hair—quite gold-like! and such a lovely white skin! I seed him through the window as he took off 'is 'at, agoin', so polite to the ladies; I'm sure they liked him.'

And John Bromby said, 'Yes, he was a nice young gent, so he was, and rode a nice nag too; but the winner of that 'ere match wouldn't have hair of the colour of young Gryffyn's, he reckoned.'

Mrs. Tebbits, the housekeeper, who did not descend all at once to the gossip of the servants' hall, when she heard what had happened, said, Miss Barbara was as keen as some older folk, and was a bird that would take a good deal of catching, if Mrs. Tebbits knew anything.

And pretty, graceful Miss Primrose Barbara's maid, who, without offensive pride, shyly held aloof from the rest of the household, thinking, it may be, that she was likely to know her mistress's mind as soon as that young lady knew it herself, having heard all, said nothing, but tripped lightly up the stair, singing—

Mayhap the lad will fancy me, and disappoint ye a'.'

CHAPTER V.

'What's that, Bosola?—I knew him in Padua,— a fantastical scholar.'—WEBSTER, *Duchess of Malfi.*

'Sectarians have said much about our incumbents being in the commission of the peace or fox-hunters ; thoughtful men have shaken their heads, and come to the conclusion that it cannot be helped ; the English are an active, not a studious, race. And Divinity professors have been for years doing what they could to revive the taste for reading. Now, it is strange that, amid all this accusation, all this regret, all this endeavour, it seems to have been forgotten that reading implies books. . . . There is no sense in reading nonsense ; and we may be sure, if men make up their minds to sacrifice society, and outdoor amusements, and active employments, that they will not do so for the drudgery of reading newspapers, periodicals, novels, annuals, Exeter Hall Divinity *et id genus*, unless they be very ascetically disposed. . . . They will read Hooker, Taylor, Barrow, etc.'—J. H. NEWMAN.

'How do you do, Captain Golightly ?'

'And how does Mr. Martel ? Why, how you have been knocked about!' added the captain, looking at his friend's disfigured face.

'I am not so bad as I look ; 'tis but a scratch of the lawyers, as some one said.'

'I don't know any scratch so venomous as the real thing. Don't get your head in Chancery—keep clear of that, whatever you do; better have your eyes scratched out in bullfinches—eh? But what is this—my old grey!'

'A neighbour's—Mr. Gryffyn gave me a mount.'

'Aye, to be sure—that's the name, Gryffyn. He bought her—I should say begged her—of a small dealer that I set to sell her. He got her far too cheap. I think I saw the son on a nice, well-bred light-weight chestnut at the meet—a neat-looking lad, in brown; I have not seen him since, though. I should like to sell him another horse. I suppose he will have all old Gryffyn's tin?'

'I'm sure I don't know. Mr. Gryffyn has a daughter or two, I believe, by his first wife, married to gentlemen in your profession that emigrated to Canada in the large way.'

'They tell me the father is as rich as a Jew—has no end of money.'

'No doubt he is well off; but he knows the value of money, and does not care to give too much for horses.'

'Ah, that's a shame! Worth a couple of hundred thousand, isn't he?'

'I should have supposed about fifty or sixty; if you count himself in, he is worth any sum you like —more precious than rubies.'

'But he is an agent as well as farmer, isn't he? And agents and thistles, you know, thrive everywhere. You know Lord Tomblemere? Well, he is about done up, and has to sell his horses. He called on his agent t'other day, and the man of business was rising in a hurry to receive his lordship. "Sit down, sir, pray sit down ; as you rise I fall," said my lord. Uncommon sharp that, eh ? I take it old Gryffyn mints money.'

'I dare say he does ; but he never told me more than he tells every one else—that he started in life with a borrowed capital of seven thousand pounds.'

'Oh, bedad ! credit is capital, sure enough ! I'd like somebody to lend me seven thousand ; I'd be as rich as "Crazes," as Paddy says. Or if I were only an agent ! Those are the lads to get money, like your good Gryffyn. He soon payed off his seven thousand, I'll be bound for it.'

'I dare say he did ; but he does not think of agencies as you do. He bawled out to me one day, rubbing his hands with glee, as eight waggons were hard at work carrying off his wheat crop, " That's what I like to see, parson ! Rot the rubbishing agencies, I say !'

'And what I say is, that he ought to have given me more for my grey. I only got fifty for her, and she is thoroughbred, with hackney action, and can do anything—walk, trot, gallop, what you like.'

'Yes, she is a prime hack—can gallop all day any pace, and her style is like going on velvet, captain, and she never refuses ; but—let these honourable scars bear witness—does she ever rise at her fences above two feet and a half ?'

'Ah-h-h !' laughed the gallant captain, 'you have found it out, have you ? She does NOT rise at her fences ; if she did, she would not have been sold for fifty pounds. As it is, I pitched hard into the cad who sold her for me, or rather sold me.'

'Gryffyn tells me the man did the best he could. He was a fellow of infinite fun. He first put the young un upon some rips of his own, and at last brought out your nag. " There, sir," said he, as he mounted the Gryffyn on the gallant grey, " now you look noble and grand; there's no hearl hin hall Hingland looks more 'andsome!" " She has not string-halt, has she?" asked little Gryffyn doubt-fully. " Yes, sir, she 'as string-'alt hall round, sir; can pick her teeth with her fore-feet, sir—leastways could if she had fingers as well as nails." '

' Well, well, a joke is a joke; but he sold her and me too:—that is no joke, though she did scratch your face. The fact is, between ourselves, she IS BETTER for the road and for harness than for hunting.'

'You see, captain, if she had been kept to her trade I should not have had the felicity of meeting you to-day,' said Martel. 'Good-bye! I see my friend; I am off. We have a few miles to ride home.'

' Fare you well; and take care of your beauty!' cried the horsey captain.

When they got to Fulmere, Martel packed off his friend to the public-house, to provide a night's lodging for his horse. By the way he had been sorely perplexed about providing the night's lodging for the rider. To ask him home was easy and pleasant; but to make comfortable a young gentle-man, who was in the habit of spending on himself some eighteen hundred pounds a year or more, was not so easy. So thought Martel, as he stood con-templating his primitive bedroom, far worse than

most garrets, and his thin, loose, ill-filled bed of
chaff, and nothing more. ' No,' thought he, ' the
swell could never sleep on that. It would not be
fair to ask him.' He had forgotten the differences
and fitnesses of things. What was to be done ?

In the village lived one Mrs. Rudge, who now and
then took in for him the stray visitors that came to
the curate at rare intervals. Mrs. Rudge was in her
way a wonder of a woman. She was once maid-of-
all-work in the small public-house. As she was
riding home upon a load of hay in harvest, her un-
adorned charms took captive the heart of a gallant
ex-colonel of cavalry. The world, in its wisdom and
virtue, had pronounced him good-for-nothing; but
he showed himself good for more than it thought.
He married the buxom, tattered young maid, and
made her an excellent husband. She had a good
head, but outwardly uncombed and inwardly un-
furnished : he combed and furnished it. She had a
good heart, and he cherished it, and, in so doing, reformed his own life. He was past middle age when
he married; and dying, in his appointed course, he
left to his relatives what was due to them, and to
her enough to live on comfortably, without tempt-
ing fortune-hunters into mad pursuit of the widow's
hand and purse. She, wise woman, married among
her own people a worthy cousin of her own; and,
as she had by her neighbours, who with good cause
respected her, been in her first wifehood and widow-
hood invested with the half-military title of Mrs.
Colonel Gruggen, so, when she married again, her
second husband was honoured, in right of her, with

the full military title of Colonel Rudge ; being, in
fact, a retired copying clerk, and a most upright
man. Together, the pair did a vast deal of good ;
and, among the rest, relieved now and then the
cubicular needs of the curate's more fastidious
guests.

To Mrs. Rudge, then, wrote Martel thus :

'A friend of mine is come, and I have nothing for
him to pig in but my own litter of straw, with et
cæteras to match, which are good enough for me,
but not for him, who has lived in the lap of luxury
upon the fat of the land. I would ask you to take
him in for a night at your own house but for
reasons that will keep. If you will kindly lend
me a bed, with the appurtenances thereof, and
send it down by the bearer in his donkey-cart,
you will oblige

   ' Your fleeced and fleeceless pastor,

       'C. MARTEL.'

By dint of borrowing wine from Mr. Gryffyn, and
other accessories and appliances here and there, not
quite a lord mayor's feast, but a cosy hermit's dinner
was set out, and it was eaten with hunter's appetite. Old times furnished talk, old memories
opened both hearts. At last the pair, well-pleased,
turned to the fire (the poorest had a fire in those
days), and took two high-backed, wooden chairs,
which were the nearest approach to ' easy ' that
the cottage afforded ; for the curate rather piqued
himself upon being hardy—

'Like some that cannot sleep on feather-beds,
But must have blocks for pillows.'

'So here you are, my dear old friend,' said the host, rubbing his hands, and gazing on his guest, as if to make sure of his identity. 'The sound of your voice made my heart leap this morning; for, living much in solitude, I am one to ponder over the days of yore, and the friends that adorned them. I ever felt that we should meet again, and discuss poetry, philosophy, and fox-hunting once more.'

'And I,' said the other, 'was very delighted to pick you up, as it were, my dear Martel, and to find you, after all, hard at the old sport, in spite of those financial difficulties which, as I remember, used to trouble you, in anticipation, long ago.'

'And you, Franklin? What are you about now beside hunting? What is your line?'

'Well, you see, my friends, being a strict sort of people, thought it right and respectable that, since my bread was ready buttered for me, I should do something by way of seeming to earn it. I was paid for my work beforehand, they said; and so I was—for more than I shall ever do, I am sure, and paid far too much, I dare say. So acquiescing, like a good boy, in their reasoning, I went to Lincoln's Inn to study law, with a view to practising as a barrister some day, should I ever get a chance, and so to make my farthing candle shine in the world. But, you see, it would only be living a life I don't like for money I don't want. Who is it says that for a barrister bad port and bad jokes are the

rule till forty—or is it fifty ?—and then success is—
gout and a coronet ?   In short, to be a lawyer you
must cease to be a man, live like a hermit, and work
like a horse. Now though I like bad jokes, and even
bad port, when I can't get good, I should not like
gout, and I don't care a rush for coronets, or county
courts either; but I do like hunting, and I have no
taste for a hermitage, unless it be one like this, where
I find a Friar Tuck. Freedom and moderation in
all things for me, and a humane and sociable life.
Upon due reflection, therefore, I did as so many of
my betters have done before me—read law three
years, and then shut my books, took a tour abroad
to enlarge my mind and polish my manners, as you
see ; and then, like a giant refreshed, I resumed my
study of the free and noble science of fox-hunting.
And on the strength of my vast legal acquirements,
I believe, and my agricultural importance, I have
been made a magistrate; and so my farthing candle
is to give light to the world, after all, with other
farthing candles. Why not ?'

The guest paused, and the host, eyeing him with
something like good-humoured envy, asked, with a
sigh :

' Now, you that live in the world, what news can
you tell me ?   Do you ever see any of the old lot ?'

' I have no news of much interest, though I have
been knocking about ; I am stupid : and somehow
the old set have not come in my way. I did
stumble on Redgate t'other day. He had thought
proper to re-educate himself at the sister University ;
and, as his brain was not so capacious as to need a

new course of books to fill it, I have a horrible suspicion that the red hood, on the beauty of which for
processional purposes he descanted largely, had something to do with his migration. He has contracted
very prim—I beg your pardon, I ought to say very
ecclesiastical—manners, and very unlike yours, my
friend. Otherwise, I do not perceive much change
in him. He told me that Hookey Walker was at
last going into holy orders, after your example.'

'And Bromage, have you seen anything of him?'

'Not for an age; so I fear we must conclude that
poor old Brom still sticks to the downward course,
which doubtless he finds agreeable. I should immensely like to see him all the same.' As the guest
spoke, his eye was roving round the room. It took
in all the seven and a half feet of whitewashed wall,
and the red-brick floor with the two yards square of
carpet under the deal table, and the scrap of rug before the wee fireplace. 'Rather different this, old
fellow, from your rooms at St. Jerome's, eh?' was
the summary of his observations.

'Aye, indeed,' replied the curate. 'They won't
stand brick floors in national schools; but you see,
I, a graduate of a great University, am a hewer of
wood and drawer of water to the Church of England
as by law established.'

'Yes, old Marty; those times are bygone when a
hunting day cost you five pounds by the time your
dinner was eaten and paid for. I suppose you now
earn five pounds in about three weeks. I declare I
am astonished to find such wretched pittances contenting the working clergy; it is a complete proof

of the unworldliness of your cloth in a country like this, where poverty is held infamous by the world at large.'

'I do not think some of us, any way, are very worldly. The grandees say that they assimilate our circumstances to those of the Apostles; only they forget that the Apostles' education came by a miraculous gift, and did not cost two thousand pounds. Well, well, when I entered the ministry I knew its conditions, and that, having no interest or rational hope of advancement, I was taking a vow of perpetual poverty as surely as any·monk ; and so far as the external conditions of the ministry remain the same, I have no right to complain of them. My eyes were wide open to the fact that I was sacri ficing all my worldly prospects.'

'You thought you had a " call ?" '

'What I considered a providential call ; and, rightly or wrongly, I gave up my own views to the demands of those to whom Providence had given claims upon me. God calls us now, I take it, not by voices or visions of the night, but by daily events and circumstances. That was my view, and I do not repent of it ; on the whole, I have been and am happy. I am proud of the *past* of our Church, at all events.'

'I see ; there are your ecclesiastical chiefs, like penates in little engravings, upon your wall.'

'Not chiefs ; I stick to my order, which embraces nearly all the heroes from Hooker to Keble.'

'Who is that jolly, bluff, shrewd-looking old fellow ?'

' Old Fuller.'

' And that lean-looking lad ?'

' Erasmus.'

' And that solid, bold, sardonic visage, whose is it ?'

' South's.'

' That grave, handsome face ?'

' Barrow's.'

' But see I not the jovial company of playwrights too ? I am sure that is Ben Jonson.'

' Yes, poet, philosopher, divine, grammarian—what you like.'

' And there is the Catholic element in miniature —Raphael's Madonna della Seggiola, that I saw at the Pitti Palace ; and there, quite promiscuous and as large as life, Herring's steeplechase cracks—Lottery, Pilot, and Sailor. Rather a scratch pack yours, old fellow, and betokening the natural and acquired tastes of the owner. But here are some more in the corner. That must be Jeremy Taylor ?'

' Yes, my one bishop.'

' And that, I know, is Swift's fine head, from the bust in St. Patrick's Cathedral. These be thy saints, O Israel !'

' As for saintliness, my friend, any old woman who cannot even read, but is true to her light, may be as good a saint as the best. Please to observe that those are not there as saints, but as luminaries who have lightened our darkness. Genius is one thing, conduct is another ; they may be joined, or they may be separate. I am taught by the wisdom of Balaam, who was no saint.'

'Well, of your Swift there I would say, he may be a genius, but he was an uncommon bad one.'

'Aye, yes, so say Macaulay and Jeffrey and Thackeray; so says *not* Grattan, or Scott, or Mackintosh, or Coleridge, or Bulwer-Lytton. I am satisfied to say, with Grattan, that "Swift was on the wrong side in England; but in Ireland he was a giant."'

'And what a muddle our friend Thackeray made of his figure!'

'A great artist may not be, after all, the man to measure giants. Swift was a thorough Churchman; if he had not been, we should have heard less of his errors. He was never forgiven for saying that "the Reformation, in every country where it was attempted, was carried out in the most impious and scandalous manner that can possibly be conceived; to which unhappy proceedings we owe all the reproaches that Roman Catholics have cast upon us ever since."'

'But wasn't he a turncoat pure and simple?'

'According to Macaulay, who could never discriminate between Church and State. Mackintosh, more discerning, remarks that Swift was always ac ecclesiastical Tory, even when he was politically a Whig.'

'I should not call him an ecclesiastic at all. Did not he take orders simply for bread?

'If you ask for information, certainly not; because a clerkship in the Rolls (at least as good as a living) was offered to him by or through Temple, and a captaincy of horse was offered to him by King William.'

'Wasn't he much fitter for either than for a Churchman?'

'Well, I don't know. The Romanists have a wider idea of churchmanship than we Protestants have; they would have known what to do with Swift, as with all men of all gifts. No doubt his right place was not in a Puritanic or in the Reformed Church. With the Catholics he would have been a Wolsey, a Richelieu, a Mazarin. "Swift was a king fit to rule in any time or empire," is the reluctant confession of one of his narrowest critics. But he was a man morbid and fitful of spirit; in the cast of his genius and in the circumstances of his life, not unlike Dante; whom he resembled too in his plain, nervous, concise style, in the, often painful, exactness of his descriptions, and in that *sæva indignatio* which has been miscalled savage misanthropy, and is perhaps almost righteous malignity. He is, I think, the nearest English approach to the great Italian. In short, he was so great and so unhappy, that I would

> ' " Be to his faults a little blind,
> And to his virtues very kind."

Mr. Fox, with that kindly wisdom which is his special charm, used to say that no one could be unamiable who wrote so much nonsense. You see you have touched a hobby of mine.'

'I know you well; nothing was ever too paradoxical for you.'

'I do like to see both sides of a question; and I confess to a weakness for genius struggling with adverse conditions and characters full of contradictions, like Ben and Sam Jonson, or Johnson and Jonathan Swift. As the representative of two attainted and ruined families, I have sympathy with infirmity and misfortune.'

'Well, who is that other stout clerical gentleman ?'

'Robert Hall.'

'What, the Baptist ?'

'I would rather call him a Catholic Christian— a man worthy to be classed with our best.'

'Your taste for prints is Catholic too.'

'You mean not over-nice, since these miserable little abortions do not come amiss to me. They are in the very small way, like my fortunes; but I do not seem to know a man until I have seen him or what is called his likeness.'

'You have a most venerable selection—I may say collection—of books.'

'Say select, for a good many of them are not to be had every day; they cost me many a weary walk, and many a shilling that I could ill spare. I have been, almost ever since I last saw you, picking them up at my price, and even then they have about tithed my clerical income.'

'Five hundred volumes, I should guess.'

'Not quite, very nearly.'

'And they do not quite hide the fair beauty of your walls, but very nearly.'

'What company have I five days out of the seven but that of dead authors ? I try, therefore, to have them select, reputable, and, though last, certainly not least, agreeable. After all, where should I go to find better company? These gentlemen are the flower of our land.'

'With all this good company at home, do you dine out much ?'

'I go for flesh and blood's sake when folk ask me; and that is not so often as they did once upon a time. I am more lazy; and society is less hospitable: times do not mend in that more than in other respects as one grows older. I fancy, though I do not see enough of it to have an opinion, but I seem to see that country society is getting cut up by railways into many distinct and almost hostile sets; I know I have not now many houses open to me that I care to enter, beside those of my early friends who are left. And so, you see, I read and think more, and eat and drink and talk—less; save when I catch a friend like you to exercise my rusty tongue upon, and then, as you perceive, there is no end of it.'

'I wonder that you, with your love of books, did not read more at college, and go in for a fellowship. To be sure, you may say the same of me; but unfortunately, so to speak, I knew that I was to come into a rude sort of plenty at some early day, and meanwhile I had enough to go on with, and so—and so— But you—had your way to make.'

'True, but every house has its skeleton; and those masterful circumstances that God calls providences, and men call mischances, regulated my finances. Nobody knows how much I was kept on promises, and how little coin I ever saw the colour of, during my first three terms. A little windfall

came to me in the second year, when it was too late
to read for honours. You know, one of the wise
ordinances of our University in our day was that a
man should not be allowed to take honours in the
classics unless he had first taken them in mathematics at an extra cost of one hundred pounds a
year for private tuition, books, etc., etc., without
which the idea of a fellowship was moonshine to
the best of men—a capital scheme for making idle
half the " Humanities " men.'

'But some of your belongings are well up the
ladder—rather grand, ain't they ? Could not they
have lent you a helping hand ?'

'They are a little too high up the ladder for me
to reach them ; and, to tell you the truth, I have
never been under the roof of one of them since I was
ten years old. Up to that time I was pretty
well cared for ; mighty little since. But it was just
the impulse of that small start that has kept me
going until now, such as I am—on the borders of
gentility. I am not just a gentleman, you perceive,
but I know one when I see one ; so you need not
be afraid you are not appreciated. As the old play
puts it :

> ' " What tell you me of gentry ? 'Tis nought else
> But a superstitious relic of times past.
> And sift it to its true working, it is nothing
> But ancient riches : and in me you know
> They are pitifully on the wane." '

'I hope to see them,' said the other, ' like the
moon, wax after waning. Shall we have you at the
boat-race in London ? That is the great place of
meeting for old college pals. It was my grand day

of the year when I was "sapping" mildly at the Bar, and I go there still to see every one I know or have known. I hope to see you there; you were a boating man before I knew you.'

'Yes; you know ours was a small college. We did famously my first year: won six places in two races, got up high on the river, and covered ourselves all over with perspiration and glory; and I, rowing number seven, thought myself no less than a University swell. Next year we were short of hands, and it was all down hill with us. I was a goose ever to have given up cricket to row on a muddy ditch. Well, I made my bow to the boats, and just then came the little windfall, and I took to horses, so far as a poor man could, and far more than he should. However, I had the happiness through that respectable introduction to become acquainted with your virtues.'

'But you were great at the gloves, were you not ?'

'If to be buffeted for an hour or two a day by professors of the noble science, and to drink porter out of pewter with Dutch Dick and Black Sambo, our tutors, is to be great, then was I great. Ah! but we were in racing condition in those days, and trod the earth as light as corks, or, rather, walked on air;—physically, Greeks; intellectually, very much the other thing. But what are boats and gloves to horses and hounds, and hunting, of all recreations the cream ! Not short, and violent, and partial, monotonous and damp, like boat-racing; nor stuffy and dusty, and, though neat, cribbed, cabined, and confined, like boxing; but varied and continuous, wholesome and airy; stretching, not straining every muscle of the frame, flushing the whole system with fresh, sweet air, delighting the eyes and the ears, exercising the wit, bracing the nerves, cheering the spirits, and making a man of one—for the time, anyway.

> ' " Better to hunt in fields for health unbought,
> Than fee the doctor for a nauseous draught."

says Addison, quoting Dryden; and I say, with Addison, " For my own part, I intend to hunt twice a week, and shall prescribe the *moderate* use of the exercise to all my country friends, as the best kind of physic for mending a bad constitution and preserving a good one "—not to speak of the good company, the sharing our pleasure with our friends and neighbours, and the joy of meeting with old friends like you. Here's to you once more.'

' And to you. No more, I thank you. You smoke? No? Then do you mind my smoking? Have you such a thing in the house as a cigar or a pipe?'

' Both for friends.'

' Pipe, then, for me, and we'll be jolly,' rubbing his hands.

Tobacco was brought, and a pipe found and lighted; and then, like a German armed for philosophic encounter, Mr. Franklin leaned back in his uneasy chair.

CHAPTER VI.

'Theology is a rich storehouse for the glory of God and the relief of man's estate.'—BACON.

'Now, father, tell me, is not theology very dry?' said the smoker, resting his pipe, which had been for some time in full play.

'That depends on the sort.'

'Well, controversial, then.'

'I am nearly omnivorous; but, not being ascetically inclined, I leave controversy alone. Do *you* know anything about it?'

'Not much, you may guess by my question. But I told you I was in chambers at the Bar for three years; and perhaps you remember that some of your dignified ecclesiastics put it from the platform to us young briefless barristers that we should take up the study of theology, since you young curates had no time for reading. The idea was delicious; I was tickled like a trout. So, living alone, and not having too much to do and some curiosity, I thought I would just try a little divinity. I soon had enough of it. In fact, as I said, I cut London and

the Bar altogether, and returned, with fresh zest, to
country pursuits and our old honoured sport, so soon
as I had polished myself by foreign travel. Now
you have the history of my craft in theology.'

'I call theology good reading when your theolo-
gians can write. *Omne tulit punctum qui miscuit
utile dulci.*'

'Which means,' said the lawyer, 'that whisky
is a good thing; but I like it best mixed with suga
and hot water: this water is cold. But here is th
tea, which is better still.'

'You talk like a toper and act like a member of
the temperance society. A pint of sherry between
us, and a glass of toddy! What would the last
generation have said to my hospitality? Well, if
you won't drink, tell us your story.'

'"Story, God bless you! I have none to tell, sir."'

'What do you read, then?'

'I never read.'

'What do you do?'

'Go a-hunting.'

'You cannot always go hunting.'

'No, but as often as I can; when I can't I shoot.'

'You can't shoot all the year round. Do you
farm?'

'Ah, no; I cannot afford to bury my money in
the earth, and never see it again.'

'Farmers do both; bury it, and find it increased.'

'Yes, but they look after their labourers; and if
they did that more and better, they would be able
to pay better wages—they would give more wages,
and get more work. But labourers would do little

for me or for you—that is, nine out of ten of them—
because you and I would not look after them ; and
they would reasonably suppose that what we took
no trouble about we could not care about :—that is
human nature.'

'Do you fish ?'

'Never.'

'When you don't hunt or shoot, what do you
do ?'

'Dine out.'

'Aye, in the evening ; but what do you do with
the day ?'

'Oh, I have a fine faculty of doing nothing.'

'That won't do ; I know you too well. What is
your occupation ?'

'Well, if I do anything, I read Robert Browning.'

'That is a great deal to say. I must read Robert
Browning too.'

> '"And," quoted Franklin, "still persist to read,
>   And *Browning* will be all the books you need."

But for myself I am bound to say, after this
vapouring, though I am ashamed to say it, that I
have not counted, and could not count, the novels I
have swallowed or tasted.' Here a long whiff and
an elaborate cloud-compelling puff.

'I call that speech unhandsome, downright mean :
from a man of honour like you I could not have expected it. "Clear your mind of cant, sir"—the cant
that all we Anglo-Saxons live, move, and have our
being in ; get quit of it for once, and praise the
bridge that carries you over, and the books that

pass the time. Why be ashamed of novels if you cannot get along without them ?'

'Because I could employ my time better.'

'No doubt; but, after all, novelists worthy of the name are moralists. What does stout Ben Jonson say of the dramatists ? " Poets," says he, " are not born every year, as are aldermen; there goes more to the making of a good poet than a sheriff. Though I live in the City, I will do more reverence to him than I will to the mayor—out of his year."'

'Ahem! that might fit Tennyson or Robert Browning; but it is your novelist we are talking of.'

'True; but the rightful successors of the Elizabethan dramatists, Jonson's " poets," are in fact the nineteenth century novelists—the great ones, Miss Austen, Scott, Dickens, Thackeray, Bulwer-Lytton, Kingsley, Miss Brontë, to say nothing of others far too many to name: these do more to right wrongs than all the aldermen, sheriffs, and lord mayors, with all the ministers and legislators of their time. Dickens, who was a lover of equality and a real liberal, has somewhere said, in the very spirit of "rare Ben," that " few debates in Parliament" (and he had been a parliamentary reporter)— " few debates in Parliament are so important to the public as a good picture ; and any number of bundles of the driest legal chaff would be cheaply purchased for one meritorious engraving."'

'A painter, you know, is not exactly a novelist : but you are on the old tack, I see, of artists literary, pictorial, and all the rest.'

'Well, I know some high and mighty ministers give out they have no time for literature, but pass their days and nights in "*severer*" studies. A man of plain sense, clear of cant, can see what Dickens meant by saying that "the National Gallery contributes as much to the good of the empire as Westminster Hall and Downing Street."'

'Dickens is an awful democrat,' said the barrister.

'What do you mean by democrat?' asked the curate. 'I know he would not accept rank or title, if that is what you mean.'

'No,' said the other; 'but he had no sort of sympathy with gentlemen—never could draw one.'

'As to sympathy, I think he very finely teaches little boys, in his "History of England," that one example of a finished gentleman like Sir Philip Sidney does more for the good of man than any number of solemn Poloniuses, lord-deputies of Ireland, or M.P.s.'

'Ahem! couldn't you say Polonii?'

'Certainly, if you think it better English. But to return to Dickens, he evidently felt, more than other writers of his day, that humanity is brotherhood, irrespective of circumstances or condition— "a man's a man for a' that." And as to the drawing of gentlemen, the hero of the "Tale of Two Cities," who saves at the cost of his head, for the lady of his love, the life of her preferred lover, I take to be a very perfect gentleman, if to be a gentleman is the honourable thing I think it—a gentleman of the purest type, to be classed with the Philip Sidneys and George Herberts. Mind, I grant you that Lord

Frederick Verysopht and Sir Leicester Dedlock are
not clever men ; but I maintain they are gentlemen
—they have the " gentle " spirit of honour and self-
sacrifice even to excess, if that be possible.'

' Why did he make them so stupid ?'

' I suppose to mark, what is not always recog-
nised, but what is a very sure distinction, that it is
not so much the *intellectual* as the *moral* quality
that goes to the making of a gentleman—not what
men get at school, but what they get at home.
Compare Verysopht and Dedlock with Bounderly
and Gradgrind, and you will see what I mean.'

' I know what you mean very well,' said Mr.
Franklin.

' And this,' pursued the other, prosing on regardless of interruption, ' this is, I suppose, what Coleridge means when he says, " You may depend upon
it that religion is in its essence the most gentleman-
like thing in the world. If unalloyed by cant, it
will alone gentilise ; and I know nothing else that
will alone." The truth is, so far as it is alloyed by
cant it is not religion ; for cant is egotism, and religion—the religion of Christ, I mean—is self-sacrifice.
By the way, talking of Gradgrind and Bounderly, it
seems to me that " Hard Times " is a specially good
book ; as a plea for sanitary reform, and some other
reforms too, it is better than a thousand politico-
economical speeches in the House and on the stump.'

The smoker smoked on in silence.

' What have you to say against Bulwer Lytton ?'
asked the talker, whose tongue was let loose for a
holiday. ' Is he a democrat ?'

'Far from it; he runs too far t'other way—a dandy aristocrat.'

'But his is the aristocracy of culture. "From literature comes all that makes nations enlightened and men humane," is what he says. He "loves literature the more because her distinctions are not those of the world—ribands, stars, and high places: hers is the great primitive church of the world, without popes, or muftis, or hierarchies; her servants speak to the earth, as the prophets of old, anxious only to be heard and to be believed." His is an aristocracy not of title, but of talent; and I, for my part, hold with him and with Sir Humphry Davy, and many another good man and true, that artists, artisans, agriculturists, men of science, and men of letters, are the true civilisers and benefactors of men, the unacknowledged legislators of the world —police grows out of the improvements wrought by them. "A stout constable and a clear highway," beef, and beer, are all we want; oratory and party politics are luxuries for those who are

> ' "Like the stars; so brightly shining,
> Because they've nothing else to do." '

'Well, now, Martel, I should say that to be an orator gives a man almost absolute power of doing good in a free country.'

'And to the man resolved to ruin or to rule the state, quite absolute power of doing mischief,' replied the clerical. 'Besides, oratory is but a public sort of flattery; it is not an attainment that ranks high in the estimation of men of sober judgment.'

'You know the culture of it made Athens famous.'

'I know it made Athens fall, after a very short career of glory gained by better arts. Neither orators nor politicians do much good to any one. That country is best governed which is least governed; the world will manage itself in less than the eight hours a day which a busy bishop used to boast of inflicting on his diocese. Lord Melbourne's was the true wisdom for a statesman—" Could not you let it alone?" Of almost any minister we may say, as King Henry said of his Earl Percy, " I trust we have within the realm ten thousand good as he." Pitt's lament over the loss of himself to his country is as ludicrous as anything that Swift has put into the record of those "who have cut a poor figure in some circumstances of their lives." " Do you know all the consequences?" and " Can you not let it alone?"—those are my political watchwords.'

'Are they?' asked the stunned and astounded auditor, when he could get in a word. 'What do you think, then, of political economy?'

'I think it means just " Cannot you let it alone?" But I see that under the direction of a dogmatic science, which is not that of Adam Smith, the discoveries that should have lightened have added to the burden of the poor people : the extremes of luxury and want are exasperated—the rich are made richer, the poor poorer. And this is the "prosperity" of the yearly budget; it has increased, is increasing, and ought to be diminished, for it is not Adam Smith's " wealth of the NATION." '

'Not to exhaust you,' said the lawyer, laughing,

'suppose I grant the politician does little good : can the novelist do more ?'

'I think he can. He holds up a mirror, in which folk, and especially young folk and idle folk, who are many, may see themselves, while your politician just fools them to the top of their bent with his tongue in his cheek.'

'A beautiful figure of speech, which you have done right to borrow; but get on.'

'While the politician trades on the faults of his fellows, the novelist shows then up ; and now and then, by turning the eyes of the public, as the policeman flashes the bull's eye of his lanthorn, upon the evildoers, extorts redress.'

'Fine ! very fine ! especially the bull's eye : but what novels have done this ?'

'Two of the last you would suppose—" Paul Clifford " and " Night and Morning." See the prefaces.'

'And take the writer's word. Suppose I do. Can Dickens say that he did as much with Chancery ?'

'Ah ! Chancery is a first-class fortress : lines upon lines of circumvallation, vested interests all round, and a very staunch garrison : all the old judges, (who, in stuff and silk gowns, bawled and blustered for reform,) get up, one after another, to tell the people, with dauntless courage, that " to delay justice " is not " to deny justice," and that " Chancery is just another name for perfection." What is it but flesh and blood, that a real law-reformer should have against him all the lawyers and most of the rich men that fill the two Houses of Parliament ?'

'Hah! traitor, I have you! You touch me to the quick. Have I not heard politicians vilified, ministers vilipended, economists held cheap? and am I further to sit still, I, a member of her Majesty's Bar, and hear the majesty of the law questioned—aye, flouted? Forbid it, gown and wig! Forbid it, mace and seals!'

And the barrister brandished his pipe, and puffed from mouth and nostril shadowy volumes of typical disdain. Then rising, like another Erskine, he asked, in appalling accents:

'Do you dare to say to me, a member of her Majesty's Bar, that the law is not open to all—I repeat it—to all men, rich and poor alike, sir?'

And the other replied, like a second Horne Tooke:

'Do you mean, sir, to say that the Clarendon Hotel is not open to all—I repeat it, sir—to all men—who can pay its bills?'

'Upon my word,' said he behind the pipe, 'you have, for a novice, a very pretty idea of forensic tragedy. It is my opinion, sir, that in course of time, by unremitting assiduity, you might learn to do Brougham pleading "on his bended knees" before the House of Lords the purity of Queen Caroline; which, I suppose, is the finest piece of legal heroics on record. But, joking apart, you are an awful radical and railer.'

'I scorn the imputation. I am simply a constitutional stick-in-the-mud and political sceptic, who sing, with all my heart and voice:

'" Confound your politics ;
  Frustrate your knavish tricks ;
  God save the Queen." '

'But, padre, tell me, what made you so bad?'

'Why, you see, I have been behind the scenes.'

'Oh! ah! what! come! Behind the scenes! In the most rustical of parishes, squatted behind a dirty little public-house! Oh! I say, parson, that is too rich! Oh! your acting bangs Brougham's and Keeley's to boot! Behind the scenes! Oh, monstrous! Behind the scenes! Come, tell us how it was.'

'Well, you see,' said the other, amid volumes of smoke from the excited pipe, you see, in my pagan obscurity, I have had what you in your metropolitan and templar splendours had not: I have had time (as I had the honour to intimate to you) to peruse at my leisure, to read, mark, learn, and inwardly digest endless volumes of political speeches, memoirs, and correspondences — none of your panegyrical or abusive biographies, but the men's own letters, words, and thoughts; and they have just landed me (as I had also the honour to intimate to you) in the safe and unambitious maxim, "Cannot you let it alone?" There is Pitt, "heaven-born," "*cui nec quidquam simile aut secundum,*" and all that sort of thing. His cousin and coadjutor, Lord Grenville, a very competent judge, tells us how " he went into office with a fixed determination to improve the finances of the kingdom, and—how greatly he injured them," I hope it is not high treason to add, as empirics are apt to do.'

'What a radical you are!'

'Do you call "Can't you let it alone!" a radical cry? If I do not believe in this man or in that, I

do believe in the people at large and their common-
sense *customs*. I believe in old England ; I believe
that she is, like her oaks, the growth of a thousand
years, and not created by cotton or by mechanism
yesterday. In short, I put my faith in *growth*, and
slow growth.

> ' " A thousand years scarce serve to form a state,
> An hour may lay her in the dust ; and when
> Can man its shatter'd splendour renovate,
> Recall its virtues back, and vanquish Time and Fate ?" '

During this last harangue, the gentleman with the
pipe, though silent, had not been idle. He said
much in dumb show ; he performed many curious
feats expressive of his regard for the argument.
He emitted columns of smoke, sometimes from one
nostril, sometimes from both ; he blew beautiful rings
of various sizes, which rose from his pipe and hung
about his head like halos ; and then he executed
other quaint and graceful devices, acquired by long
and sedulous practice, and such as betokened an
adept in the unsubstantial science of smoking, all
shadowing forth pictorially the facility with which
he puffed into thin air the parson and his theories.
At the last sentence, delivered, as became it, with
fire and emphasis, he exploded into a peal of un
seemly laughter.

'Why, old man alive !' he cried, choking with
irreverent emotion, and throwing up his pipe and
hands, and, it must be added, his legs also, high above
his head, with sad failure of forensic decorum ; ' Why,
man alive ! who'd ha' thought it ! You are as full
of old saws and modern instances as any justice of

the peace among us all. You ought to be on the bench instead of me. And I—well, no, I ought not to be in the pulpit instead of you. You have a 'gey' turn for preaching.'

'Thanks; 'tis my vocation, Hal.'

'Pity you did not go to the Bar in my place. You are, so to speak, a fine, free galloper, and can get over anything; while I am rather sticky in tongue and in conscience, don't you see ? But as for you, why you might talk on for a week on end, it seems, like any Attorney-General in private practice. If I had only known that I was in for this sort of fun, I would have brought my old gown and wig; we would have done it in state.'

At this juncture was heard a tap at the outer door, followed close by a step in the passage; and, as the inner door was opened, Martel, whose spirits, happily for him by nature elastic, the talk of old times had raised to youthful jollity, exclaimed :

'Ah, then, is it you? "Thou wast my Dick ; thou art my diamond !" '

'Neat historic allusion and pastoral address!' said Franklin smugly, his sly eye glancing to the new-comer.

'Come, my lad of romance,' said the hilarious host. 'You seek a hermit; you find Friar Tuck entertaining a royal guest on the tobacco plant and cold water. Let me make known my friend Mr. Gryffyn to my old college friend Mr. Franklin. And now sit down, and unfold your tale.'

'The tale of a skirt,' put in Franklin, who had heard in the hunting-field something of Miss Palmer's accident, and of Gryffyn's connection with it. He was much inclined to poke fun at the adventure, and to be not a little free in his jokes upon the heroine. But Dick told what he pleased of his story in a short, dry style, that did not encourage liberties ; and Martel, resuming his gravity, and approving the youngster's reluctance to make a young lady's mishap the subject of jesting with a stranger, helped the lad to parry Franklin's ridiculous questions and broad gibes.

' And so it all ended in your going to a *tête-à-tête* luncheon with your Belphœbe ?'

' *Tête-à-tête!* no. Her cousin, Miss Fisher, was with her.'

' Miss Fisher, do you say ? I have a first or second cousin of that name visiting at this time, I believe, in this county, hereabouts. Do you know her Christian name ?'

' I did chance to hear Miss Palmer call her Kitty.'

' The same! the very same !' said Franklin. ' By Jupiter! (excuse my heathenism, your reverence), I will call upon my cousin, and see this heroine that you are both so close about. Alas ! though, my time in these parts is up next week, and I cannot spare a day's hunting, if the weather keeps open. Well, well, I shall hear all about it, in spite of you.'

After this there followed much tall talk about hunting, and horses, and difficulties, and exploits,—

> ' And thrice they leaped the leaps again,
> And thrice they ran the run :'

and each performance was better than the last.

Then Franklin vainly tried to tempt Martel to
London for the University boat-race. But young
Gryffyn was going to it; so Franklin asked him to
the rooms that he still kept in the Temple, since
Martel positively declined to occupy them.

As the little legal squire went up the narrow
stair to his little whitewashed chamber, the curate,
following him with a light, could not but overhear
him muttering:

'Good fellow! very good fellow, Martel! But he
won't do. If my living were to fall vacant to-
morrow, as it is not unlikely to do, I could not give
it to him—could not. He is an awful Radical—
awful! And,—besides,—he *hunts !*'

The curate saw his friend into his room, and bid
him good-night. Then, having retired to his own
den, he indulged at last in a fit of suppressed
laughter.

'What fun!' quoth he. 'But that he chiefly
drank water, I should have said, " *In vino veritas.*"
What an absent little beggar it is! and always was,
I remember. Right though, I dare say, quite right—
from his point of view ; not from mine, though, not
from mine,' he repeated obstinately, and as he got
into bed, inwardly resolved, weather permitting, to
hunt the next week—TWICE.

CHAPTER VII.

'In a land of liberty it is extremely dangerous to make a distinct order of the profession of arms. No man should take up arms, but with a view to defend his country and its laws : he puts off the citizen when he enters the camp, but it is because he is a citizen, and would continue so, that he makes himself for a while a soldier.'—BLACKSTONE.

' Among us, but not of us ; valuing their rights as citizens chiefly as instruments to their powers as churchmen ; ministers of love, to whom the heart of a father is an inscrutable mystery ; teachers of duties the most sacred, which they may not practice ; the sacerdotal caste yet flourishes, the imperishable monument of that far-sighted genius which devised the means of Papal despotism.'—SIR JAMES STEPHENS.

'The clergyman is with his parishioners, and among them : he is neither in his cloistered cell, nor in the wilderness, but a neighbouring and a family man, whose education and rank admit him to the mansion of the rich ; while his duties make him the frequent visitor of the farm-house and the cottage. The revenues of the Church are the only species of *landed* property that is essentially moving and circulative.'— S. T. COLERIDGE.

FOLK who fancy that what whatever is, is wrong, are wont to say that the squire and the parson divide the parish between them. The eldest son has the lion's share, and reckons his income by thousands; but the younger son has his share too, and reckons it by hundreds, and sometimes he comes, by succession, into the thousands as well. We then get that well-known compound called the black squire.

The foes of the Church of England say that to abolish purchase and lay-patronage would break up the recruiting-ground for the black squires; would alienate the class who, having left it for a while, return to the Establishment when they have made fortunes; and so would strike a heavy blow, and cause great discouragement to all Conformists.

Patronage in the Church is the exact equivalent to purchase in the Army, say—rather in-exactly— these unfriendly critics. Yet, 'if every squire in England wore a black coat, who would be the worse ?' is Bishop Berkeley's very pertinent ' query.'

Few people have considered how many squires actually do wear black coats—not those who, having come into large private fortunes after seeking and receiving ordination, appear to be, for some inscru- table reason, ashamed of what they have done, and retire from the exercise of their calling; but those, rather, who, starting with private fortunes, choose at the outset of life to devote their fortunes and their services to the ministry of the Church, regarding it not as a mercenary profession, but as a calling of honour, and desiring no other title in it than that of plain priest. They will serve it all for love and nothing for reward; just as in the one other specially unmercenary vocation a gentleman of ripe military experience and approved military skill would once upon a time be content to pay down seventeen thousand pounds for the honour of commanding a light cavalry regiment, satisfied with receiving for pay little more than the interest of his money, and perhaps volunteering to spend an additional thousand a year in promoting the comforts and smartness of the corps under his command. If he lives to be too old for service, he may sell out, put off the soldier's uniform, and return to civil duties, thus bridging over the gap between the soldier and the citizen. As it is with a regiment thus commanded, so is it in a great degree with many a parish. Its parson, in return for his two or three hundreds a year, gives to it the use of a private fortune of ten times that amount, along with his own services. His wife works for the parish; his servants run errands to and fro on its business; his weight and influence as a man of fortune and social standing serve it in numberless ways, much as its members serve the interests of a borough.

It is the pride of the Church of England to be able to say that it has ever had, in time past and now, many hundreds, aye, thousands of men of good birth, of complete education, of fair scholarship, and easy means, settling themselves down in entire content as priests of small, secluded hamlets, with no other aim in life than to make all their advantages and talents serve to the religious, intellectual, and temporal good of the labouring villagers.

A person not long since took the trouble to count the number of clergy of considerable private fortune who held livings, great or small, in a given district with which he was very intimately acquainted. The tract of country experimented on was about twenty miles long by ten broad, speaking roughly. Within that space lived, in villages, seventeen beneficed clergymen, of whose private fortunes the least exceeded two thousand a year; three of them possessed over seven thousand a year each; the several fortunes of four exceeded four thousand a year; and of the seventeen, only five had livings that could be called large—that is, amounting from six hundred to eight hundred a year. Of these large livings, none were in public patronage, and two out of the five had been purchased at great outlays of eight or ten thousand pounds. For the remaining twelve incumbents, the income of their livings ranged from two hundred and seventy to four hundred pounds a year, and did not in all amount to four thousand pounds.

Many, or most people, seeing their style of living, used to say, 'Ah! what fat livings have those parsons! how red are their noses! How rich is the Church!' Just as the same penetrating, reflective, and scrupulous folk see the gay and expensive fine gentlemen of cavalry regiments on high-priced hunters, or on smart drags, and cry, bursting with envy, 'What pay those aristocrats get out of our taxes! What scandalous waste of our money!'

Like the Queen's Army, the Church of England partakes largely of the nature, not of *the*, but of *a* 'voluntary system,' wherein those who serve are paid mainly out of their own pockets, and are left to maintain themselves on their own private re-

sources.   In this sense the Church of England is by
far the largest 'voluntary' body in the country.
The case is tolerably plain.   There are thirteen
hundred 'livings' (that is the word) in England; of
these, eleven hundred are under two hundred a
year.   An incumbent dependent upon one of these
for maintenance would find it hard to perform his
pastoral duties in the independent manner that he
ought to do.   He would be to the rich parishioner
but as one to be classed with mechanics and day-
labourers, and, as standing alone and helpless, much
less to be feared than any of them; the rustling of
his gown or of his surplice, or of the leaves of his
sermon, would be censured in plain-spoken language
as disturbing to the fine nerves of the rich man's
lady, or the sermon would be condemned as too
long or too short for her convenience, and the hours
and the order of Divine service would be dictated
by her judgment; and the labouring class, noting
all this with curious eye, would be equally docile to
its teacher.

   'Was it ever yet known in the world that men
sucked in instruction from those whom they despised?' is the pertinent query of Cobbett.   To be
sure, the Apostle was poor, and was not despised.
But why?   Take the record as you find it; it gives
the fact with the reason.   While he said, ' Silver and
gold have I none,' he could say to the lame man,
' Rise up and walk;' or he could say, ' The feet are
at the door which shall carry thee out dead.'

   As for dissenting ministers, they do not live
among their parishioners—they have no parishes.

Having, then, to do with our day and its ordinary circumstances, it may be confidently asserted that were it not for the vast amount of private means possessed and expended by the clergy, computed at six times more than they receive from the Church, the problem of Church finance would have brought the Establishment to a standstill long ago.

Homely common sense, looking out over the country, argues thus: I see a vast number of parishes that gain, through the old and complex and patched machinery of the Church Establishment, more or less of the advantages of a resident educated squire, who, in putting on a black coat, submits himself to a good deal of wholesome extra restraint, and to not a few absurd and vexatious and even derogatory bonds— ambiguous too, and liable to be strained by power to this purpose or to that; and he is, further, compelled to so much of extra education and continuous study, that he is more cultivated and softened than the average lay squire. For the most part he resembles other gentlemen of his own rank; where there is difference, it is in his favour. More carefully trained and more refined, and more self-restrained than his lay brother, the black squire is also above the average of the *clerical* character: liberal and open, with the sentiments and feelings of a gentleman and man of honour, and being mixed up in so many important ways with the laity, he is freer from clerkly *finesse*, and from other faults which beset an isolated caste.

The class, whether from the lay or the ecclesiastical point of view, is a superior class. 'The black

squires are the flower of the squirearchy. Their
households afford the best examples of Christian
regulation and habitual decorum ; and, so far back
as 1840, when there was less of caste in the clerical
profession than has since been imported into it, the
noble and accomplished lay author of ' England and
the English ' remarked how ' the report of the Poor-
law Commissioners showed that nine times out of
ten, when the poor-laws had been well-administered
by a neighbouring magistrate, that magistrate had
been a clergyman.' That three-fourths of the edu-
cational provision on the voluntary system has been
made by, or through the influence of, the clergy,
none but the most uninformed are unaware.

To those who are aggrieved at the anomalous composition of the twenty-two thousand clergy of the
Church of England this is an answer.

The small fry of squires and independent landowners, except in a few favoured districts of
England, as, for example, Norfolk, are rapidly dying
out. They are absorbed by the leviathans of capital,
commercial or landed ; and it is a fact, as certain as
it is ill-boding, that there are fewer freeholders in
England in the reign of Queen Victoria than there
were in the reign of Queen Elizabeth.

Now to those afore-cited seventeen parishes (and
much the same proportion is observable in some
other parts of England that have been tested) those
clergymen of fortune are as resident squires, who
wear black coats, emblematic of stricter discipline.
And if these also are to go, after the majority of the
smaller lay squires and freeholders, who are to take

their places ?　Some inferior sort of capitalist turned
farmer, who, with no love for country life, little
education, and trading habits, is addicted to the exclusive worship of the dollar.　He is not a farmer
proper, he is not a gentleman-farmer; he has no tie
to any place such as bound the old-fashioned, bred-
and-born farmer, whom it is the cockney fashion now
to mock at.　He just comes to double his fortune as
soon as he can, and be gone : what sort of village he
leaves behind is nothing to him.　All he knows
about education is that it did not help him to make
money.　Is he the man to promote it ?　He is just
a speculating trader, who makes the country for a
while the scene, and land the subject, of his opera-
tions.　Can one of this sort in any respect or degree
fill the place of the resident squire, who lived on his
patrimonial estate, whose father lived there before
him, and who hopes that his children for many generations may live there after him ?

The black squire, of necessity resident, and having
both a temporal and a spiritual interest in his parish,
will, one way or the other, contribute to enlighten,
relieve, and assist those who need his help, in all
classes; and by his silent influence, exerted with
social tact, in a discreet, quiet, and unobtrusive way,
will do much to protect the poor against oppression.
He continues to do what the lay squire, the Alworthy
or Coverley of the days of his forefathers, used to do,
and what the new-made man often does not attempt
to do, and never could do so well.　These black squires
are men who ' go their warfare at their own cost.'
They bring back into parochial life the older patri-

archal times, when the eldest son, in virtue of his birthright, was the priest of the family and the wealthiest of his race.

But all this time we are keeping a company waiting who are assembled in the drawing-room at Finchdale Rectory, ready for the announcement of dinner.

There is the new law-peer, Lord Whittleseamere. Irish peers, it is said, take their titles from play-books, English peers from the land; but mostly, nowadays, from land that is not their own. Lord Whittleseamere chose his watery title, as he said, because almost every spot of dry land was pre-occupied by some lord or other; and the mere, which was just being drained, offered one more resting-place for the title of a new peer. With him came a Mrs. Delafield, a lady who set up for fashion, and was fast.

Then there was Sir Alfred Ashwood, a county baronet, and Lady Ashwood, his wife. Born and bred in the county, schooled at Eton, and graduated at Trinity, Cambridge, Sir Alfred was to the county as a Hebrew of the Hebrews. He knew instinctively by use, as by a second nature, all county matters, and he knew them the better for that he knew not much else—had no theories, nor even much general knowledge on other subjects. Country life was his speciality. Of some dozen descents, and born to twenty thousand a year, he was quite content with his lot, and had no desire beyond transmitting to his descendants the property, with its rights and duties, and the principles which he

had inherited from his forefathers. In a shifting,
unsettled, and empiric age, the property and principles of such as he are the ballast of the State in
every county of England. The minds of such men
are turned to no land of promise; to them 'the
thing that has been is that which shall be, and
there is no new thing under the sun.' Such as
Sir Alfred was, such was his lady, allowing for the
difference made by petticoats.

Besides these there were present Mrs. Mallinders,
fond of music and driving; and Messrs. Donald
McDonald and Duncan McFarlane, very fine gentlemen of the Stock Exchange, faultless in dress and
lofty in manners, far-off Scotch cousins of the
Palmers; also Miss Fisher, and her half-brother,
Lieutenant Fleming, of the 29th Red Dragoons,
familiarly termed 'the Flamingoes.' He was recommended to the ladies by his height, which was
six feet two inches, and by his good looks, which
were even more remarkable, and to some by his
demeanour, which was that of a bold dragoon,
easy and free to a fault. With Miss Fisher we
have made acquaintance already.

There remain to be mentioned Mr. Sloan, the
elderly rector of a large college-living adjacent, his
wife, and their friend Mr. Cumber, an illustrious
University professor. Mr. Sloan, tall and gaunt,
and, bating the wig, a Dr. Syntax in appearance,
was, in truth, a noble specimen of one of the best
species of the Anglican clerical genus. A Fellow of
St. Luke's, and first-class classic, he was full to
overflowing of Oriental learning. Some, who knew

him not well, said that he had accumulated a vast mass of undigested lore, but those who knew him better admired his liberal spirit even more than his vast erudition. If his boundless stores were poured forth at times without measure or method, they always flowed at the prompting of good-nature, under the wish to communicate knowledge. Of gentle blood, and sufficient, though not large, private means, an ardent Christian, he lived—as, through several successive generations, his forefathers had lived—for the Church of England in its ministry; holding, without doubt, that there is no better life upon earth than that of an English country parson. He was gentle, deliberate, and careful. His wife was, as a wife should be, her husband's complement —sensitive and enthusiastic. He was all forethought, she was all impulse. And then she dressed her part to admiration : the material handsome and new, the colour grave, the fashion antique and formal, as became the help of a sober and learned minister of a church which used to boast that it never changed.

Their friend, the Reverend Frederick Spencer Cumber, was much younger and yet a better known man. He was of high mark in his University, and had great expectations. The son of a gentleman distinguished in official life, he was supposed to be destined for dignities himself. He was the author of some lectures of great merit and of almost European reputation ; an able writer of articles for reviews, with not a little political zeal and knowledge. With unusual academic accomplishments he had the usual academic failings, and was inoculated in no slight degree with the donnishness which seems scarcely separable from academic notabilities. In appearance five-and-thirty, in figure he was fat. Pointed at as destined for high place, he was at present the examining chaplain of a bishop who had a good deal of patronage, over the disposal of which the clever and rising chaplain was supposed to exert influence—the more, perhaps, that he stood above the need of it himself.

Besides, and in contrast to these academic and clerical dons, were the host's particular friends and associates and their wives, the Reverend George Lawrence, and the Reverend Finch Adams, men of the same stamp as Mr. Palmer. These three friends, and not distant neighbours, afford illustration of that which was said at the commencement of this chapter. In them we see men of precisely the sort there spoken of, very far above the common level of small squires in accomplishment; three clergymen whose private fortunes, taken together, amount to nine thousand a year; whose means and whose services, with the services of their wives and households, are put at the disposal of three small, secluded country parishes, for the respective yearly stipends of three hundred and fifty, three hundred and five, and two hundred and ten pounds—in all, eight hundred and sixty-five pounds a year gross.

They were birds of one feather, and in describing one of them you would more or less describe the other two. The many prepossessions—and prejudices, if you like—that these three gentlemen had

in common with their squarsonic class were, no
doubt, the bonds of their friendship. They were
purely patrician in every fibre, and, as true aristocrats of the patriarchal type, they were full of clan-
nish feeling: seldom changed their servants, shook
hands heartily with them after any long absence
from home, and with new-comers on their arrival—
in short, the servants of their houses, and the poor
of their parishes, were to them as clansmen. The
new, moneyed idea that a man's dignity is hurt by
contact with his poorer brethren, could never enter
their heads except as a source of amazement or
amusement. It was the firm basis of their social
creed that a lord, a duke, or a prince is, as such, en-
titled to respect, but, socially considered, can be no
more than a gentleman ; and this feeling leavened
their minds with a certain sense of equality in all
worthy people of all classes. They never changed
their tradesmen : each of the three dealt still with
the same excellent tailor that he employed when he
was at college. It was a sacred principle with them
never, under any circumstances, to cut or drop
friends once made, if by any stretch of reasonable
toleration it could be avoided ; and as they held it a
crime to drop old friends, they were slow to take up
new ones. They were self-restrained, wary, reserved,
and cautious. In short, they were aristocrats to the
core—not of the new-fashioned flashy sort, with
which they had no sympathy, but of the antique
patriarchal species, of which they were fine specimens, with all its faults and all its virtues.

Thus in the drawing-room of Finchdale might be

seen a sample of the working of the Church of England in the pastoral economy of its parochial system. Some of its finest links would be detected there by the eye of an initiated observer. At one end of the chain he would see Sir Alfred Ashwood, the great lay squire; at the other, connected with him by intervening black squires, the Reverend Charles Martel, who, sinking the sad fact that the old French marquess his grandfather had to turn dancing-master in England, was a man better born than the baronet, and poorer than Job in his curacy of one hundred pounds per annum.

Neither he, nor yet Mr. Sloan, with his small private income of a few hundreds a year, and his large college-living with some ten or dozen more, would seem at first sight to have anything in common with the great county landowner of many descents and born to at least twenty thousand a year; but there was, in fact, a close connecting-link afforded by the influential class, of which Messrs. Palmer, Lawrence, and Finch Adams were representatives, in their two-fold nature of squire and parson—squires wearing black coats, as Bishop Berkeley puts it. Sir Alfred is bound, possibly by ties of blood, certainly by all the interests of property and county business, to those black squires, with whom Messrs. Sloan and Martel, as clergymen and men of like education, have also many ties and intimacies. Thus, through the squires who wear black coats, like our host and his two allies, the wealthy landowner and the poor clergyman are (such was the state of things then) practically bound together by countless common sympathies and interests, light as air and unseen, but stronger than bands of brass. The chain of society thus reaches the heights and the depths; and as there are no barriers more impassable than the impalpable barriers of society, so are there no ties more effectually binding than the thin-spun threads of social connexion.

The squires who wear black coats exert great influence in both their capacities, but their action is social, quiet, unobtrusive, and not much seen by the outward world; among the squires they are clergymen, among the clergy they are squires. If they be of distinguished families, they are not the least distinguished members of their families : and generally they are of the class described of old as ' *bene nati, bene vestiti, et mediocriter docti*'—that is to say, not pedants, but well-read and well-bred gentlemen. They compose the crack regiments of the Church's army. It is a large army, numbering from twenty to twenty-three thousand men of all arms. It has its patrician corps, its 'Guards' and its 'light cavalry,' its 'scientific corps,' and its 'marching regiments,' which in the Church's, as in the Queen's Army, do the rough work.

One of the most valuable features of the Church of England, and the most savouring of the old Saxon jealousy of Rome and centralisation, is the great degree of independence enjoyed by the beneficed clergy, which is, perhaps, the chief *temporal* attraction it holds out to men of talents or birth and fortune. And the want of unity of purpose, which might be its most inconvenient consequence, is suffi-

9—2

ciently remedied by this social chain of sympathy
running through the whole body of the Church, and
embracing its laity with its clergy, many of whom
are poor gentlemen connected not very remotely
with the most distinguished families; many of
whom also belong to families which, though very
amply provided with material resources, cannot
be said to have any other claim to the title of
gentry; not to speak again of black squires, upon
whom so much has been said already, nor of an
equal sprinkling of good men and true drawn from
the yeomanry, the shopkeepers, and the peasantry.

Is this view of the very *mixed* and *national* character of the Church of England as by law established
sufficiently understood and insisted on ? Perhaps
too much here; generally not enough or not at all.
How well the system has worked is plain in this—
that from a small and distracted body, terribly de-
pressed and weakened by the Rebellion or Revolu-
tion under Cromwell, the Reformed Church, which
never did include the whole or nearly the whole of
the nation, has grown up to her present stature,
with her clergy from twenty-two to twenty-three
thousand strong drawn from all classes of the State,
and her eighteen thousand chapels and hospitals;
while her works of charity extend over every spot
where flies the flag of England.   And if it must be
confessed that great numbers professedly dissent
from her now, as great numbers always have done,
it must also be admitted that they do her the honour
to copy her pretty constantly and closely, to their
own very great advantage.

'Well, Tom,' said Mr. Palmer to Mr. Finch Adams, 'what's this I hear about Arthur Clifton? You have him for a neighbour now.'

'No, I never see him; he has not returned my visit. That's not much; but what do you think he gives out? Why, that he cannot visit me because I hunt! Think of that!'

'I think the fashion of things is changing—in that matter for the worse, and in some other things for the better,' said Palmer.

'And I,' said Mr. Lawrence, with a demoniac frown, 'think it the greatest impertinence I ever heard of! The young puppy!'

'The best of the joke is,' said Finch Adams, 'that, for a consideration, he let his rectory last winter to Lord Malvoisin for a hunting-box! There's consistency for you—pelf and pocket *versus* principle! He cannot plead poverty, for his living is a good twelve hundred a year, and he got it when he was but seven-and-twenty.'

'Ah!' said Palmer, 'depend upon it, he does not see it as you do. He is one of those fellows who are always splitting straws. He is full of scruples: has his four-and-twenty reasons all in a row for and against everything, and cannot square the account, gets bothered, and then does what your over-scrupulous refiner mostly does—follows the line that makes for his own interest, without being conscious of corruption. He is not at the bottom a bad fellow. He has a nervous, ambitious temper, and a shallow, sophistical mind, which has not been improved by the canting, confined set he has lived in. I have known him ever since he was a boy at school; in fact, he is a kind of connexion of ours—at least, he is nearly related to our relative Lady Selina Wadhurst, whom you know.'

'I suppose the truth is,' said Finch Adams, 'he is set a little above himself by coming so young into that very large college-living. How is it, by-the-way, that a young man, even of good birth and breeding, who comes into a large living without merit, is always much more stuck up by it than he would be by inheriting a large estate? You see, the fellows of those colleges that give their fellowships not to scholarship by examination, but solely by interest, as does Sandford College—those fellows are the most absurdly donnish and bumptious of any. I have seen the case a hundred times.'

'I suppose,' said Palmer, 'they measure their merits by their pay, as is natural.'

'And a man with a large living is the same as a man of large understanding. Eh?' laughed Finch-Adams.

'Or, to speak according to the "*Simony*" scheme, is a man with large "*spiritual gifts*,"' sneered Mr. Lawrence.

'One thing, any way, is clear,' said Mr. Palmer; 'which is, that it is better for us, if we have it, to take money into the Church than to take money from the Church. In that way, as in others, it is more blessed to give than to receive.'

'Well,' said Finch Adams, 'be the cause what it may, Clifton, who is a gentleman, and should know better, gives himself, I am told, for I never see him, such airs as would be preposterous even if his fellow-ship had followed a double-first, instead of dropping into his mouth like an over-ripe plum. Donnishness is, we know, one of the academical vices—contemptible in a man of parts and learning, but unpardonable in an ignoramus. Rafferton, who is a fellow of the college, told me that, out of friendship to his family, he had canvassed for Clifton, and secured him the votes that made him a fellow. You know, they vote in their friends, as vacancies occur ; and, as they are not required now to take holy orders, very few of them do, and that is the way such very young men get such very fat livings ; and the youngsters wax fat too, and kick. I don't see such absurd fellows anywhere ; but they lay on a thickish varnish of cant, mind you.'

'I have been told,' said Lawrence, 'that if Clifton goes to the school while his curate (who is a priest old enough to be his father, and is a gentleman and a far better scholar than Clifton will ever be) is reading prayers, he will snatch the book out of the curate's hand, and finish the reading himself, by way of asserting, as rector, his *civil* and *legal*, though he chooses to call them *ecclesiastical* and *priestly*, rights. And then the daily prayer he talks so much about he does by deputy three months out of every year ! So that daily service is with him a matter of two hundred and seventy-five, and to his curate a matter of three hundred and sixty-five, days a year ; for the elderly curate gets no holiday, having to take the young rector's duty, if, indeed, one man can take another's duty. All that is of the earth, earthy, is it not ?'

'Aye, aye,' said Palmer. 'There is a good deal of dirt and dross in human nature, and your saint is but a man after all.'

'A clergyman,' put in Finch Adams, 'especially if he be a youngster and holds a large living, must get over his own engagements very lightly, if he is not too conscious of shortcomings to hazard censures on his brethren, who do, and for years have done, nearly gratis that, which he, a mere boy, is uncommonly well paid for doing.'

'Well, Tom, I'll tell you what we'll do with Clifton. He shall come here to meet you and George, if you will, and we elders will try and shame him into more modest manners.'

'With all my heart,' said Adams; but Lawrence was silent, and Palmer proceeded :

'There is nothing like meeting your neighbours for rubbing off the angles of egotism, and taking the starch out of a don.'

'Starch or egotism,' said Finch Adams, 'whichever it is, "the gentleman doth protest too much, me-thinks." He is one of your people of uneasy virtue —talks of high views, that is, of turning English clergymen into Irish priests, barring hunting, by the way; for you know, Palmer, many an Irish P.P. hunts to the full as much as we do, though not with such smart packs, but without a word of blame from pope or parish. Our friend Martel there often reminds me of "Father Fitz on a wiry weed." They have better times than he has. I grieve to think his sport will stand in the way of his promotion, and his chance is bad enough without that. As to

Arthur Clifton, the worst I wish him would be to put him upon my horse Kangaroo, and start them after the hounds on a burning scent from Wilderness Gorse. He enlarges a good deal on mortification, as I hear. He would get more of it out of that than by drinking tea without sugar, or eating toast without butter, or refusing roast goose now and then. He would be mortified doubly, in flesh and in spirit. He would be well laughed at, and not able to sit down in comfort for a week : it would save him the need of the scourge. That is all the harm I wish him. He is welcome to his opinions, such as they are, and to visit me or not, as he thinks fit. But I do not like his going through the country gabbling about his fellow clergy, and putting his foolish ideas into the heads of still weaker people, who take him for a saint because he is a goose, and of still worse-conditioned people, who like to hear the clergy abused, and most of all by one of themselves. Barring that, he is free, for me (since there is no precept on the subject), to follow what course he pleases. I am content to follow the example of one of the best and truest men the Church of England ever reared, good Bishop Juxon, who followed the hounds, and kept them too, and stuck to his master to the end of the worst of runs.'

'Oh !' said Palmer, 'with all his straw-splitting and scruples, Clifton is one of your "sorry-to-think" gentlemen. His answer to any unwelcome argument is always of the same sort : " It gives me pain to hear you." '

'That, for a self-mortifying man, is an absurd answer enough,' said Finch Adams.

Mr. Lawrence had been listening with a scowl on his dark, handsome brow. He did not seem to approve of this easy way of taking things.

'You will have to fight these men for your gowns, or your skins for aught I know,' said he; 'but if you have, it will be the fault of your own folly or cowardice. It is all audacity and encroachment on the part of these men, and tameness on ours. We stand still to be insulted; they know it, and act accordingly. But if these Raca-ites—as, copying their abusive ways, I call them—if these Raca-ites, I say, succeed in infusing such a spirit into the Church that its clergy cease to observe towards one another the courtesies of gentlemen, then gentlemen must quit the stage, and it will be all over with the Church of England that I have known and cared for. For myself, I can only say that when these men get the upper-hand I know very well what they will do with us, and that it will be time for me to make my bow and retire into private life. To be sure, the loss of me is not likely to be much lamented; but you, and all the like of you, will have to follow, and the Church will be handed over to another twenty years of religious jars, such as rendered the Commonwealth intolerable to every man of rational mind and peaceful temper.'

'As how, George?' asked Palmer.

'Why,' replied Mr. Lawrence, 'the English laity will build showy churches fast enough, but they will

not now give the clergy a proper maintenance—
livings that are livings in deed as well as name.'

'Indeed, Lawrence, I do not think they will;
but what then?'

'They will find out some day that they want
men more than *buildings*. Men of means will be
afraid to take orders. It will be of no use any
longer for episcopal or lay patrons to ask, as usual,
"Has he private means?" And a clergy without
means will either be as compliant as any political
weathercock, or they will be half-starved, and
over-worked, and worried into a state of chronic
febrile excitement, which will drive them to rant
and to rave, and to take up every sort of mad
and violent enthusiasm.'

Palmer shook his head.

'You will see; the joker's joke will be no joke.
People will have to play "cribbage in the cellar,
and lock themselves into their closets when they
drink wine;" and we shall be, or, rather, I hope
those who come after us, will be ruled for another
twenty years by spiritual pride and besotted fana-
ticism, until the young generation gets sick of it
all, and has another Restoration, and another
Charles the Second, and a new Prayer-book.'

'Ah! George, zeal and devotion count for something.'

'H'm! your Thug is a zealous and devoted
fellow enough, but I should not like to come
across him,' replied Lawrence.

'Do you carry that argument out, George?' asked
Finch Adams.

'I carry nothing to extremes, I hope ; to do that is the trick of fools, Tom.'

'Then how far do you go ?'

'I just stop short of the Irish candidate for the butler's place, who was asked, " Are you a Protestant ?" and answered, " No, but I'm a mighty bad Catholic; and that, your honour knows, is the next best thing." '

'Talking of butlers,' said the host, 'I am glad to see Trimmer come to tell us of dinner.'

'I cannot compliment your cook upon punctuality, Palmer,' said the more exact, and exacting, Lawrence, looking at his watch. Mr. Lawrence was always looking at his watch.

CHAPTER VIII.

'Feast then, and merrily together sit,
And please yourselves with stories.'
HOBBS—*Odyssey* bk. iv.

IT was Martel's lot at dinner to sit next to the young lady whom he had not long since, with irreverent jocularity, called 'Bones.' She opened fire at once.

'Is not it strange, Mr. Martel, that, often as you and I have been here, we never chanced to meet before ? I suppose you took me for a myth.'

'Not exactly; I saw you once at Mudford—sat behind you at a concert—and was convinced of the solidity of your existence.'

'Though our acquaintance is so new, Mr. Martel, do you know, I had a letter all about you this morning.'

'Indeed ! No harm, I hope ? If you will tell me from whom, I shall be prepared for the worst.'

'Can't you guess ?'

'Never guessed a thing right in my life, not unless I knew it, as the Americans say.'

'Do you know a thing they call Jem ?' asked the lady.

The gentleman shook his head.

'No ?   Little Jemmy ?'

Another shake.

'Do you give it up ?'

'Yes.'

'Not know little Jemmy Franklin ?'

'Do I not! So well that I wonder at his writing to you a letter all about me. Was it quite all about me ?'

'Well, not quite. It was rather an inquisitive letter.'

'That's more like him; wants to know how you are, and all the rest of it, I suppose ?'

'Oh me! it is little Jemmy Franklin cares for poor me! It is all Barbara—his letter is crammed with questions about Barbara! Every one goes mad about Barbara—every one who has seen her, of course; but he has not even seen her. Don't you think her lovely, Mr. Martel ?'

'I have thought so ever since she was height of thumb, when our acquaintance first began.'

'And Barbara is constantly quoting you. She is rather blue, you know; she is reading now some books of your recommending.'

'Oh, ah ! I am a sort of father-confessor to her in the book way. Mr. Palmer never reads the literature of the day; he has Shakespeare at his finger-ends. And how well he reads! It is as good as a play to hear him.'

'Do you know Uncle Palmer is a first-rate actor ? Being a clergyman, he never does act, except in the very most private theatricals among his own family.

They are all fond of theatricals. There is a theatre at Rowanshaw, and has been these hundred years. I have heard papa say that it was thought at Cambridge Uncle Palmer might make a fortune on the stage. He is not my uncle, you know, but I always call him so; papa and he are cousins, and were at school and at college together. Some said that uncle was the best actor off the stage, and others said he would be the best actor on the stage. Is not it odd that so quiet a person should be so good an actor?'

'I don't know. You see, he is not pre-occupied with himself; he can throw his heart into the feelings of others; he is very sympathetic. I have often heard and admired his reading, but I have never seen him act, and I should, above all things, like to see him in some of his very private common domestic performances,' said Martel.

'Well, it is a secret as yet,' said the lady, lowering her voice, 'but I am sure they will tell you soon, so I think I may tell you now, that we are all in delightful excitement expecting to go to the private theatricals that our cousin at Rowanshaw is getting up. I am to go there, and I believe you are to be asked. And oh! have you any friend that is clever in genteel comedy? Perhaps you are? I believe you are.'

'Of course I am—in the very genteelest.'

'Ah! you laugh. I am sure you are. They are talking about "The Rivals," and they want one more actor. Can't you help them?'

'Perhaps I can; it depends on the part. If it is

not a very onerous one, I have a young friend who is thought rather promising in that line. He has taste, and acts with spirit, and throws himself like a man into his part; but he has little experience, and is not a showy stage figure—small and not handsome, but a nice-looking lad notwithstanding.'

'You provoke a lady's curiosity—and make me wish to know who this accomplished young gentleman may be that is not good-looking but nice.'

'I think you have seen him. His father is a parishioner of mine whom Mr. Palmer knows well—Mr. Gryffyn.'

'Oh indeed!—I almost guessed it—the hero of Barbara's horrid adventure in the hunting-field. I assure you she gave so flattering an account of her deliverer, that I have the greatest wish—that is, curiosity—to see—well, more of him.'

'You have seen him, then?'

'I did get a glimpse of him when he gallantly escorted Barbara back after her escapade. But Uncle Palmer was not at home, and I believe Mr. Gryffyn felt unprotected in the dangerous company of two spinsters, he was so silent, and made off in such a hurry.'

So spoke the lady. If the whole truth had been told, round and unvarnished, Martel would have learnt that the prospect of that young man's calling to inquire after the lady's health had been made for two whole days the incessant joke between those virgins, and, 'Oh, he's coming, he is coming! You told him you hoped he would come to inquire after you; he'll take you at your word.' 'Oh! it is he!'

rung changes in the girl's morning-room as the sound of each horse's hoofs reached their ears, till, on the third day, he did call, and the two ladies were out, and missed him—whether to the mortification of either or of both, it is hard to say at present.

Something like that would have been the whole truth; but Miss Fisher merely said, that 'Barbara was sorry not to have seen him; she often talks of her deliverer and her mishap.'

'I am glad he has made so good an impression,' Martel replied. 'And as to his acting, I think him, for a secondary part, likely to make a good, serviceable little actor, should it turn out that such an one is wanted.'

'Barbara thinks him handsome,' said the lady.

'And you ?'

'Oh, I am no judge.'

'Nor am I,' replied he, 'but I should not have thought him a beauty; though no doubt he is, if you ladies think so.'

'I do not think about it, Mr. Martel; I merely gave you Barbara's opinion.'

'Well, well, though I have not known him very long, nor made up my mind about his loveliness, I am very sure that he is a nice fellow. And so he ought to be; for he has received a liberal and, indeed, a very costly education, and his father, though of the old-fashioned, bluff, country sort, is one of the very best men that ever wore top-boots—he is a real, though a rough, diamond.'

'That is just what Uncle Palmer said when Barbara was praising her preserver; and he said, too, that, if it were not for the distance, he would go and have his talkee-talkee with Mr. Gryffyn almost every day. 'Mr. Gryffyn is very rich too, is he not?' asked the lady.

'Who knows what another has, unless that other likes to tell it? which, of course, he won't. But the old man is said to have made a good deal of money, and there are all the signs of it. To be sure, he is not like your newly-enriched speculator, who, having no culture, sets what he calls his mind upon eating and drinking like an alderman; and, with John the footman, makes flaring liveries and showy carriages and horses his beau-ideal of refinement.'

'Ah! don't speak of it,' hastily broke in Miss Fisher.

Martel did not understand her emotion, and passed on to say:

'Mr. Gryffyn is plain, not to say homely, in his habits; but as a specimen of shrewd simplicity and prosperous content in rural life, I know not where his match is to be found. In his son's education he was really munificent, and allowed him four hundred a year while he was at Oxford. Before that he had as much as possible kept him away from home, and at very expensive private schools—"houses of lords," in fact;—until he sent him to France, for tuition at Nancy.'

'To Nancy! Why not to Paris?'

'In order that he might acquire the best French with the best accent.'

'Ah, Mr. Martel, you must have been born at

Nancy. You are like that fond son of the modern Athens, who would have it that the purest English is spoken in " Id-in-broo." '

' I was not born in France at all, Miss Fisher.'

' Well, I thought, Mr. Martel, that Paris was the only place to acquire good French in.'

' I am, though French by recent extraction, not Frenchman enough to offer my own opinion, with the confidence with which many fine ladies offer theirs, upon purity of French and accent. Of course, in Paris you will find all sorts of French—good, bad, and indifferent. I have heard some Parisian French classed with cockney English. Lord Mercia, who knows French and Paris as well as most Englishmen, recommended Nancy as the favourite resort of the gentlefolk of the *ancien régime*, where the purest French was sure to be got.'

' Young Mr. Gryffyn is an only son, is he not?' asked Miss Fisher, in reply.

' Yes ; but his father had by a former wife two daughters, who have married military men, and are settled in Canada in a largish way, I believe. My friend Dick is the only child of the second marriage, and his father is a widower this long while.'

' And what is young Mr. Gryffyn to be ? Not a clergyman ?'

' No ; he has not, you see, taken his degree; though that will soon signify little, for bishops will be glad to take any recruits they can get. Dick had just passed his Little-go, when his father lost, I believe, a good deal of money in some corn speculations ; and then he put it to Dick whether he would be a

10—2

clergyman or not.   Dick decided not, and proposed
the army, which his father in turn declined.   Law
and physic do not seem to have occurred to either
of them as eligible alternatives ; so Dick is to be a
farmer, and no doubt an agent, to fill his father's
boots if he can—no easy matter.   The family have
been, father and son, for several generations, agents
to the Earls of Mercia.   Little Dicky is a bit of a
count, you know, thanks to his peculiar education,
but a very good little fellow all the same. And now
you have the whole history of the Gryffyns of Fulmere Grange.'

' I see,' said the lady, ' you wonder at my curiosity.
I beg to inform you, Mr. Martel, that my cousin,
James Franklin, tells me in his letter of having met
Mr. Gryffyn at your house, and that they have forgathered several times since in the hunting-field,
and have, in short, struck up an intimacy ; so that
Mr. Gryffyn is to stay with James at his chambers
in London for the boat race. My cousin's letter was
full of questions about Barbara and her adventure
and young Mr. Gryffyn ; in fact, I may say he scarcely
wrote to poor me at all.'

' Well, Miss Fisher, you know now all about the
incipient, Francised, Oxfordised agriculturist.   Oxford theology is supposed to save the risk of his
being made in France atheistic or superstitious, or
any way pert.'

' Is that speech patriotic in a Frenchman, Mr.
Martel ?'

' I am no Frenchman, as I have said, Miss Fisher ;
I wish I were.   I am but the grandson of one, who

in France was a marquis, and in England a dancing-master or fiddler, or both. In 1792 he lost his country, his rank, his place—all but life and honour, I may say; hence am I a pauper, with an education and nothing more.'

'A profession, Mr. Martel.'

'No, Miss Fisher; the Church is no " profession," except perhaps for bishops and big-wigs. In general, it is like those " *livings* " advertised for sale to " *suit gentlemen with private means—income very small.*" Ah, well! what does it matter? I heard Lord Mercia say not long since, quite gravely, that a gentleman of his acquaintance, with fourteen thousand a year, could not afford to marry. I have food,' said the curate, looking at the well-spread table, 'and raiment,' looking at his own dress-clothes. Why not be content? as St. Paul says.'

Miss Fisher sighed, and Martel relapsed into silence and his own reflections; then said, after a pause :

'I suppose, Miss Fisher, you know all the people here ?'

'I should suppose that you do also, Mr. Martel.'

'Not quite. Who is that not just pale, but as it were neutral-tinted and sunburnt, rather distin-guished-looking man, there, to the right ?'

'That is Colonel Denny, some relation of Barbara's mother—I never understood what. They think very much of him here. He was in the Guards, and was once in Parliament; has travelled in the East, and has just come home. He is thought very clever and refined, and all that. Between ourselves, *I* think him rather " *fine.*"

'Oh! Colonel Denny, is that? And who is that very tall, amazingly handsome young man? He, I mean, with the dark hair and yellow moustache, brilliant complexion, and blue eyes?'

'That,' said Miss Fisher, looking amused and pleased, 'that is my half-brother, John Fleming— my big brother Jack, you know. He is in the 29th Red Dragoons—the Flamingoes I believe they are called. Not very like me, is he now?'

'The family likeness is not strong, but there is a likeness. You are not six feet two inches high, as I should guess he is.'

'I know what you would say, if you dare.'

'What would I say, Miss Fisher?'

'I need not tell you, Mr. Martel.'

Here the reader may be told that Miss Fisher is small, slim, skinny, and sallow, with dark hair and very fine grey eyes; her face is long and narrow, her features are regular and high, and rather bony. But her countenance, despite its outline, is not hard: it is a very sensitive face, and one to win many men's admiration. She has admirers in plenty, but she has not the ten thousand charms that provoke men to declarations of their love. Her father, a clergyman, had lost a good deal of money that he had invested in a commercial firm who were relatives of her mother—speculating, showy, extravagant sort of people, whom she dreaded.

'I seem to know your brother, Miss Fisher,' said Martel.

'He is very accessible, very *affable* indeed,' said she, laughing. 'You know all the rest? Mr. Sloan; Lord Whittleseamere.'

'Yes, I know them very well. They are bookish folk ; so am I.'

'That is one reason why you were specially asked to meet them.'

'Aye, Mr. Palmer is always very kind about that ; he knows the sort of people I like to palaver with. If it were not for the pity that he and a few others take upon me, in giving me a chance now and then to rub off the angles of my rusticity by contact with civilised swells, I believe I should soon sink into a beast of the field.'

'Not quite that, I think, Mr. Martel.'

'It is well for you not to know what a banishment is a poor curate's life! To be sure, I individually cannot complain ; for hitherto I have been most fortunate, thanks to my vices rather than virtues. My hunting, more than anything else, has kept me out of Coventry. When people do not see you, they forget you ; and how can they see a man buried in the darkness of a country parish ?   Not that I have found mine dull, thanks, as I said, to the Palmers and the foxhounds.   But how do you like these horsey and doggy counties, Miss Fisher—the happy hunting-grounds of the rustic blessed ?   You who come from the fair south-west, the land of rocks, and sea, and cockney tourists; do you find us very dull and drowsy ?'

'I! not at all.   I am of Uncle Palmer's mind and Barbara's.   They think a good neighbourhood the worst of all places to live in.   I cannot imagine what uncle would do with visitors flocking in to interrupt him all day and every day.   From breakfast till dinner we seldom see him, unless he pops in for a minute at luncheon, looking bothered by his morning's work; and then he never sits down with us.'

'And you ladies, how do you kill the time?'

'We kill no time; it flies fast enough. The morning goes in a little reading, a little music, a little stitching, or a little drawing, or a little daubing perhaps; and Barbara inspects the household affairs, with a big bunch of keys at her waist, and sees the old women who come up to tell their wants and their woes. And after luncheon she and I visit in the parish at large, if we do not ride or drive out to make visits to our neighbours. In short, we make the most of our hours, and have not a minute to spare.'

'And do you hunt?'

'No, Mr. Martel; I would not upon any account.'

'And you do not find country life monotonous?'

'I do not find it so when I am here.'

'And Miss Palmer's hunting breaks the monotony for her in the short days of winter?' put in Martel.

'That is one reason for her hunting,' replied Miss Fisher. 'Another is that she may be company to her father. He likes to have somebody to ride to cover with; and he likes to have somebody to talk with in the evening about whom and what they have seen. He also likes Barbara to have horse exercise and a little change from the Finchdale air. For the hunting Barbara cares not one jot; and she despises fast talk about horses and hounds, especially when it comes from ladies. But little

Miss Barbara, with all her quiet tastes and country ways, is fond of seeing what is to be seen, you must know; and of course she knows that she is admired, and she likes to be very charming, and is used to be flattered and petted, and have music wherever she goes. She will have a great fortune, and that is a great matter, you know, Mr. Martel.'

'Oh, you women!' said Martel mentally; and, aloud, 'Yes, she is very charming; and, as I told you, I was her admirer from the time she was the height of my knee. But now she has got beyond me, and I give her up to my betters.'

And so they gossiped on through the dinner and the dessert; and some who did not know them were sure that they were flirting desperately, and some went so far as to say, in sweet slang, that it was 'a case.' But the last subject of their disinterested conversation deserves description in a chapter to herself.

CHAPTER IX.

'Such a rural queen '
All Arcadia hath not seen.'
MILTON—*Arcades.*

OF the middle height, and finely formed, Barbara
was plump and upright as a partridge. Her small
head rose gracefully upon a slender neck, tapering
up from sloping shoulders.

'Neat-handed, fairy-footed,
Well gloved, and well booted ;'

all about her was trim and sleek, without tight-
lacing or harsh constraint; and every beauty appeared 'free to sink or swell as nature pleased.' But
though softly rounded, the figure was firm-set, nor
did it suggest unwelcome suspicions that time would
ripen it to undue luxuriance. Full-proportioned,
nicely balanced, and graceful, she was a delight of
the eyes, from the sole of her arched foot to the
crown of her classic head, and to the tips of her
dainty fingers,—not pretty, pudgy, pointed fingers,
on tiny hands of boneless fat: no, her hands were
nervous and shapely, as they were small and soft;
and pussy's velvet paw promised to give a smart

pat to any dog that vexed her. Rich as a tench in colour, her clear, smooth, fresh skin was shaded with olive and warmed with a tint of rose. Glossy, and thick, and long was the dark-brown hair, braided so smoothly over her broad, low, brow, that not a pile was [out of place. It was usually dressed with a knot behind, in the Greek fashion, that well became her head's faultless shape, and showed

> ' Her white and polished neck,
> With the lace that did it deck.'

Barbara, choosing to call herself a country girl, indulged her own fancy in many a little whim. Her head was her own in the country, she said ; when in London, she must make herself a monster, like other people. Her eyebrows, though not meeting, spanned her broad brow in one dark pencilled arch, beneath which her eyes looked out from their deep orbits, clear and brown, like the waters of a highland loch. They were neither large nor small, and were more noticeable for expression than for shape. Her nose was of the straighter sort, and rather long than short, well-cut enough, but not with an outline hard or sharp. Red and ripe as cherries were her lips, like to pearls her teeth, and her chin was pointed. Without being by any means a showy beauty, taken altogether, she was, as the dames of the village used to say, 'a sight for sore eyes.'

If any reader wishes for a better idea of her than words can give, he may enjoy the delight of seeing a passable, though perhaps over-favourable, representation of her in the picture of Mary Queen of Scots, that is, or used to be, in the Bodleian library at Oxford. At all events, there is the same broad, low brow over a face tapering to a pointed chin, the same rich colouring, the same hazel eyes; and, better than all, the same sweet, winning, womanly expression.

Add to these charms of flesh and blood good breeding, good temper, amiable and gentle manners, a high and lively spirit, and the certain inheritance of some two thousand pounds a year, in her own right, and probably as much more; and you may be sure that she met with a great deal of admiration, disinterested and other;—which, being a tolerably shrewd young lady, she took for just so much as it was worth. But her good-nature disposed her, in return for attentions that were pleasant, to make herself to every one as agreeable as she could; and, having great capabilities, she became a very general favourite. Used to admiration, she looked for it, as her cousin has hinted, and received it very graciously by whomsoever offered; and if by any chance it was withheld, she only viewed with curiosity one so different from his fellows as to 'withstand unmoved the lustre of her charms.'

For her habits, the fair Barbara was tinctured with letters, and, in an engaging way, somewhat 'blue.' Cultivated and grave elderly gentlemen gladly spent an hour in chat with the very pretty girl, who was able and willing to entertain them with conversation suited to their taste. Nor had she any difficulty in exchanging with younger heads that lighter discourse, which is called 'chaff' between

young people of different sexes, and in fact borders
pleasantly upon flirtation. If she liked riding to
see the hounds, she also could draw and paint with
taste, and was an enthusiast in music. For some
years it was her advantage to have in her governess
a musical genius ; and she had profited by her opportunity, having patience and perseverance, as well as
a fine touch and a true ear, and what is better than
all else, plenty of feeling with the gift of expressing
it. Her voice being low and sweet, and clear and
flexible, she sang ballads very well; and did not hide
any of her talents in a napkin, but played the organ
in church, and trained the village choir, as few choirs
were trained in those good old days of flute, flageo-
let, and bass viol. In short, this young lady had
within herself a world of resources ; and, though
her home was of the quietest, had no wish for more
excitement or society, quite sharing her father's
opinion, (which her mother had neither shared nor
tolerated), that a good neighbourhood is a great
nuisance, and only fit for folks who know not what
to do with their time.

On the whole, the world was agreed that Miss
Palmer was a model heiress, brilliant and amiable, who
wanted nothing to make her perfect but marriage ;
'and *that*,' said some good ladies, whispering and
nodding at one another, 'that would do her a great
deal of good.' But she had not showed herself in
any hurry to exchange the liberal and assured admiration of the many for the more stinted and less
certain worship of one. Indeed, she was a very
dainty miss, always obliging, and generally frank,

but something freakish ; the result, mayhap, in her merry and managing mind, of being monarch of all she surveyed.

A little pentagonal room was hers, that had been her mother's, built to gratify one of her many whims. It opened into the drawing-room, from which it was screened by rose-coloured curtains, that usually hung festooned on either side of the carved and arched entrance. This wee, pentagonal snuggery, which she called her book-closet, and which her father called her conjuring-den, was charmingly fitted up to the ceiling with book-cases of carved ebony, beneath which were ranged luxurious rose-coloured settees and easy-chairs. The ebony shelves were fitted with choice and valuable books, richly bound in bright hues. A small writing-table, ingeniously-equipped and furnished with a cleverly-contrived library chair, and a few more of fanciful shapes, scattered over a carpet of brown and green and pale yellow, made to resemble the mossy carpet of the woods in primrose-time, and a sprinkling of lady-like minutiæ, unknown by name to man, but adding much to female comfort, completed Barbara's bower, or in the paternal phrase her den, the sanctum sanctorum to which she would carry off her victims of the lettered sort, to indoctrinate them with her views, or pick their brains at leisure, whilst whist and small talk were prosecuted in the profane precincts of the larger drawing-room.

Such was Barbara, and such the sacred retreat, into which, if we look, we shall be sure to find a selection of the guests inveigled after dinner.

CHAPTER X.

'When dinner's done,
And body gets its sop and holds its noise,
And leaves soul free a little. Now's the time.'
                    ⸱R. BROWNING'S *Blougram.*

IF we stand at the entrance of this lady's bower, we shall hear the conversation of the company within, composed chiefly of elderly gentlemen.

'I must tell you, Mr. Martel,' says the lady of the place, 'that I have been studying criticism and history, at your instigation, in Macaulay's essays.'

'And you are full of gratitude to me for the pleasure I have secured you ?'

'Well, no; I cannot truly say that I am. I was very much entertained at first, and had a perfect feast; but I soon got nauseated, as though I had been living on plum-pudding:—he so overloads one with superlatives. His first-form boys and school-girls are miracles of knowledge; half his fellow-creatures are mountains of infamy, and the other half pure angels. I don't believe in one or the other one bit. For the future, when I want to improve myself, I shall go back to my old oracles the poets, and dear old wholesome Walter Scott; they make me feel happier and better. I will have no more of your Macaulays and critics; I wish to avoid stimulants, and to preserve my health of mind. I do not like caricaturists.'

'I am quite with you, Miss Palmer, about critics in general, such as kept a whole generation from reading Wordsworth, and killed Keats. But there are critics and critics: we have Dryden and De Quincey, and Lamb and Coleridge, and Mackintosh and Hallam, to set against their opposites. About my great Mac I have felt just as you do. He certainly does "lay it on with a trowel" in the matter of praise and blame, and his facts want sifting: but I have learned to do him justice, and I cannot give him up. Though I grant you Scott is miles before him, I hold my Mac to be a mighty genius, with a vivid imagination and plenty of strong common sense.'

'Very *common* indeed,' muttered Mr. Cumber, who was standing in the gangway, listening with all his ears, and a sneer upon his shrewd, sleek face.

'And a very honest man,' proceeded the Macaulay advocate.

'If you call a man honest who never scruples to attribute dishonesty or stupidity to any one who is not of his faction,' retorted the examining chaplain.

'Wait till we get his history,' said the curate.

'I put more faith in Scott's romances,' said the bishop's chaplain.

'They use largely the same materials—ballads and popular literature; and work in much the same way—by imagination and picture-drawing,' replied Martel.

'But Scott has the heart of man, and a good word for every one,' retorted Cumber.

'I grant you Scott has the larger humanity,' said Martel. 'Macaulay has managed to kick off the Puritan fetters, but they have left their marks on him; he is as narrow as honesty and genius will let him be.'

'You mean that he can see no beauty in any bird that is not of his feather; that nothing is too bad for him to think or say of Wilson Croker and Brougham; that he all but *hates* Wordsworth, and has no love for Sydney Smith, or Moore, or Byron, or Scott, or Coleridge, and is far from fond of Lytton-Bulwer, or Dickens, or of any author else that is alive in flesh and blood, except his Jeffrey, if you call him one. Your Macaulay is a Turk; he is a book; he has no sympathies; or if he has, they begin and end at home.'

'Oh! but,' rejoined Martel, 'he has strongish likes and dislikes. He has a strong distaste for the Reverend Robert Montgomery, and he has a strong regard for the Very Reverend Henry Hart Milman. He is, in fact, very jealous of the honour of literature. He did not devote himself to literature because he had failed as an orator or as a statesman. A man of letters to the marrow, he puts heart and soul into his work.

' " It is not *his*, by false connections drawn,
At splendid slavery's sordid shrine to fawn ;
'Tis not for *him* to purchase, or pursue,
The phantom favours of the cringing crew ;
More useful toils his studious hours engage,
And fairer lessons fill his living page,
Above ambition and above disgrace,
With nobler arts he forms the rising race." '

Martel stopped, and Cumber was silent, in grim disgust.

' Have you done ?' asked Mr. Sloan, looking amusedly towards the former.

' I have done,' replied he, with a grin.

' Then I suppose I may be allowed to say that I quite agree with Miss Palmer about Sir Walter Scott and Macaulay. But we live in unpoetic days : no more Scotts, or Byrons, or Wordsworths for us. The race of poets is, I fear, dying out naturally, for want of subjects suited to the muse ; we are too sophisticated and scientific—too materialised, in short, for poetry and high thinking.'

' No poetry—no poetry !' almost screamed Martel, all alive for the fray again ; ' no poets, Mr. Sloan ! Have we not one walking in the steps of Wordsworth, and, some say (of whom I am not one), excelling him in all but his unapproachable " Ode to Immortality ?" Yet Keble is an apt pupil, and has, no doubt, exerted a far more general and popular influence than his master. He has even trained people into a taste for Wordsworth. But think of Tennyson ! than whom, I contend, no greater poet has arisen since Milton.'

' Yes, Mr. Martel,' struck in Lord Whittleseamere ;
' and I contend that Tennyson is a greater poet than

Milton; of this at least am I sure, that Milton could not have written " Enoch Arden." '

And then it was delightful to hear the old judge, despite his dry studies and his threescore and ten years, fire up like a boy, and set off repeating passage upon passage of that most pathetic of poems.

After a respectful pause, and perhaps because old lawyers have seldom quite lost the trick of hard and sharp hitting, Mr. Sloan said to Martel, who sat next him, in a subdued tone, not meant to reach the ear of his lordship, who was a trifle deaf:

' Tennyson is a mannerist, and has wrought the taste of this generation into a liking for a false style.'

' Oh ! but, Mr. Sloan,' whispered Martel, ' Lord Whittleseamere is of the generation *before* Tennyson, who therefore cannot have moulded *his* taste.'

' H'm !' said Mr. Sloan, ' lawyers' tastes are peculiar. I found my objection to Tennyson on his conscious affectations.'

' Conscious affectations !' repeated Martel; ' I don't know about that. Great critics have taken exception to what they call the affected phrases and un-English inversions of Milton ; yet who, unless (as our friend says) Tennyson, surpasses,—how many equal,—him, in the exquisite art of twining short, homely, natural Saxon words into "linked sweetness " ?'

' Yes, yes. It is not of Milton's, but of Tennyson's affectations that I complain.'

' And I must beg to maintain that what you con-

11—2

demn as conscious affectations are natural to him,
and that you are "calling his flower a weed."
Secondly, as we used to say in sermons——'

'And as I, being an old-fashioned man, say now,
when I want to be clear,' interposed Mr. Sloan, with
dignity.

'Secondly, then,' proceeded Martel, 'if I might
indulge such egotism before my betters, I would
attempt to prove in my own proper person that the
taste for his writing is not an acquired taste like
that for port wine, but a natural and, I hope, a
healthy taste like the taste for beer. When I was
at college, and leading an idlish life——'

'More shame for you!' remarked the college don.

'Yes—the unprofitable thought entered my head
to read through all the prize poems. Only one
seemed to repay my idle curiosity, and the subject
of that was "Timbuctoo," and the writer was Alfred
Tennyson. "Who is Alfred Tennyson?" asked I.
A friend, in reply, brought me from the University
library a volume of poems written by the prizeman
in question. In my youthful, unacquired, and un-
cultivated and unsophisticated appetite—for I will
not presume to call it taste—I devoured the volume;
and even yet I think that neither in Tennyson, nor
in any other writer that I am acquainted with, is
there anything sweeter than what I then most admired—the "Œnone," the "Ulysses," the "Lotus-
eaters," and the "Dream of Fair Women."'

'H'm! I think I remember he is a bit of a Turk
in his tastes,' commented Mr. Sloan. 'Well, well, I
may be wrong, for I have scarcely looked into his

books; but since his lordship and you agree in saying so much for him, I will try, some day when I
have time to throw away, to read him and his " fair
women " with more care and less prejudice.'

'Then will you,' said Martel eagerly, 'let me call
your attention as a scholar to a fragment of translation from the " Iliad " ? Compare it with Pope's, to
which I owe very much, and which I loved and had
by heart as a boy, or with Cowper's, or even Chap-
man's, or with any of the many other translations
by lords and by commoners, and tell me some day
whether you would not regret with me that, amidst
the endless recent attempts to re-translate the old
bard, Tennyson has not been induced to make one.
Among the greatest of his many, in my eyes immense, merits I count his having recovered the lost
secret of Elizabethan and Jacobean art in writing
the most difficult of all metres—musical, well-
jointed, and natural blank verse, wherein the rhythm
flows with the sense, and marks it, and the syllables
are not counted on the fingers. This charming art,
with that of using to magical effect short, simple
Saxon words, mostly monosyllables, went out with
Milton and Dryden.'

'I think, Mr. Martel,' said his neighbour, 'that the
restoration of the old poetic diction you speak of,
and the old poetic treatment, was wrought syste-
matically by Wordsworth, Southey, and Coleridge,
and that Scott, though he did not preach it up, and
Byron, though he rather ran it down, used it to the
full as effectively as did the other three.'

'True; but neither Wordsworth, nor Southey,

nor Coleridge, nor Byron, nor Scott found the magic that could do it, though they all tried to awaken the slumbering harmonies of the old blank verse. Shelley and Keats did the most for it, but the great restorer of all was Tennyson. Dr. Johnson, whose criticism has more in it than some people are now willing to allow, remarks, in his "Life of Waller," that the poets of England had attained an art of "modulation," which was afterwards neglected or forgotten. It seems that art of rhythmical melody was first wrought into completeness in what Ben Johnson called "Marlow's mighty line." It was modified and invested with fresh power by the supreme and solitary genius of Shakespeare. From him it was transmitted in glorious, though unequal, succession through Ben Jonson, Beaumont and Fletcher, Webster, Massinger, and a host of lesser lights ; and, mind you, to that so carefully elaborated art we owe, under God's providence, the harmonious fitness and musical chime of our authorised translation of the Bible. The balance of its rhythm was made perfect, though the character of its diction was not changed, in the process of revision by King James's divines, who were trained in the fulness of the dramatic time. Its cast of phrase, the ebb and flow, the unbroken roll and wave-like beat of its short, clear, uninvolved sentences, depend for their effect upon the emphasis and pauses of the understanding reader. Sense and sound are so entwined that if the reading be lame or unmelodious we may assume the reader has failed to catch the drift of the passage. "The uncommon beauty and pure English of the Pro-

testant Bible is one of the strongholds of heresy in
this country," says Father Faber; "it lives on the
ear like music that can never be forgotten, like the
sound of Church bells." So great is the use of style
and melody, and so much do we owe to all those
who helped to make it perfect in its revision at that
particular period.

'But, my good sir, the style was in the air in James
the First's day, and at the latter end of Elizabeth's.'

'To be sure it was in the air. But how did it
get there?—eh? How did it get there? Why
through the theatre, the great school of the nation.
As Scott, who understood such matters if ever man
did, has remarked, "The audience must have had a
stronger sense of poetry in those days than in ours,
since language was received and applauded at 'The
Fortune' or the 'Red Bull' which could not now
be understood by any general audience in Britain."
The fact is, we have lost in the fall of the theatre
an enormous educating instrument. Yes, the style
was in the air when James's bishops revised the
Bible translation. But it was not in the air when
Sir Thomas More, and Cranmer, and Latimer
wrote and spoke, any more than it was in the air
when Stillingfleet, and Burnet, and Tillotson wrote.
Scarce a grain of it lingered in the atmosphere
after the days of Taylor, Barrow, and Dryden. If
any subtle touch of it remained with Addison and
South, certainly Pope and Swift had none of it,
perfect as they are in a style of their own.'

'What have you to say to Clarendon?' asked
Mr. Sloan.

'Well, Mr. Sloan, though Mr. Hyde was one of Jonson's "Tribe of Ben," his literary art seems to have been derived rather from Hooker than from the dramatists.'

'Ahem!' put in Mr. Cumber, who had been listening with visible impatience. 'I had fancied till now—I suppose I was wrong—but I had fancied it settled that Hooker built up into perfection our prose construction, and that he had caught the cadence from Cicero.'

'I think, with you, if I may be allowed to have an opinion, that the style of Cicero was the model for the rather long-winded prose of Hooker and of our Prayer-book. But the blank verse of the Elizabethan and Jacobean dramatists [whose rhythm depends as much on the sense of the words, as would the construction, if they were not writing in metre at all,] was derived not at all from Cicero, but, through Surrey and Wyatt, from the line and period of Virgil; who arranges his words naturally and properly as in prose, every one just where it ought to be. From his pupils, the dramatists, was caught not only the style, but the phrase, or expression, also, in which James's revising divines recast for the last time and perfected the old English Bible—a style as different as possible from the long, involved, exhausting, and Latinised, though not unmelodious, sentence of Hooker and of the Prayer-book.'

'Ah, then,' spoke Mr. Sloan, 'the English Bible is indebted, not only for the music of its movement, but for the purity of its phrase also, to your friends the Elizabethan dramatists! Is that what you would say, Mr. Martel?'

'Indeed, yes; I say the style and the diction were in the air, and that same most competent judge, Sir Walter Scott, seems to give us a good hint how it got there, when he says that, "Worthless as were many of the plays of what is roughly called the Elizabethan era, they are almost all *written in good tune*. The dramatic poets of that time," he remarks, "seem to have *possessed, as a joint stock, a highly poetical tone of language*, so that the worst of them reminds you of the very best." But, though the revised translation of the Bible by the Jacobean bishops and divines is past improvement, the *whole* credit of the work cannot be set down to their account; certainly not its Saxon diction, which traces back at least as far as Wyckliffe. It is not, indeed so much the work of one, but the growth of many, generations, to which King James's men were called by Providence to put the last finishing touch, when they had learnt from the dramatists the perfection of their art.'

'H'm! I never imagined till to-day that we could trace our authorised English Bible back to the playhouse,' said Mr. Cumber, with all the combined severity of a college don and an examining chaplain.

'That sounds very like rebuke,' said Martel. 'But this world's work is curiously and inextricably interwoven; and how can I tell all that the Elizabethan drama, with Shakespeare at its head, owes to the setting free and making public of Hebrew inspired books and their draughts of human life and character, which might at once show to those great minds the way to fulfil their mission as half-inspired teachers of their brethren. One thing seems plain enough, any way; and that is, that poetry, prose, and the drama all together, as at one birth, leaped into maturity. The Book of Revelation was unveiled to the nation at large by the publication of the " Bishop's Bible;" the truest delineation of *mixed* human character in the Old Testament, the picture of its *perfection* in the New, the noblest poems the world ever saw, by Moses and Job and David, by Isaiah, Jeremiah, and Ezekiel, and Daniel, and all the prophets, were publicly read in English, and incessantly commented on in every English town. It was reckoned disgraceful not to study them even so as to commit much of them to memory; their then novelty and freshness prevented careless reading; men talked of them by the way, and when they lay down, and when they rose up. Where is the wonder that, in such a flood of light, our poets should catch some of its rays, and kindle with the sacred fire. How could they miss it?'

'I am learning much that is new to me. The old dramas, it seems, were religious works, and the old dramatists religious men,' said the don.

'That is more than I said; and you need not assume either the one thing or the other,' replied the curate. 'But perhaps you will admit that no great and popular works of literature, produced in a country where Christianity prevails and its Scriptures are studied, can be strictly and absolutely secular. If the plays so speak to the heart of the people as to become their favourite recreation, it can only be because they reflect, in a measure, the moral tone, the sympathies, and antipathies of that people.'

'A pretty *moral* tone they must have had, if we are to suppose it reflected in most of their plays,' sneered Cumber.

'We must not judge one age by the standard of another,' replied Martel. 'We must keep in mind that the spectators of the bull-baitings and bear-baitings became the audience of the theatres, and took some of the old flavour with them, to the detriment of the drama. But the theatres emptied the bear-gardens ; and was not that a gain ?'

Here our curate stopped short.

'Go on,' said Cumber.

'No, thank you—no more in the face of my betters; I have just recollected myself.'

'Go on.'

'No, no. I have not the grace of reticence, I know, but I have the grace to be ashamed of my loquacity.'

'Go on,' said Mr. Cumber ; 'I want to hear the end of this.'

'You have heard it; I have finished.'

'Nonsense ! I want to know what you have been driving at.'

'Nay, I had no further object.'

'A man must have some object in saying so much.'

'Not I.'

'You began something about the dramatist's
sacred fire, and you have only told us they emptied
the bear-gardens.'

'I said that the dramatists, with Shakespeare at
their head, owed more than could be told to the
publication of the Holy Scriptures.'

'As how, pray? That is a very loose statement.
Explain.'

'Please go on, Mr. Martel; I am very much in-
terested,' put in Miss Palmer.

'Well, then, Miss Palmer, let me ask you who is
the most original of writers? Shakespeare, you say.
Well, and his most original play—is it not, perhaps,
" Macbeth " ?'

'Granted—" Macbeth,"' said Cumber; 'I do not
know where else is a character like his. What
then ?'

'Did you ever consider the character of Saul ?
What is the history either of Macbeth or of Saul
but a record of the gradual fall and ruin of a highly-
gifted soul ? To describe in short the career of Saul :
He first excites admiration ; then, in his struggle
with temptation, he draws our sympathy, and in his
remorse our pity. Step by step he grows worse and
worse, until the only vestiges of virtue left are his
anguish of spirit and his valour. Compare him with
Macbeth. In the outset Macbeth is a valiant soldier
and an accomplished man. He is great ; he would be
greater. But he is too " full of the milk of human
kindness " to take the nearest way : he would not
play false, yet would he wrongly win ; he dreads to
do bad deeds, does them with reluctance, and wishes

them undone. Like Saul, he excites, as I said, first admiration, next sympathy, then pity; and then, step by step, he wades deeper into blood and crime, till at last the only marks of manhood left are his desperate courage and the unquenchable remorse that still keeps count of and tells over, in burning words, his terrible sins and his awful sorrows.'

'Aye, that is all very well so far as it goes; but your outlines are so loose and general that they might be made to fit almost any wreck of greatness by sin and self. I want to be shown more clearly the several points of identity or similarity of cha- racter,' said Cumber.

'Another time. You must be tired; I can tres- pass no longer on the patience of the company.'

'No, no; go on, man, now that you have begun,' reiterated Cumber.

'We are listening with all our ears, Mr. Martel, and we must not be baulked of our expectations,' put in Miss Palmer again.

'Well, well, recluse though I be, I am tired at last of the sound of my own voice.'

'Pray go on—you have made ample apologies— pray go on to your conclusions,' cried Cumber.

'If I must, I must,' said the curate, trying to look modest. 'Roughly, then, the victorious military character, and the prophecy of a kingdom, are com- mon to Macbeth and Saul; so is the jealousy of a rival. David and his line are very much to the one what Banquo and his line are to the other. Mac- beth murders his benefactor, the gracious Duncan; Saul would slay his preserver David. Macbeth

murders Banquo; but Fleance escapes. So David escapes; and Saul attempts the life of his own son, the
friend of David. Saul is haunted by an evil spirit;
and "full of scorpions is" Macbeth's "mind." The
voice of conscience in either is smothered, not silenced;
in each is peace of mind poisoned by the rancours of
remorse. Their struggles are frequent, terrible, and
unavailing; for self still continues the ruling spirit
of each through all their dire regrets and tremors.
Wracked without respite by the indelible writing
on the brain, both are bent to know the worst, and
by the worst means: Saul seeks to his one witch,
and Macbeth to his three. Both resolve not to go
back, but to wade on still in blood. Ahimelech
shelters David, and Saul slays Ahimelech and all
the company of the priests at Nob, and smites with
the edge of the sword both men and women, children and sucklings; Macbeth seizes Macduff's castle,
and gives to the edge of the sword his wife and
babes and all the unfortunate souls that trace in
him their line. To each the end is to fall in battle
sword in hand, seeking death in blank despair.
Cruel and insatiate they both are—all but remorse-
less; the spark of good left in them is the spark of
conscience, causing ceaseless agony—the unextin-
guished light of the spirit of man searching the inward parts. It is this, and this alone, that retains
the shocked sympathies of our common nature, and
keeps up our interest in these two bad men even to
the last. Gentlemen of the jury, that is my case,'
said Martel.

'A word more yet,' replied Cumber. 'Supposing

we admit all you say about Macbeth's likeness to
Saul, you will tell us, maybe, that Lady Macbeth
also is not an original.'

'Original! yes, as much as any work of art ever
is or can be. But your poet is not really a maker
in the sense of a creator out of nothing—he is rather
a re-creator; and I should say that Lady Macbeth
has her archetype as evidently as her lord has
his.'

'And where, pray?'

'In the same place.'

'I do not remember much about Saul's wife.'

'No. But of the character of Macbeth one feature is borrowed from Ahab, whom Jezebel, his wife,
stirred up; and the hint for Lady Macbeth is furnished by Jezebel herself. The prelude to Duncan's
murder has so strong a resemblance to the scene regarding Naboth's vineyard, that the same words may
describe the prime actor in both. Jezebel pours her
spirits into Ahab's ear, and chastises him with
valour of her tongue, if not in the very accents,
quite in the tone, of Lady Macbeth. It is a rather
far-fetched fancy, but I think the banquet-scene
and the appearance of the spectre to the king have
their origin in Belshazzar's feast: at the writing
on the wall "the king's countenance was changed,
and his thoughts troubled him, so that the joints of
his loins were loosed, and his knees smote one against
another"—a description that fits Macbeth at the
banquet. In short, I know I have not converted
you, and "by your smiling you seem to say so;" but
I hold fixedly "Macbeth" to be in a measure, and

at the root of it, a scripturally-founded play, and
that the spectacle of Macbeth loaded with blood-
crimes, struggling against accusing conscience, and
haunted by the furies of remorse, is an inspiration
drawn from the Divine record of Saul's sin and sorrow, and eked out by other hints drawn from the
same sacred source.   I am as sure of this as I am
that Shakespeare took much of his " Antony and
Cleopatra " bodily (*verbatim et literatim*) from Roger
North's translation of " Plutarch's Lives." '

'Come, come, this is too much,' said Mr. Sloan;
'don't tell me about North and Plutarch.   Shakespeare's gorgeous picture of Cleopatra on the Cydnus
is one of the many marvels in his unapproachable
delineation of that bold, bad woman—a portraiture
ranking, in a certain way, as among the finest and
most felicitous of all his wonderful works.'

'There, now you have hit it; that is the very
mark I proposed for you.   My dear sir, pardon me
if I say that you are not the first great man that
has fallen into that trap.   Miss Palmer knows what
I mean, and will permit me to take from her shelves
North's " Plutarch."   I know its place; here it is;
and here is the life of Antony.   Shakespeare never
does mere work for work's sake; he uses everything that comes handy to him.   Here he has found
need to do no more than readjust the order of
North's picturesque words, and turn splendid prose
into more splendid verse.   *That* is Shakespeare's
way; and in the same easy way the fire of his
genius, with much more magical power, transmuted
into the pure gold of his historical plays the rude

ore of the old chronicles, which the first playwrights
had already stitched into scenes ready to his hand,
and had further garnished with unpolished dialogue.
That is what humoursome folk mean by saying that
Shakespeare is "a botcher up of old plays," and "an
inspired adapter for the theatre." I take it Homer
did with rude ballads just what Shakespeare did
with rude plays, and that is, gave them unity by
his genius. And now that I am upon my hobby, I
must again proclaim my belief that the very greatest
works are in some sort *growths.* Our authorised
English Bible is a growth; the "Iliad" is a growth;
the historic, if not all the other, plays of Shakespeare
are growths; Raphael's cartoons are perhaps growths
—certainly some of the *figures* are adaptations, as,
for example, from Massaccio, *Paul* preaching at
Athens; and so our England is a growth—"A thousand years have scarce sufficed to make our blessed
England what it is; an hour may lay it in the dust;
and can you, with all your talents, renovate
its shattered splendour? can you recall back its
virtues? can you vanquish time or 'fate?" asks
Sydney Smith of Lord John Russell, adapting, by
the way, four lines from "Childe Harold."'

There was a pause, which Mr. Sloan broke thus:
'Before we quit this subject, if Miss Palmer is not
too tired of us, I must, after praising Shakespeare,
out with what I have often felt, but never, that I
remember, ventured to express. Admitting and admiring his mighty gifts, I do say—and our sixteenth
century friend will forgive me—but, as an old
clergyman, I do say that there is prevalent an

idolatry of Shakespeare's works that I do not understand. Freely and gladly I grant that, when he chooses to imagine a virtuous and exalted character, he throws his whole soul into it, and gives a perfect picture of an admirable man ; but he has a licentious taste that is at home in Falstaff. Milton I like the best of all ; he is, in my opinion, more poetical than Shakespeare, and he is a good man.'

'H'm !' said the curate, ' I do not deny the "good man," Mr. Sloan, when he is not controversial; and as to the poet, I only say that his minor poems, which are inspired, I suppose, by Anglicanism, are more to my mind than the "Paradise Lost," bating some delicious scenes ; and I confess to a love of his play, the "Samson Agonistes." '

'Aye; but I want to know, Martel, what you have to say for Shakespeare ?'

'Oh, Mr. Sloan, you have opened a boundless ocean, on which I should soon lose myself. But, to say truth, I think Shakespeare a more religious man than Milton. You may look surprised. What I mean is that he has more of "reverence, that angel of the world ;"* he has less egotism, or rather none at all ; he is never impatient of fact and truth, nor unconscious of the mystery of Providence and of spirit, and he has ever a feeling of the brotherhood of mankind, such as we find no trace of in Milton, who is a partisan always. But the subject is as much out of my depth as it would be beyond the limits of conversation, which I have unpardonably transgressed already.'

* ' Cymbeline,' act iv. scene 2.

'Not at all, Mr. Martel, not at all; indeed you have not,' said Miss Palmer.

'Yes, I tread on folk's toes, and they like it, I know, Miss Palmer.'

'Now for the rest of your attack or defence—which is it?' asked Sloan.

'Oh, I will not pretend that I am a stranger to the impeachment, or that I have not seen a, to me, satisfactory defence; but I must refer you to the Schlegels and Hallam and Coleridge, and many other good men and true of the gigantic breed. This only would I say—with Keble, mind—that "Shakespeare gave play to the real sympathy he seems to have felt towards all natural and common affections in a degree hardly conceivable by ordinary men." "Out of the fulness of the heart the mouth speaketh;" and when Shakespeare painted to the life *just* men, "out of the good treasure of his heart he brought forth good things."'

'Aye, aye; but the evil things?'

'Well, you know, Shakespeare is, as I said, a "friendly genius." Nothing in the form of man came amiss to him: neither "Jew, Turk, infidel, or heretic was 'unspeakable' or inhuman in his eyes; his sympathy embraced them all. Like David in the cave of Adullam, he takes to him every one that is in distress, every one that is in debt, every one that is discontented, and becomes a captain over them; he feels their sorrows, knows their crimes and their wrongs, and comprehends their quarrel with society."

> ' " These banished men that I have kept withal,
> Are men endued with worthy qualities : "

That is Shakespeare's view always. He could, if ever mere man could, enter into and search hearts, to find many an unsuspected corner of good within.

> " 'No soul of man he worthless found ;
> But all were precious in his sight."

He was not a man to wonder that *one of those thieves suffering justly upon the cross had a good heart, prepared to receive the good seed;* and Falstaff—poor old dying Falstaff!—this great heart-searcher makes to play with flowers, and smile upon his fingers, and babble of green fields, and call upon the Universal Father, who never fails to hear the cry of the poor penitent. But the two thieves of the Gospel story had different ends; and another departure is assigned to Cardinal Beaufort. Shall I quote the passage ?'

'No—yes, go on.'

> ' " See how the pangs of death do make him grin !
> Peace to his soul, if God's good pleasure be !
> Lord Cardinal, if thou think'st on Heaven's bliss,
> Hold up thy hand : make signal of thy hope.
> He dies ;—and makes no sign : O God, forgive him !
> So bad a death argues a monstrous life.—
> Forbear to judge : for we are sinners all."
>   *Henry VI.*—Part 2, Act 3, Scene 3.

I will, by way of sheltering myself respectably, sum all I would say in words of Sir James Stephen that I well remember: "Shakespeare has written nothing in any of his dramas to confound or impair the eternal distinctions between good and evil; but he has written much to render virtue infinitely lovely, and vice unutterably hateful, and he has completed the noblest literary monument which it has ever been permitted to any uninspired man to erect for the illumination of his brethren of mankind, and for the glory of the Giver of every good and perfect gift."'

'"And now," &c.—Shall I go on, and give the Ascription?"' whispered Lieutenant Fleming, who had been flitting to and fro between the whist-table and the book-room like a great gaudy butterfly, not knowing what flower to settle on.

'I should be glad to hear anything so gracious come out of your mouth,' whispered back Martel; and the séance was dissolved.

'"Falstaff, good-night!"' quoth Sloan to the curate, with playful emphasis, as they quitted the little apartment.

Martel was standing with his back to the wall, resting perhaps after his excess of talk, when Miss Palmer, who had been looking after her guests, came sailing up, point-device, rejoicing in her beauty's pride, and anchored herself before him. This he affected to take as a challenge to admire, and proceeded, accordingly, to review her from top to toe with an air of dumb amazement; while she, on her part, stood stoutly up to inspection, and finally turned round that the survey might be completed, after which she made him a little curtsey, and he made her a little bow; and the preliminary ceremonies being thus concluded, the lady, lowering her voice, began:

'Now, I must tell you, I am so pleased; Mr. Sloan has just been saying to me how charmed he was with our little talkee-talkee. He had never ima-

gined you cared so much for literature. How little
he knew! But you are so close, you know—not with
us, to be sure—I wanted him to know you better.
He is such a good man; that is why I brought you
together in my little den. In short—don't be angry
now—but I was trotting you out on your hobby,
meaning to do you good. You know, Mr. Sloan and
his friend Mr. Spencer Cumber have a great deal of
influence with our bishop, particularly Mr. Cumber,
who is, I hear, to be made something great—a dean,
or an archdeacon, or archbishop, or a rural dean, or
an honorary canon, or something of that sort. I am
sure Mr. Sloan thinks very well of you. I saw him
very attentive at our little gathering, though he
does not generally like to lose his whist; but I
made him come.'

'Did you though? How amazingly kind of you!
I am immensely flattered and obliged.'

'You may just be as ironical as you please; but
one must make friends at court, or nothing will be
got, however deserving a man may be. I am sure
Mr. Sloan has taken to you, and will speak up for
you—as he ought to do—and will make his friend
your friend.'

'Oh, I am sure of it! Shall I tell you what his
friend said just now? I happened to be planted
close behind, and could not help hearing it.'

'You don't say so! How nice not to be able to
help hearing!'

'Very nice indeed to hear Mr. Spencer Cumber
say to his friend:

'"I suppose that fellow is so buried that he

seldom gets a chance of opening his mouth; and when it is once open, he does not know how to shut it. To think of his haranguing you and me for the best part of an hour!"

'"Well," said Mr. Sloan good-naturedly, "he had something to say for himself, hadn't he?"

'"But did you ever hear such trash?" asked Cumber. "Could you endure the slatternly inaccuracy of the man?"

'"There were *lacunæ* here and there, I fancy, in his argument," said the good Sloan; "but where was he so very inaccurate?"

'"Argument! Didn't you see he had not an idea how much or how little was done in the revision of the Bible? And as to Shakespeare, he evidently did not know the late researches into the originals of his plays, or that immortal Will was a very partial Lancastrian, and, as such, sadly maltreated poor Cardinal Beaufort, who was by no means a bad man. And, by-the-way, the death-scene is, I believe, only Shakespeare's by adoption. If I were this fellow's examiner, I would certainly pluck him!"

'"H'm! you do as much for most of the men you examine, don't you?" asked Sloan slily.

'"I dare say," went on Mr. Spencer Cumber, too lofty to regard the imputation, "I dare say he is loose in his theology—a foggy fellow like that is sure to be. If he came into our diocese, I would insist upon examining him."

'I had heard quite enough, but I could not get past that fat Lady Ashworth, so I heard kind old Sloan say:

' " But, if he is inexact, you will allow he has some cleverness ?"

' " Oh ! he is a clever fellow," replied Mr. Spencer Cumber" [Here Miss Palmer smiled and nodded, as much as to say, ' You see '] "a very clever fellow : he knew nothing at all of what he was talking about, and he had a very clever way of showing it." '

' No ! did he though ?   Did he say all that ?'

' Them was his wery words.'

' Horrid, dry, fusty old fogy !' said the lady, grimacing, and half-laughing at the utter discomfiture of her plot. ' But did he know you heard him ?'

' I fancy he did ; I was wedged in close behind. Anyhow, he did not seem to care. I dare say he thought it might do me good ; he is just the sort of lad to think all his words pearls and diamonds.'

' But he is very clever, isn't he ?' asked the lady.

' I don't know. These wooden fellows are petrified by their devotion to verbal criticism and logic, and the like of that ; they are mere stones, incapable of the feelings of flesh and blood. The Dean of St. Austin's has reduced his mind to such a state—I beg his pardon, *elevated* his mind to such a height— that he can read nothing with relish but a Greek lexicon ; and this Mr. Spencer Cumber is just such another, I dare say.'

' But that was an amusing joke of his, was it not ? —he, he, he !' laughed the lady.

' Very entertaining indeed—ha, ha, ha !' laughed the gentleman ; ' I always liked that joke. It is as old as the hills; it has been made so many times that no one knows whose it is—Charles the Second's, Sir Charles Sedley's, or Sir Thomas More's.'

She peered into his face with a roguish smile, that seemed to say, 'Oh, I declare he has made you quite angry!'

Martel's chin had been thrown well up, and he sniffed in disdain the air; then, as he looked on her merry, quizzing face, his eye twinkled, and he burst into a hearty 'Haw, haw!' which was echoed in a silvery tinkling 'He, he!'

'Old musty, dusty, fusty college don!' said the lady.

'H'm! not so very old,' said the gentleman.

'They are all old,' said the lady; 'rusty, crusty, fusty fogies, one and all—not a pin to choose between them,' tossing up her shapely, shining head, and pursing up her ripe, rosy lips, with a smile in her eye. 'Just a horrid set of people, every one of them. Never mind, we shall do better without them. I had hoped to have called you rector before this; but you know we can't kill any one off to make room for you, can we? Ah me!' sighed the kind little lady at this reflection, and turned away to be merry with other guests.

'Who was that talking there with Miss Palmer?' whispered Ronald MacDonald to Duncan MacFar-lane.

'Some curate on £80 a year. I don't know the fellow's name,' replied the gracious Duncan.

'Did you ever see such coolness?' said Ronald: 'to monopolise the conversation for the evening! I wanted to have some talk with little Barbara myself.'

'So did I,' said the other. 'I wonder Palmer likes to have such fellows about her!'

And the superb stock-jobbers shook their arithmetical heads, and calculated that the world had come to a pretty pass!

Martel, who had observed them, and rather suspected that they were talking of him, 'for they laughed consumedly,' took an opportunity to ask Miss Palmer who they were, remarking that he had never seen them before, but they seemed to be at home there.

'Oh, so they are,' said Miss Barbara. 'That one there, tall and sandy, is Mr. Ronald MacDonald; and the other, short and dark, is Mr. Duncan Mac-Farlane. I do not precisely know their exact degree of kinship to us. Our great-grandmothers were sisters, I believe, and that, you know, is a rather close Scotch relationship, though they are more nearly connected with Ralph Gibbons; only you don't know him either.'

Martel fancied the lady sighed in saying this.

'However, we do honour to our common blood by mutual presents every Christmas. Papa sends a Stilton cheese, and they send a bag of oatmeal, or something in that way.'

'They live in the land of cakes, then?'

'No; they take us on their way to or from Scotland once in two or three years. They are in some business in London; they are by way of exchanging tenpenny nails for old chairs, or something of that sort. That handsome antique chair over the way there—don't you think it handsome ?—papa bought of a broker, I know.'

'You don't mean they are stock-brokers ?'

'Ah ! yes, that is it; they are stock-brokers. They are on the Exchange, whatever that is—" men on 'Change." I don't know the least what it means, but that is the word, stock-broker. How I have muddled it ! I am not a business woman, you see. Stock-broking is a very respectable thing, I am told. You have no money of your own, but a great deal of other people's, and all that. Papa says they make a very large income that way : and to be sure they talk a great deal about money and grandeur, as if they were very rich, and they are by way of being very fine. But they are not at all in our way; only you know how dear papa sticks to everything that is old—all his old connections, and old friends, and old tradesmen too. He has the same tailor and bootmaker that he had when he was at college, and I believe his father had them before him, that is, the same firms of course. He thinks it wrong to change a tradesman, and he never drops a friend; that is the reason why he is so slow and cautious about making new ones.'

'All very good, old-fashioned principle, Miss Palmer, and I enjoy the benefit of it, you know.'

'By the way, Mr. Martel, that nice, good old Mr. Gryffyn is a dear old friend of papa's, though he rarely comes here. He does not care for our ways, you know. But if you would bring over young Mr. Gryffyn—" my deliverer," as Kitty Fisher calls him — to luncheon some day, papa would so much——'

'How much?'

'Ever so much like to talk over with him the theatricals that my cousin told you about, and pappy will be able to judge whether we can make Mr. Gryffyn useful. For my part, I feel quite sure that he will do remarkably well, so quick, and ready, and nice he seems; but papa manages all for us. He thoroughly understands the thing. There now, go and talk to Mrs. Delafield, like a good man. She is sitting all alone by herself. Johnnie Fleming has made her very cross by something he has said, or done to her—or—left undone.'

And this was it. Tall as a poplar tree, and beautiful as the day, Lieutenant Fleming, of the Flamingoes, had lounged up to Mrs. Delafield's chair, and, leaning on the back of it, had sighed.

'Don't you hate poetry,' said he, 'and philosophy, and all that kind of thing?'

'Oh, Mr. Fleming!' sighed the lady in response. 'Oh, I think the way that some ladies go on about poetry is quite shocking! Not a word of it true, you know. And then to mix plays and the Bible together, as that man did! It was positively dreadful! The church, you know, is the proper place for serious things. Such desecration! And all that talking about poetry is quite wicked; it gives such false ideas of life. And old history, and all that reading! What is the good of it? What does it do for one? Such waste of time! In a clergyman too, who ought to be writing sermons or visiting the sick in his parish—so improper!'

'Ah!' said the bold dragoon, with a meaning and not very respectful smile, 'you and I know how to spend time properly, don't we, Mrs. Delafield?'

The lady, who was generally supposed to spend more time upon dressing and flirting than upon anything else, had settled herself for an amicable and confidential discourse with the handsome young cavalry officer; but when, after making this friendly remark, he turned, lounging away to bestow his pearls of speech upon another dame, Mrs. Delafield observed to her next neighbour:

'How completely barrack-manners and their haw-haw tone spoil young men! Mr. Fleming, before he "joined," was really a very promising boy; and you see what he is now—a perfect bear!—and dissipated, I fear;' she added, with unction.

'He is very good-looking, though, is he not?' replied the other lady demurely.

No wonder Mrs. Delafield was cross.

CHAPTER XI.

'Ettericke foreste is a feir foreste
  In it grows manie a semelie trie :
There's hart and hynd, and dae and rae,
  And of wild bestis grete plentie ;
There's a feir castelle bigged wi' lyme and stane,
  O ! gin it stands not pleasauntlie !'

'In Alfred or the Norsemen, one may read the genius of
English society; namely, that private life is the place of
honour.'—Emerson's *English Traits.*

'No, upon review it was not satisfactory,' was Dicky
Gryffyn's reflection upon the visit that he had made
to Rowanshaw.   Yet it had gone off better than he
could have hoped.   He had made his *début* on the
stage and in society, and had greatly succeeded ; but
he was not one jot the happier, quite the reverse.
A restlessness, quite new, had come to him.   There
was something wanting to him that he had never
felt the want of before : in the memory of Rowanshaw the sweets were rather more than flavoured
with bitters.   The house had been full; some hundred
and fifty people, counting servants, had found har-
bourage there, and on each night all the grandees,
and more who were not grandees, within driving

distance, from the Duke, the Lord Lieutenant, downwards, had gone to see the theatrical performances; and many an humble spectator, if so minded, might 'see how the duchess conversed with her cousin, the earl.'

Dick, who had never stayed at a house of that kind before, had, as it were, taken his degree *per saltum* under the part of Fagg, in 'The Rivals,' which he played with fine spirit and humour, amid general applause. Excepting our friends who introduced him, nobody knew or cared who he was; the Palmers were his friends, and that was his voucher. Marriageable young ladies, and match-making old ladies, and gossiping bachelors made, indeed, guesses about his wealth : some said he was the owner of a coal-mine, others of a diamond-mine; but most, for some reason best known to themselves, were inclined to pronounce him a young manufacturing millionaire from Manchester, Leeds, or Bradford, or Stockport, or some other hideous, unhealthy, ill-built, crowded, pestilential, and profitable place, smelling of smoke, filth, grease, and money. But its supposed savour did him no harm; he was looked on as a possible *parti*, pump, or pigeon, as the case might be. His dress and address were those of a gentleman, his spirits good, his conversation cheery, and, what marked him as much as anything, his French, which peeped out now and then, was for an Englishman unexceptionable. Rehearsals and green-room business had set him on easy terms with many of the young folk of both sexes; the elders approved his acting, and observed his modest and obliging manners. On the whole, his essay was a complete success, and he had spent a pleasant, even an exciting, week.

But the excitement has passed off, and left languor behind it, and he has not come back light-hearted as he went. And yet his home was a very comfortable one; only he had conceived new ideas, and all things go by comparison. The rooms, not really small, seem closets; the men he meets in them appear to him clowns. He had seen no finer fellow than his father; that was certain, and consoling. But the ladies—oh, the ladies! ah, the ladies!— there was the change. His enlightenment was, as usual, purchased at some cost: Rowanshaw was looked back to with regret, though he sometimes wished he had never seen it.

And yet it was better worth seeing than many show places. The mansion was a genuine old country house of the grand order. Descriptions of the interiors of such places can be new to no one; they are done to perfection and overdone. As to the doings in them—

> ' Haut Ton finds her privacy broken ;
> We know all her ins, and her outs,
> All the very small talk that is spoken
> By very great people at routs.'

So let it be understood of Rowanshaw that inside it everything was commodious and comfortable, if not very modern.

The outside and the situation of it are worthy of more notice. The Hall stands on an eminence. Built of an enduring stone, that had withstood the

damps and frosts and storms of centuries, and tinted
with rich hues by moss and lichen, it is a venerable
and well-preserved relic of the olden time, being, in
fact, no small part of a once famous abbey. Doves
coo about its ancient roofs and embattled towers,
and wheel in airy circles above its cold flagged
courts and grassy quadrangles. The park in which
it stands, rough with many a rugged rock and frequent heather, and many a tall fern, promises venison
of high flavour. There scud the mixed progeny of
the dun-deer of old England, and Norway black-
deer of James the First, and the dappled Indian deer
of Meynell; crossed and re-crossed, and crossed again,
they still retain the original distinctions of colour,
and, it may be, other distinctive qualities. A broad
brook runs riot through those lands, and a bridge of
ancient masonry, solid and quaintly carved, spans
its frothy and babbling waters. On the hither side,
the hill breaks with frequent slopes, and swells in
sweet acclivities towards the sun, and, coursed over
by flitting lights and shadows soft, dimpled lawns
laugh in the landscape; while on the farther side,
below the hill, amid beeches, pines, and walnut-trees,
nestles and peeps the village, under shelter of the
solemn grey church-tower.

The lord of this ancient seat and the broad lands
that pertain to it is an English country gentleman,
belonging to that class of long-descended and landed
but untitled nobles which is peculiar to Great Britain
and Ireland. He was nearer to sixty than fifty years
of age. In the outset of life he had been a member
of the set of the dandies; then, when he was about

thirty, he stood for and won a seat for the county, and sat through one Parliament. Though he somewhat distinguished himself, he soon grew sick of political life and of public men and the fine arts of the hustings, and decided that he could spend his days with more pleasure and more profit out of Parliament than in it. An enthusiast for the literature of Italy, he went abroad, and lived at Como, Florence, and Rome in succession, till, despite a preference for the way of life in Italy, a patriotic longing sent him home. After his return, he lived chiefly in the country, at Rowanshaw, and passed among men for a model of that pleasant combination of plain good sense, easy temper, and gentleman-like feeling, which is by their admirers supposed to belong pre-eminently to the English gentry.

He kept a hospitable house, much frequented by men of letters and foreigners of distinction. His sister, a feminine and older likeness of himself, lived with him, and thought everything that he did wise and good, and would have thought so still if he had thwarted her wishes, which he never did.

He was often invited to come forward again for the county, but his unvarying answer was: 'No, thank you; I shall not be caught repeating in mature age the follies of my youth. Life is worth something more than that. Pray go to some gentleman who is ambitious of making his mark in history, or at least in the newspapers.' To this he would sometimes add: 'There is only one object worthy the ambition of a man of sense, and that is to do, according to his light and his power, God's will in his generation; and the business and temper of political life seem to me rather to obstruct than to further this.'

He had inherited a good, and had collected a still better, library, which was to him a club he much preferred to the House of Commons. Abundance of recreation and of useful occupation he found in discharging county duties, in attending to the tenantry on his large estates, and in preserving and shooting a reasonable quantity of game, proportioned to the terms on which his farms were rented; in taking care of the foxes, subscribing to the hounds, and finding easy work for a couple of hunters by meeting his neighbours in the field. There he had a seat in perpetuity, without canvass or stumping, or hurting his conscience by party pledges.

In his social character, though of the old school of the dandies, he was a stranger to the new school of fashion whose glory it is to be showy and stingy, profuse and greedy; but as a well-principled man, of simple tastes and manly habits, who abhorred waste and disorder, he sat long uneasy under the legion of men-servants that his fine fortune, his immense house, and the custom of the country imposed upon him. Of the quarter of a hundred or more petticoated functionaries of all professions he was tolerant enough; but the crowd of idle male fellows bored and annoyed him, men in livery and out of livery—butlers, powdered footmen, valet, groom-of-the-chambers, porters, pages, errand-boys, gardeners, under-gardeners, coachmen, stablemen, grooms, pad-grooms, helpers, gamekeepers, park-keepers, helpers

again; there was no end to them. He now and
again had essayed to prove the half of them useless,
but prescriptive right was too much for him. Once,
after asking this man and that what he had to do,
and receiving unexceptionable answers, he turned
short upon a huge British monster six feet and an
inch high, full-fed with beef and beer, powdered,
and silk-stockinged.

'Pray, sir,' said he, 'and what may be your
work ?'

"Me, sir ? Work, sir ?   I carry missus's clogs, sir,'
stoutly replied the giant, looking down in serene
pity upon the ignorant querist, who felt himself
answered, and retired once more ignominiously.

The giant, looking after him over his shoulder,
shook his head and muttered:

'That cock won't fight nohow; wittles is wittles,
an' wages is wages, an' work is work, old gen'leman.'

The easy old gentleman made no more ado, and
no more tyrannical attempts on the liberty of his
servants.

'Cousin Brandon,' said Miss Barbara to Martel,
'is a dandy still.'

'As how ?' quoth he, something surprised. 'I see
no signs o't, rather t'other thing. Look at that bit
of common string tied to his watch for a guard!'

'Yes,' said she, with a lady's quicker penetration,
'that is just it—a bit of the old dandy's affectation.
Most people would not wear such a thing: that is
why he does. He is by way of being above common opinion, you know. It is a little weakness of

Cousin Brandon, as it is of somebody else that I
know. But indeed I like Cousin Brandon the
better for it: otherwise, he is so good I should be
afraid of him. Yes, he is a very dear old dandy,'
she repeated, shaking her wise little head at Martel,
who looked hardly convinced. Dandy or no dandy,
on artistic subjects Cousin Brandon was exact and
exacting.

Something was 'all a matter of taste,' Martel said,
as the squire was walking him and Dicky Gryffyn
round the house to look at the gardens.

' No, no, Mr. Martel, begging your pardon, not of
taste; of fancy, if you like. Most of us have our
fancies, very few have taste. I don't dispute yours,
mind; but it is a plant of slow growth, and needs
cultivation.'

Altogether to Dicky the scene and people formed
a new page of life, affording fresh standards of
judgment, that were useful in the end, though their
immediate effects were not sedative or contenting.

' I think every one ought to marry before he is
five-and-twenty,' said he, soon after his return to
Fulmere, where he sat swinging his legs in Martel's
room.

' What's that you say ? Marry !' quoth Martel,
looking up from the disorderly pile of papers before
which it was usually his pleasure to sit, pen in hand.
' Marry, while your father lives! which we hope
will be for ever. What are you to marry *for ?*—we
won't say marry *on.* Oh, fortunate young man ! if
you did but know when you are well off! You
have a home that is Liberty Hall, a liberal bache-

lor's allowance, bachelor's freedom to go hither and thither, and wander, like Wordsworth's river, at your own sweet will; as much occupation as you like, and no more; good introductions to start you in life, and good prospects to look forward to. What more can a sane man of two-and-twenty wish for? We must leave spoilt children to cry for the moon. See the world first, man; and then, when you come into your property, marry, and have an heir, and give your country as many pledges as you will.'

'I doubt your advice on this subject. Why don't you act up to it yourself? You have had time to see the world, and are old enough to marry, if you ever mean to.'

'Ah me! too true, too true, ingenuous youth; but, don't you see, the Church of England, as it were, forbids the banns.'

'I know the Church of Rome does.'

'Yes, she says plainly you shall not marry; our good Church of England says you may marry, if you can. To me, as a curate of I won't say how many years on full pay, what is the difference? And if I were a rector, with my services munificently acknowledged by £200 a year, minus rates and taxes, with meat at a shilling a pound, and the gardener's wages at £1 a week, and dilapidation overhanging me, would it not be much the same, thou uncalculating advocate of a married clergy?'

'Why not marry a little money, as my father says?'

'Why not marry a great deal of ugliness? Why not marry one eye and a hump, like that of the intended of Captain Absolute, in whose service you have made yourself immortal?'

'I do not see why a lady with a fortune should not be as handsome as another,' replied Dick sharply.

'Oh, aye, the lass wi' a tocher, to be sure! And, since handsome is that handsome does, I don't see why she may not bestow herself upon somebody who may pair with but cannot match her. But if the lady be rich and handsome too, tell me, why may not eldest sons, and lads with a plum, be as agreeable suitors as those who are not so well gilded? Handsome young ladies, with handsome fortunes—like our friend Miss Palmer, for instance—may just take their pick and choice of the lot. Your Lydia Languish marries not the landless Sir Lucius O'Trigger, or the clod Bob Acres, but the very agreeable and rich young heir of Sir Anthony Absolute; and sentimental Julia finds her Falkland. Why, man, your play is the moral of life; and it is pleasanter to learn life from Sheridan's wit than at the cost of one's own feelings: that is my philosophy. Hence you behold such a lump of me left with heart unbroken and digestion sound. Eh! young un?'

'Your heart was never very soft, I guess.'

'Like butter, man, or—what is it?—"wax to receive, and marble to retain." Only I got my wax petrified before it took any impression.'

'I have not observed that you are so very insensible to the charm of ladies' society.'

'That is the very reason why I remain unmarried. What has a beggar like me to do with well-nurtured women, except as a non-marrying monk? To talk tall, I may say that to my family nothing is left but honour. Folks soon understand me; and, as an assured, if not professed, bachelor, I, like any real monk, have fine times with the ladies. You know Lever's song:

'"An elegant life the friar leads
With his fat round paunch before him;
He mutters his prayers, and he tells his beads,
And the ladies all adore him."

Like my friend, the friar, I have no wife to claim my homage, and many a matron, and many a maid, that wants safe convoy, is handed over to me. By the way, I had a funny adventure in my capacity of escort, when I was at Rowanshaw—not this time, but for the great amateur concert last year. Miss Palmer wanted to call upon a friend who lived near, an Honourable Mrs. Somebody, who could not be of the party in the house because of a recent death in her family. Every one at Rowanshaw, servants and all, for once in their lives, were engaged and busy. So my poor services were put into requisition, and I had the pleasure of riding with Miss Palmer—all alone by ourselves, my boy,' said the narrator, looking at Dick with amusement, that was not reflected in Dick's face. 'Well, we slipped away through the park, among branching oaks, and bucks with branching horns, and does and fawns scuttling through the fern; for our nags were used to deer, and not afraid of them, as many horses are. And when we got to the house, as it was in grief, I, a stranger, of course could not go in. So I sat still on my horse by the door, and held Miss Barbara's, while she scampered in unannounced. Presently out comes John Footman, with a jug and a glass in his hand.

'" Yo'll like a drain, fellow-servant," says he. "This hale 'll make your 'air curl till your hat tumbles off yer 'ead; you see if it won't."

'And do you know, young un, I had not the presence of mind to accept his jolly invitation! So my new friend had to carry his ale away untasted, and, no doubt, drank it all himself in sheer and dry disgust. When Miss Palmer and I told the story to the squire in the evening—

' " Well, Mr. Martel." said he, " Barbara certainly paid a very high and unusual compliment to your good-nature in leaving you to turn groom, and hold her horse ; but," shaking his head—you know his way—" but you should have taken the ale."

' You see, Master Fag,' continued the elder, ' no one is without his troubles and wants, and no one need be without his consolations. I have mine. An unmarriageable man, I am a squire of dames, as trusted as any friar.'

' So great an admirer of the sex may be trusted once too often. We shall hear of some fine runaway marriage one of these days,' said the youngster, tired of being preached at.

' When you have known me longer you will know me better, young man,' said the elder. ' Again to parody vilely a great man's words, " I could not

love the dears so much, loved I not honour more."
You see, I am not quite goose enough to fancy
that heiresses will fall in love with my virtues,
and I should be still more of a goose to fall in
love with theirs, not to speak of the breach of
honour in a trusted man.'

'Honour! hum! ha! That is an old-fashioned
and worn-out idea. We talk of high principles and
religion in our day!' said the boy glibly.

'I know,' said his senior, 'there is a new religion that allows a man to stab with the tongue,
but not to strike with the hand; that is called
parliamentary chivalry, and all that sort of thing.
But honour is a good old horse, that will carry you
a long way, if you ride him fairly; good enough,
any way, for an old-fashioned fellow like me. When
men repudiate honour in the name of religion I trust
them so far as I see them. I am all for like mating
with like, my boy, and heiresses with heirs. By
the way, did you hear how our high-principled
friend Burgoyne, late Buggin, in his sly way, set
on, no doubt, by what he heard at your father's
dinner-table, contrived, under cover of clerical business, to make his way into Finchdale Rectory?'

'No! you don't say so! Impudent beggar!' cried
Dick, disgusted.

'Did he not? But what is the matter, my dear
boy? How pale you are! you must be ill.'

'Ill!—I! oh no! it is nothing. I had been smoking
a cigar before I came here; it always serves me so,
sooner or later. I can't smoke, you know. But go
on. What about that scamp Burgoyne?'

'Well, with or without pretext, he made two or three calls, and seemed quietly slipping into visiting terms with the Palmers. One day he was going there again, all fresh as paint, on a new nag far too good for a tailor like him, with bran-new bridle and saddle all complete and tailor-like, when old Launce, coming home from a ride, happened to overtake him. The old gentleman pulled up quite polite, and they rode on together like father and son, talking as pleasantly as you please, till they came to the cross-roads. "Here," said the old boy, "is my road ; there," pointing with his whip to Burgoyne's way home, "there, sir, is yours. I wish you good-morning;" and, bowing him off, he rode away, leaving our fortune-hunting friend to his own reflections. The fellow's audacity! Would nothing less do for him than the very pick of the midland counties ?'

'Why, for the matter of that,' said Dick, whose colour was coming back to his cheeks, and whose mind seemed to have come round with it, 'Burgoyne has fifteen hundred a year, I fancy.'

'And if he had fifteen thousand he would hardly be a fit match for her. Why, lad, she is an embryo duchess, depend upon it. "*Non cuivis homini contingit adire Corinthum ;*" which means, it is not every gay bachelor that will be permitted to pay court to Miss Barbara. Old Launce is in the common way as quiet as a lamb, but in guarding his golden fruit he is a regular dragon to the whole predatory tribe of you young unmarried dandies—Bugginses and Franklins, Gryffyns, and all the rest of you.

You are a Shakesperian, and remember poor Helena's
Bertram—

> ' " It were all one,
> That I should love a bright particular star,
> And think to wed it, he is so above me." '

' I remember that he married her, for all that,'
snapped Dicky.

' 'Twas a tyrant's act to make him,' quoth his
friend.

' Why should he not marry her ?' asked Dick.
' All the critics agree that he was a proud, contemptible fellow for needing to be made marry a true-
hearted girl who was dying of love for him.'

' But that, you know, was not the point of view
from which he, as a young nobleman of *that age*,
could regard her ; to him she was just a dependent
in his family, neither more nor less.'

' Snobbish, feudal aristocrat !' growled Dicky.

' Our days are not feudal, my boy ; but Mr. Macaulay, who is certainly not an aristocrat, sneers at
Swift's Stella as a " waiting-maid," though she was
in precisely the same position as Helena. There is
a good deal of lordly pride in the *bourgeoisie*, as the
French workmen will tell you. And Helena's character, you may understand, is a good way from
delicate, and her love perhaps is not quite clear of a
very vulgar ambition. You should read Coleridge
on " All's Well that Ends Well." '

' I need not read Coleridge to understand what is
delicate and what is vulgar; I fancy I know that
well enough without him or his opinions. And I
was not aware that you thought it " indelicate " or

" vulgar " to admire ladies who are rich, or, as you choose to put it, who are "above you."'

'Oh! I! I admire them immensely. Do I not? But you perceive, as I told you just now, I am a humble and safe admirer—safe in my age and in my insignificance; I could never rise into a lover, don't you see?'

'I see,' retorted the young one savagely, 'the truth of what Franklin remarked when I was with him at the boat-race—I see that you want to keep the lady to yourself.'

' Nay, my lad of pepper, how is that? You have the *entrée* as well as I; mind you keep it by good behaviour, and never heed Franklin. You are a juvenile bachelor; take an old one's advice. Enjoy your liberty, young un, for the next eight or ten years, and see the world and what turns up. You have capital quarters, a free leg, and the best of fathers. What would you more, my dear lad?'

Dicky, who had seemed very ill-at-ease through-out this dialogue, though the subject was of his own introducing, grew silent and glum, till, cheering up with an effort, he said:

' By-the-way, do you know who he was that played the part of Sir Anthony Absolute the second night? I could not find any one to tell me; all that I asked said they did not know. Somehow he was kept quite as a dark horse. Can you guess who he was?'

' I guess there are not many men in England who could play that part as he played it.'

' His name?'

'His name—let me see—Sir Anthony Absolute—
his name—by-the-bye, do you know that the Abso-
lutes, father and son, are borrowed characters?'

'Borrowed! From whom? But I dare say you
won't tell that either.'

'Oh yes, I will—from Cowley's old and young
Trueman, in his "Cutter of Coleman Street;" and
other parts of "The Rivals" can, I think, be traced
to the same source. But Sheridan borrows like a
man: what he takes he makes his own——'

'No doubt of that,' quoth Dick.

'Makes his own, I say,' proceeded Martel, 'by his
inimitable treatment of it.'

'Brougham, in that volume you lent me,' said
Dicky, 'does not rate him so very highly: he says
that Sheridan is more prone to repeat with variations the combinations of others, or to combine anew
their creations, than to bring forth original produc-
tions.'

'Originals! creations! Very fine words! Does
he mean that there is any new thing under the sun?
Is it not with mind, as with matter, all that the
creature can do is to re-arrange the primary elements? It is not in the mind of man to imagine
anything absolutely new; man's originality is not
shown in creating fresh matter, but in stamping his
own impress on the old.'

'H'm! in plain English, then, the greatest plagi-
arists are the best writers?'

'Mr. Fox used to say, "If plagiarism be a fault, it
is a fault of which the greatest poets are the most
guilty." Take Milton and Pope—they savour of

their predecessors in every line. Of painting, Sir Joshua Reynolds says much the same: "The daily food and nourishment of the mind of an artist is found in the great works of his predecessors." So much for Sheridan and Lord Brougham's sneers against him. I'll back Lord Byron, who says: "Whatever Sheridan has done has been the best of its kind: comedy, comic opera, farce, address, oration, he has tried, and *is* supreme in all." After hearing Pitt, Fox, Canning, Peel, "Sheridan was the only orator" Byron ever "wished to hear at greater length."'

'Well done you!' cried the junior. 'Then what do you say to him as a statesman?'

'What says your friend Brougham?'

'He says: "It would be flattering to call him a bad, or a hurtful, or a shortsighted, or a middling statesman; he is no statesman at all."'

'And I,' said the elder, 'against your Brougham and his opinion, will pit Mackintosh: "In judgment," says he, "no man formed a more just estimate of the result of public measures: he would have dissuaded his party from all the measures which proved unfortunate to them. But the union of fine genius with delightful talents, an excellent understanding, a generous temper, and incorruptible public character, was insufficient to support him against the depressing power of dissipation. Had he possessed discretion in conduct he might have ruled his age;" that is what Sir James Mackintosh says of "Poor Sherry."'

'I observe you often shelter yourself under your Mackintosh,' said the junior.

' I do think him a man of the right stuff, of vast
knowledge, wide sympathies, and singular fairness.
However, you are welcome to your Brougham and
his virtues, too.   As for Sheridan's faults, I say with
Grattan, they were the excesses of the generous
virtues.   " Solvitur ambulando."   Shall we stroll
and criticise the critics ?   I am a peripatetic always,
and fresh air will cool your blood, which smoke and
some other unwholesome vapours seem to have
heated,' said the elder, smiling as he looked kindly
into the troubled depths of the young man's eyes ;
' take the good that God provides thee ; my son, my
son, enjoy and be thankful.'

CHAPTER XII.

'Ring his knell.
Hark! Now I hear them: ding, dong, bell.'
SHAKESPEARE.

THE fact must be told as patent that our poor
Dick, if he had not already quite lost, was in a fair
way very soon to lose, his freedom of mind and
heart, by falling into love past recovery. Whether
he were wise or not, time will show, but perhaps he
was not much to blame. Miss Barbara was a very
attractive young lady; and during the visit to
Rowanshaw she had by no means rejected the com-
panionship which Dick seemed so anxious to bestow
upon her, and he might, without any unnatural
vanity, conclude that she did not dislike it. Though
by some accident or management he happened to
get into her way pretty often in the course of the
twenty-four hours, she appeared to meet him always
gladly and graciously. But, somehow, neither in
the house nor out of the house was she ever to be
met with alone. Colonel Denny, who was at Row'n-
shaw (as the proprietor pronounced it), seemed to
think that his connection with the family required

that he should be always with her. Cousin Kitty
too, another of the party, appeared to be pinned to
Barbara's skirt; but, then, Kitty was not less gracious, though may be a trifle more constrained in
manner, than the ever bland and easy Barbara.
Dicky, like a moth about a candle, followed and
fluttered around this bright pair with a blind per-
sistency that provoked remark from those whose
inclinations might tend in the same direction.

'I see you are hunting on the spoohr,' said one to
him, between the whiffs of a huge cigar.

'What is that?' quoth Dick. 'Spoohr! I don't
understand.'

'You are scarce likely,' replied the other. 'It is
a phrase we used abroad for the tracking of wild
beasts. When I came back from Africa, with my
old habits strong upon me, I remember how I was
puzzled by a spoohr that I tracked, running zigzag
along every West-end London pavement. At last
I found out that it was made by the swing from
side to side of the long petticoats with which it was
the pleasure of the ladies to sweep the streets.'

Dicky was not delighted with his smoking friend's
illustration or reminiscences, but he took the hint;
and, though becoming every hour more restless in
the shortest absence of the lady of his love, he became morbidly careful to avoid any more observation of his movements.

Returned home, his opportunities of meeting the
object of his fond devotion were reduced almost to
nothing. Now and then, out hunting, he could
enjoy a few minutes of mad transport; but he felt

painfully conscious that his actions were open to all eyes, and he had a horrid presentiment that criticism would not be favourable to him. His suspicions were soon confirmed in the most disagreeable manner.

'Eh! Gryffyn; how is this? What brings you here?' asked Mr. Palmer one day in the hunting-field, as riding, Darby-and-Joan fashion, at his daughter's side, he found that young gentleman quietly attaching himself to their company. 'I thought you were the keenest of hard riders, always glued to the back of the leading hound. How is it that you are not with the hounds now?'

'I—erh—erh—can't hold my horse. I tried him in a snaffle, and he is too much for me.'

'Come out hunting on a horse you don't know, with a snaffle bridle! That's a stupid thing to do, isn't it? But a smart young man like you can do anything. It is capital practice for your hands. There are the hounds, not two fields off, in the valley; that's your line. They have just turned; you'll catch them if you make haste. Off with you!'

Thus summarily sent about his business, the young man looked as unconscious as he could; and, with a very transparent hypocrisy, pretending to be thankful for the hint about the hounds, galloped off in a bustle. He contrived, however, to use his snaffle with sufficient effect, and rode very viciously, to get away from his cares.

In short, Dick had begun to taste life, its sweets and its bitters. He was well-mounted, rode stoutly,

made friends in the hunting-field, and was received
with flattering cordiality in many pleasant houses;
but the pleasures of hunting and dining were sadly
alloyed. Martel's caution, which, for all his anger,
Dick duly weighed, had come too late; and if it
had come sooner, would it have done any good?
The poor young fellow was now never easy, but
when—after what seemed to him ominously long
intervals—an invitation to dine, or some message
from his father, which he himself had concocted,
sent him in a nervous fever to Finchdale. Not that
his father favoured his amatory inclinations, or
would have favoured them if he had known them.
He was simply glad that Dick should go to the
Palmers, because theirs was a good, wholesome house
for a young man to visit at. He had no suspicion
of the attraction that drew his son there as often as
he could find a decent excuse for calling, though he
now was not a little in awe of the rector.

The elder Gryffyn did not notice this. He had
found out what the younger had yet to learn—the
secret of happiness in this world. He was devoted
to his occupation, gave to it his time and mind, and
found unfailing pleasure in his complete mastery of
it. He held himself a steward for God and man,
and he saw in his calling his duty to God and his
neighbour. He was a farmer and an agent everywhere and always. He thought of his business when he went to bed and when he rose up
from it, when he went out and when he came in,
and while he travelled by the way. He was always
farming, always managing the estate; never an

hour his mind stood still. Every ride and drive accomplished some stroke of business, or brought some information, or furnished some calculation that could be turned to profit. Hence he was less observant of his son's ways than, from his fondness, might have been expected of him.

'He is young, and I am old,' he would say. 'We old folk must let the young uns "gang their ain gate." We have been young ourselves, haven't we, parson? But you are young now. I call you young. You'll be young these ten years. You are just the right age; you're company for young and old, for Dick and for me. So come along wi' me now.'

Mr. Gryffyn was pleased with the company of Martel, and Martel enjoyed to the full as much the society of Mr. Gryffyn, and was always ready to jog about with him in his old-fashioned gig. And as they went along together, he would listen to the veteran discoursing of business, and descanting, as was his wont, of cattle, and crops, and the qualities of land, and the cost of working each different soil.

'Now, parson,' he would say, 'you see those ploughs and horses, and the men and boys with them. What could you plough that field for? How many acres are there? What rent could you afford to pay?' and so forth, with many a shrewd story told by the way.

It was mid-Lent; the season when God, revealing His love in nature, renews the face of the ground, and pours forth bounties with open hand, scattering broadcast over the bosom of earth sweet fragrance, fresh flowers, and all young things.

The curate remembered for many a spring afterwards some of the least circumstances of that season. During the week he had gone to a neighbouring town about the trusteeship of a village school endowment with Mr. Gryffyn, who had then said :

'I would be a trustee myself, but that my life is not worth an hour's purchase.'

On their way home the old man got out of the gig to walk up a hill, whip in hand; and, discovering an urchin hid in the hedge by the pathside, he, full as usual of boyish fun, lifted his whip over the youngster, and cried, in his jolly way :

'Now, my boy, what do you think of me ?'

'I think you are a fool,' squeaked the impudent urchin, as he bolted through the fence.

'Ho! ho! ho!' laughed the tall elder, till the tears ran down his cheeks. 'Did you hear him ? He thinks I'm a fool! and I think so too, an old un, the worst of any. Ho! ho! ho! ho!'

On the next Sunday morning the sermon was on repentance.

'Yes,' said he to the neighbours about him, as they left the church together, 'we must repent, as he tells. We must all repent. I know he made my old eyes twinkle.'

And then, as Martel came up to him in the churchyard, he said :

'Parson, you'll dine with us to-morrow.'

That morrow never came. The next day was a Lent, indeed, of dust and ashes, and darkened

windows, and bruised hearts. Then came the funeral
—'ashes to ashes, and dust to dust'—and folk flocked
to it from far and near, of every degree, in every kind
of conveyance; carriages, gigs, dog-carts, light carts,
donkey-carts, bread-carts and coal-carts, market-
carts and carts simple, choked the street of Fulmere
and the adjoining roads; and not a few came on
foot—some poor, perhaps, with their natural sorrow
blending the no less natural fear that young ' Gruffun'
would reclaim the cows which old ' Gruffun ' had lent
them so very long ago.

Martel, who, sorely loath and hardly able, had yet to
preach to this mixed multitude the funeral sermon,
thought much more of the friend he had lost than
of improving the occasion to the edification of those
who had attended his funeral. He said just that
which is usually said, and which, therefore, is probably the best to be said upon such occasions. There
are some, but it is to be hoped not many, who think
that these are times in which true friends have the
heart to make laboured orations; but it is then, if
ever, that heart speaks to heart in words few and
plain: the tone and manner say more than the
language.

And Richard Gryffyn, a week ago, as he looked
at his lot, because he had an ungratified wish, was
full of repining; and now that he looked back upon
it, he thought how blessed he had been, and how
regardless of his blessings! how greatly favoured,
and how ungrateful! Now his father was all to
him and everything, and every one else as nothing
in comparison. The suddenness of the blow bowed

him to the earth in pain and shame and self-reproach.
Happily for him, there was much to do—much that
had to be done at once, and would brook no delay :
his father's place was empty, and he had to take it.
As Homer sang in the olden time, so it is still :

> ' Like leaves on trees the race of man is found,
> Now green aloft, now withering on the ground ;
> Another race the following spring supplies,
> They fall successive, and successive rise ;
> So generations in their course decay,
> So flourish these, when those have passed away.'

Sorrow he had much ; anxiety the young man had
none. His circumstances, when his feelings would
allow him, and when business compelled him to look
into them, were found to be equal to men's expectations. Twenty thousand pounds, and all the house
stuff, and the farming stock and implements, worth
at least ten thousand more, were left to him ; to
each of his sisters, in lieu of the allowance of three
hundred a year which they had hitherto severally
received, fifteen thousand pounds, to revert to
Richard or his heirs after the death of themselves
and their husbands, in case they should fail of sur-
viving issue.

CHAPTER XIII.

'The end of it was that the superior clergy got a good deal, and the inferior clergy got little or nothing;—which has also happened since King John's time, I believe.—CHARLES DICKENS' *History of England*, vol. i. p. 202.

' As you, ye sheep, are shorn by others' hands,
As you, ye oxen, plough for others' lands,
As you, ye bees, do store for others' honey ;
So starv'd priests earn for well-paid priests the money.'
Virgil travestied.

' He' (Mr. Pendexter) 'concluded by apologising for having neglected his own business, which was to study and preach,—in order to attend to that of the parish, which was to support its minister ; stating that his own short-comings had been owing to theirs, which had driven him into the woods in winter, and into the fields in summer.'
LONGFELLOW'S *Kavanagh.*

ABOUT the time of Mr. Gryffyn's death died Martel's rector, and that event ended his tenure of the curacy of Fulmere. The late rector was what is called non-resident. Some miles from Fulmere he had a living, whereat he lived and died. Why he continued to hold the former is a Church secret; since he received from it but seventy-seven pounds a year, and paid to the curate one hundred. However, his death turned Martel adrift upon the world again, and he, in his destitution, applied to the bishop for help to a cure. By the bishop's desire he called at the palace.

'So you want a curacy again, do you?' asked his lordship. 'Well, a gentleman has just written to me for a curate—though I don't know that it is my business to find him one. However, I thought you had better come and see whether his offer would be likely to suit you. If you like it, and would go to him, it might be a good thing for all parties. He is an odd sort of a man, you must know. Here is his letter, and a very strange one it is. He tells me how he spends his day, when he gets up, breakfasts, and dines, and drinks tea, and when he visits the parish; he says he cultivates the science of music, as David did, and that he spends three hours a day in *meditation*—that is a good deal for these bustling times. Well, you see, he is a queer man—a bit of an oddity; that he can't help, I dare say. This is what he says of his parish,' continued the bishop, handing the letter to Martel; 'and that I know to be correct. And for stipend he offers a hundred a year, and so forth; that is all quite right too. He is an odd man, clearly, but you will not have much to do with him; he is old and infirm. He can put you out of his pulpit, though, if he likes,' added the bishop, with a little twinkle of humour rippling over his grave face. 'I shall not license you at once in any case. Taking a curacy is like taking a wife: one question is whether it will suit you; another is whether you will suit it. The best way is to wait and see how you like one another before the license is issued. And now you will take some luncheon.

I would ask you to stay and dine with us, but we could get no one to meet you. We have had an election here, and all the people have quarrelled; they don't speak to one another. I can't tell you the number who used to be friends that are now at feud. But come; we shall find Mrs. Smith in the drawing-room.'

And so Martel, at luncheon with the hospitable prelate and his wife, was asked about this friend and that neighbour, and was surprised to find how much his simple-mannered diocesan knew about the parishes and people in his district.

At the station a vulgar face put out of a first-class carriage invited him to enter.

'No, thank you; I ride third.'

'Ah! I see; your masters ride in the first.'

'Well, no; you stockinger fellows take all the best places; the whole first-class smells of hosiery,' was the polite rejoinder.

Martel soon made his visit to his rector *in posse.* The rectory pointed out to him, as he asked his way through the village, seemed to be a plain, substantial red-brick house, surrounded by a wall. He opened a door in this wall, and found himself in a grass-field, in the midst of which, without any interval of garden, stood the house, with a flight of stone steps leading up to the front-door. The steps were all moss-grown. He mounted them, and knocked at the door; echo answered him. He knocked again and again, rousing the echoes, but no one else. Tired at last, he felt his way round to the back-door, and there a few knocks drew out the *genius loci,* in rusty black clothes of very baggy village cut. A huge unstarched roll of white neckcloth enwrapped the lower jaw, and over it blazed a round red face, with redder nose of the flat, pug pattern; the whole of this flaming visage was further lit up by a pair of large, fiery black eyes; snow-white hair, long and plentiful, with the aid of the neckcloth, made a complete and effective framework for this striking physiognomy. The person who presented this amiable appearance was, as it seemed, verging towards seventy years of age, but hale and bright. He might be the butler (if the establishment boasted one), or he might be the parson himself. Whoever he was, as he opened the door he looked at Martel inquiringly, and, as Martel thought, rather fiercely.

What did he want?

He was sent by the bishop to see Mr. Brown about the curacy.

'W-a-a-aw-lk in, sir, pray w-a-lk in; I am very glad to see you, sir,' said Mr. Brown—for he was the reverend proprietor of this very prepossessing appearance—and as he spoke he ushered his visitor into a kitchen with snow-white freestone floor that, but for its hardness, would be nice to picnic on; snow-white dressers, shelves, and tables to match, everything spotless—a most model kitchen, only rather bare of garniture in the way of cooking utensils, but still it was a kitchen—and there his reverend guide halted our friend.

It was about twelve o'clock.

'Have you dined?' asked fiery-face. 'No? That's well, that's well. Get dinner ready, boy!'

At the word, a boy appeared out of a closet, and began to set out with a very white coarse cloth the very white deal table. Upon it he set a dish containing one cold duck and part of another, a broken dish of hot potatoes, the crusty shell of a loaf of bread, and some cheese.

'Take the cheese off the table !' cried the master; 'we don't want that yet. Don't you see I have company ? Now, sir, let us fall to.'

Thereupon with glee he rubbed his hands together, and presently said grace, which he in a manner prolonged with—' Thank God I have everything I want—everything I want—everything !' rubbing, as he spoke, his hands again.

When they were seated, the host drew a chair between himself and his guest, and upon the chair he set conveniently the broken dish of smoking potatoes that was before upon the table.

'Now, sir, we can both reach it; and we have everything we want, everything we want. We took the crumb out of the bread yesterday to make a pudding.'

The ' we ' seemed to mean himself and the boy, who had again disappeared in the closet: there was no sign of any other domestic.

'You see, I have everything I want, everything I want—everything !'

This, accompanied by the rubbing of the hands, for which purpose he laid down his knife and fork, was the burden of his song throughout the dinner, at which he and his guest played the parts of men even to the cheese, that reappeared in its appointed

order for the company. After all, the guest was re-
galed with a glass of gin and water—water which was
excellent having been the sole beverage up to this
time; and the host indulged himself further in a
pipe, a luxury which the other declined. Altogether
it was a wholesome, frugal meal, that, though unusual, was not the less sensible; and after it they
were in good heart to talk over the affairs which had
brought this unwonted visitor. The discussion ended
in an agreement that Martel should take the cure
for a time, as the bishop had suggested, without a
license, to try how each might suit the other.

When Martel left the rector, he went to call upon
the outgoing curate, and found in him, to his great
surprise and joy, an old college friend. Mr. Jones,
with his wife, a very handsome and well-bred lady,
was eating his dinner off a deal box in default of the
customary and conventional table; his bedroom was
his dining-room, and he made Martel take his seat
on the bed beside him.

'We are short of chairs, you see; but this will do
very well,' said he, in perfect content and the most
radiant good-humour.

This family meal was hardly over when a gentleman, a county magistrate and landowner, who in
truth had, out of pity, given the curate free use of
the cottage in which he was thus living, came to
visit him, and was requested to take his seat upon
the box which had just served the office of a table.
The box and the bed seemed to be all the furniture
in the house, though Mr. Jones, as Martel happened
to know, was the son of a clergyman, and the grand-

son of a man whose near relatives were among the high old nobility.

But nothing had descended to Mr. Jones beyond a costly education at the University, where he had taken barren 'honours;' and he had married a lady who had nothing but beauty and gentle birth. His whole heart and soul were in his work, and, finding the Church at home did not recognise the text which says, 'The labourer is worthy of his hire,' he decided that it was better to go to the heathen: muzzled and persecuted in one place, he would flee to another. He told his story with much humour, and with a good-nature to which it is not possible to do justice.

To his dying day Martel never forgot the scene, and would always maintain that the persecuted and expatriated curate was the best specimen of a Christian that it ever was his happiness to see.

During his period of probation here, Martel met with another old acquaintance of another stamp. He also was a clergyman, of fifty years of age or so, who, having served thirty years without a benefice, had retired without a pension, to *eke* out his private resources by shooting and pot-hunting over a rented manor. He was a bachelor, and asked Martel to dine with him in his little five-roomed cottage standing in a scrap of paddock, with a cabbage-garden at the back, and a barn-like bit of stabling in front. At the door, not easily opened, a flowing flaxen wig, crowning a rosy face with a parrot-beak rather rosy too, a very long upper lip drawn to the under one so as to give the cheeks the appearance of a trumpeter's blowing hard in his vocation, narrow shoulders, a goodly girth of waist and breadth of beam, small feet, and little fat hands, whose pointed fingers were constantly spread out for the admiration of their owner—all these goodly properties, together compounding a portly figure of nearly six feet high, and overspread with an indescribable mixture of broad farce and dismal melancholy, were displayed in welcome to Martel, who knew and appreciated them of old.

'Ah, well, you are come!' with a sigh. 'I am glad to see you,' with two sighs more. 'I have asked a Mr. de Coucy to meet you; he said he would come if he could! As if a man could not say whether he would come or not—such nonsense! However, we won't wait for him. Mary, let us have dinner!' he shouted from the door to the kitchen, which was close beside him.

Martel had hardly time to look over the fine old china and handsomely-bound old books of the otherwise ill-furnished room, where 'Burton's Melancholy' and 'Montaigne's Essays,' and other respectable old-fashioned authors, were flanked by some good miniature likenesses of members of their owner's family, who looked like what they were, ladies and gentlemen, when Mr. de Coucy and the dinner appeared together.

'Oh, you are come! We were just going to dinner without you,' in a melancholy tone dashed with indifference, was the host's greeting to his daintily-dressed and very clerical visitor, whose air gave one the notion that he thought himself irresistible among women, and a great man among men.

'A beauty, but not a gentleman,' thought Martel, as he surveyed him. 'A character, but not a beauty,' he added, as he compared his serio-comic host's outward gifts with the magnificent eyes, long eyelashes, black, curling hair, and handsome features that adorned Mr. de Coucy's five feet ten inches of symmetrical manhood.

The age of this Adonis would seem to be about eight-and-twenty or thirty.

The host looked round, and his hungry grey eye brightened, but not with admiration of his guest: he was looking with satisfaction at his dinner, for though very fond of good cheer, as his face and figure bore him witness, he was of frugal mind, and would not indulge inclination to the top of its bent unless he could find an excuse for prodigality in the entertainment of company; and, indeed, he was apt to let it appear that he thought more of his feast than of his guests, though hospitable enough in his way.

'A comfortable little dinner, I think,' said he, as he eyed it from the head of the table; 'fish, soup, eh? Oh, Mary knows how to do it! Mary, give Mr. de Coucy some sherry.' (Mary was cook and waiter, butler and housekeeper, footman and housemaid, and if any other function was needed, she performed that also.) 'Martel, help yourself. It is long since I have seen you. You look older; I suppose we all do. Well, well, what does it matter? We can't help it. Let us be comfortable now, any way; it's not often one is. Ah-h-h! if I had the means, I should like to give little dinners of this sort every day.' (Those who knew him best would doubt this very much.) ' Well, well, what is the good of wishing ?' (said rather crossly). ' I may have the means some day, though,' added he pompously.

This meant that he was the next heir to an ancient and considerable estate. He used to sink the fact that the present possessor's life was a much younger and apparently a far better life than his own.

Martel, who knew intimately all his humours, was always entertained by them, and laughed at them freely, as the humourist liked men to do. Not so Mr. de Coucy, who evidently did not understand his man: he sat silent and grand, and showed a disposition to give himself airs.

The host was accustomed to be honoured with attention at least, if not with applause. His dismal drollery was, to those whom it did not vex, the more amusing in that it consisted much in affectations of manner, and the queer expression of a face which had natural aptitudes for broad farce; but his humours were not always good-humoured, and to those whose fancy they did not tickle they were often offensive. His quick vanity soon saw, and his jealous temper as soon resented, the insensibility of his fine guest.

Determined not to lose this opportunity of enjoying himself, he just ignored Mr. de Coucy and his wet blanket, and after dinner pushed the bottle with a jovial air, while he once more praised the skill of his maid Mary, and appealed to his company for confirmation.

Mr. de Coucy filled his glass, tasted, and put it down.

'Corked!' said he.

The host's cold grey eye glittered like the hoar-frost, and his wig seemed to bristle; but he only said :

'Ah! all my port is corked in the same way. Take a glass of sherry ; that is not corked—it is out of the wood. Help yourself to port, Martel; *you* will not find out that it is corked.'

Not long after this, Mr. de Coucy got up from the table. He must go ; he had promised, and so forth.

'Well, if you must, good-bye,' said the host; and he held out a frigid finger. 'I am sorry that my little entertainment is not appreciated. *You* are not obliged to go, Martel ? Handsome animal!' said he, as the door closed on De Coucy; 'though as to his face, *il ne dit rien.*'

'I should not say that,' quoth Martel. 'If it is not intellectual, it speaks cunning.'

'I don't know who he is,' quoth the other ; 'not a gentleman, any way. He has been staying these nine months with my neighbour Miller, who intro-duces him ; but if he knows anything about him, he doesn't say so, nor where the man came from. Because he is good-looking and uncommonly well-dressed, as we must allow, people say he is a man of money, or "a hair to forting." I don't believe any-thing of the sort; never saw a sign of it. He is more like an adventurer. I doubt if he has a shil-ling in the world but what he gets from Miller for helping him in his Sunday duty.'

15—2

'Then he is not his regular curate ?' asked Martel.

'No, a sort of friend, or hanger-on; lives in the house with him. I don't understand it. What does it matter ? He's gone; let's be jolly. I am sure he did not add to our pleasure.'

Martel remained some time longer, talking over past days, and the host's recent success in shooting over the thousand acres, while he lamented the thousand sixpences they cost him. At last it was :

'Well, so you must go too, must you ? It's very dark; the roads are knee-deep in mud; it's raining now. You had better take care at the foot-bridge; the brook's full and deep. If you fall in, you won't get out again. I hope you won't, though, but it's very slippery. And I say ' (this came out less glibly, and with evident effort), 'would you think it worth the trouble to take home a rabbit, if I were to give you one ? But perhaps you would not like to carry it.'

'Thanks; yes, I would,' said Martel, who thought very little about his provender at any time, and who certainly was not in love with the idea of lugging home a heavy rabbit through three miles of mud, on a pitch-dark night; but he could not resist the temptation to practise on the old pothunter's stingy temper, which he knew of old. 'Thanks,' he repeated, 'thanks ! I shall be too glad.'

'Well,' said the promiser, more than half repenting of his promise, 'we'll see. Mary, go look whether there is a rabbit for Mr. Martel to take home with him.'

Mary returned, holding downward what Martel

knew at once to be a large hare, which, as it was heavier than the rabbit, was the more unwelcome to Martel. He did not care a pinch of snuff about the state of his larder, which was, indeed, always very ill-furnished, not to say scandalously bare ; but he saw in this heavy hare a chance of pinching still harder, on his tender part, his penurious but exceedingly well-to-do friend. So he took the hare from the maid's hand without remark, vastly amused within to see his friend's gooseberry eyes fixed intently upon it.

'Will you let me look at that ?' quoth the starer. Then, taking it in his hand, and holding it out at arm's length as he gazed, 'Oh-h-h ! this is a hare !!' quoth he. 'Oh-h-h ! Mary, I said a rabbit. Oh-h-h ! I cannot—afford—a—hare !!! If—you—would—like—a—rabbit ?'

'Yes, I would like a rabbit.'

'Is there one, Mary ?'

'There is one rabbit, sir ; but there are five hares. I thought Mr. Martel would like one of them.'

'Oh-h-h ! but I can-not—af-ford a hare !!!'

As he spoke, he handed the hare back to Mary, adding :

'Bring Mr. Martel a rabbit, if he would like one.'

'Yes, I would like one.'

When Mary returned with the rabbit her master took it from hers into his own hand, held it up to the light, turned it round and round, examined it cautiously and comically ; then put it into Martel's hand, and sighed.

'Aye, there it is, if you would like it. It is a

rabbit. I wish it were a hare!' and he sighed
again.

Then, ' fat as a whale, and walking like a swan,'
he waddled to the door, with his pale eyebrows, his
gooseberry eyes, and his red parrot beak uplifted in
resignation ; while he put out three taper fingers of
his fat little hand for his departing friend to grasp,
if he pleased, and gently groaned :

' Well, well, good-night.   How it rains !'

So saying, with apparently high satisfaction, he
shut his door, and locked it.

' *Sauve mari magno !*' repeated the outsider,
laughing.

CHAPTER XIV.

'As when a Gryphon through the wilderness,
   With wingèd course o'er hill and moory dale,
Pursues.'

   MILTON—*Par. Lost*, bk. ii.

'In the marvellous merry month of May,
      When all the young buds pouted,
   In mine own heart the flower of love
      Unleafed itself and sprouted.

'In the marvellous merry month of May,
      When all the wild birds chanted,
   I sang her the song of passionate hope,
      Wherewith my whole soul panted.'

      HEINRICH HEINE, *by* JULIAN FANE.

'EVER to sit scribbling and poring over books in the dusty twilight made by four dingy walls, thinking of all the year's sweet revolutions, and tasting none; to sit and choke, and dream of balmy fresh airs breathing over free downs, of green pastures, and clear streams, and leafy nooks, which the pale primrose gilds and the purple violet perfumes; and, overhead, in the blue sky, the lights and shadows that come and go, shifting and still shifting, and the vapoury clouds, now bright and now vanished, and flying scuds of gauzy vapour, dressing the landscape in an atmosphere of all-glorious hues, from cool,

gleamy grey to orange, and purple, and crimson, and
gold! So to sit, and so to *dream* of nature's glorious
beauty, and to be *shut out* from God's great earthly
revelation of his love! Oh! it is enough to kill
man's soul within him! And that,' concluded Martel
to himself, 'is "the reason why"—in spite of all
that has been said, or shall be said, or can be said,
or thought, by good little Franklin, or by Goody
Two Shoes—so long as I have strength to ride and
a nag to ride on, I shall continue to come here. I
can hardly attend a meeting, or hear a charge, without being informed that no man following the calling of the apostles has a right to go out of his study,
unless to read prayers in church, and to visit the
sick, and make parochial visits. Of "spontaneous
wisdom breathed by health, and truth by cheerfulness," this unconvicted prisoner and commissioned
teacher is to know nothing! Let them talk, and
talk to their hearts' content. I do not believe that
the apostles ever did or taught anything of the sort.
They were adventurous travellers, most of them.
And as for Paul, whose name, in season and out of
season, is hurled at our heads, we know that at
Corinth he worked at tent-making, and "taught in
the synagogue on the Sabbath-day." We ministers
are, as we are pretty often reminded, simply men,
and not inspired men; "though we are Churchmen,
we are the sons of women." And the power of work
in man is, as all but the idle know, limited pretty
tightly. But oh, "of all the cants that are canted
in this canting world," and very canting Anglo-
Saxon part of it——

'Well, well, as old Rosy says, it is some comfort, anyway, to observe that our excellent lecturers are, one and all, gentlemen, who never omit to take out at least a fourth of the year in holidays, and many are not nice about taking the half; while I, though I "have some salt of youth left in me," have not had three months of holiday in fourteen years. Let them talk. I cannot stop them, but I can stop my ears. I know, as our worthy legislators say in August, we must have change and relaxation; and this is the way in which it suits me to take it. I have not much choice about it: this or nothing. I know my place. Rome, Florence, Venice, Switzerland, the Rhine, are not for the like of me; no, nor Cowes, nor the Highlands; but I am not going to throw away the good thing that Providence puts in my power. Some folks do not like hunting, do not approve of it. Very well, "one man's meat is another man's poison;" that is all. I have great faith in nature, and the tastes that she gave me; and I have not great faith in—well, we will say "uninspired oracles."'

Thus argued our friend, after his wont, with himself, while he enjoyed the slack spring hunting in the hilly parklands of Beauleigh.

The loud halloo, the short, sharp tooting of the hunting-horn, the hounds' challenge, and response, and full cry, rang in turn again and again, with many an echo, through the wide woods. Now here, now there, in the long vistas of the narrow rides pranked with primroses and violets, or in the broad glades that opened between the several

copses, under a sapphire sky, through the greys
and greens and golden-browns of the budding
trees, flashed and glanced sparks of light, and
deeper colours—scarlet coats and white buckskins;
long, floating habits and plumed hats, whose
wearers the charm of the season and of the spot,
and the confined nature of woodland hunting, had
lured to the sport in unusual numbers; and carriages, filled with fair forms, in gay apparel, price-
less shawls, and lovely bonnets, like moving par-
terres, rolled backwards and forwards along the
surrounding roads, now smooth and dry, and powdered with April dust, as the sylvan war shifted
its scene hither and thither in the large labyrinth
of woods.

Horses galloped, horses fretted on the bit, and
chafed to stand still, pawed the unoffending ground,
and tossed their patrician heads. There were
ladies and gentlemen that followed the sport, and
ladies and gentlemen that pulled up, and chatted,
and ate sandwiches and drank sherry, and gave
and took news, and watched the scene, or quietly
hunted foxes more cunning and more to their
fancy than the red-furred beast of the field. And
the tall beeches, all bedropped with amber gems,
and the ruddy gold of the sprouting oaks, shed a
glowing mellow light amid the fresh and tender
greens of the trees of the wood, as they rejoiced
before the Lord in the spring-time. And ever and
anon for the spectator on horse or foot, planted
on some vantage-ground, as the hounds' bell-note
and the echoing horn sounded nearer and nearer,

the chase rushed into sight across some brier-
bound ride, or flashed for a moment in the open.
The serene stillness of the azure sky, the young
loveliness of the renewed earth, the refreshing sweetness of the scented air, the budding woods, the bay-
ing hounds, the horn's shrill blast, the huntsman's
cheer and chiding, the scarlet and white of the men,
the flowing skirts and bright locks of the women,
the general landscape and view of nature, all alive,
and sweet, and fresh, in spring attire,—all went
'merry as a marriage bell,' and ministered delight
to every sense ; and, chiming in with dulcet chorus,
blackbird and thrush sang responsive ai-ai, papai-
papai, on every bush.

It was one of the golden hours of men's chequered
and exercised life. But even in this hunting Eden
human discontent found a place, and vile suspicion
lurked and leered, and trees concealed listening ears,
and bushes hid prying eyes. The company straggles
farther and wider, now joining in the chase, now
looking on, and now unobservant of the sport and
deep in gossip. The weather, beautiful and fresh,
exerted an idle influence : men and women were like
Paley's oyster ; to be inactive, and passively to enjoy
existence seemed to be the general order of the day.
Foxes were afoot, and ran from covert to covert ; the
hounds, hunting now on this scent, now on that,
were embarrassed by the multitude of riches. A
few sportsmen spurred and hustled after them, more
sat still and viewed the sport. Martel, who in his
heart set up for a hunting philosopher, and made
the field as much his study as his sport, sat apart

upon his cob on a green knoll, whence he could best at leisure survey the whole animated and varied scene, drinking in delight at every pore.

'Oh!' he exclaimed in his rapture, 'oh! what a gracious, heavenly day! What simple joys surround him when a man does not wantonly mar them!' As he spoke he started. 'Eh! what! how! is it possible? What do I see? Those two! It must be they! So far from the rest, and so very near together! What can they have to say? The old story, no doubt. Here's a pretty kettle of fish! I have been looking for this. Oh, thank goodness! she shakes her head. I hope there is as much in that shake as in the great Lord Burleigh's. There! it is not all right. I am going too fast. He takes her hand, or glove, or both; she shakes her head, and gives him her hand! How like a woman! Ruin to them both! I don't see what I can do to stop it; no business of mine. But I shall make it mine: I shall just take the liberty of cantering down to intrude my presence upon a *tête-à-tête* which can by no possibility bring good. I suspected it would come to this. One is seldom wrong who looks for mischief between young men and women. I am more afraid for him than for her, though; she is so clever, and so right always. It is all her good-nature and his infatuation. I don't believe she cares a button for him; only she is so amiable, and he is so young and warm-hearted. What will dear old Launce say when he hears of it, as he surely will, with additions and variations? There is not in the world a more gossiping place than the hunting-field.

Old John Bromby, there, is all eyes and ears, faith-
ful as a dog, and watchful as a cat. However, I'll
be a marplot for once, and spoil the sport for them
to-day, any way.'

His inward conference was brought to an end as
he cantered up to them. It seemed in a critical
moment, for the lady was, or he fancied it, evidently
relieved, and the gentleman as plainly disconcerted.
He received the new-comer's salutations with very
ill-grace; while John Bromby, who, as he was fond
of saying, knew his place, gave Martel a touch of
the hat that was more than respectful, even grateful.

That night John Bromby asked to see his master
in the library—about the horses, as was supposed.
He shut the door very carefully behind him, hem'd
a little, then turned and tried the door again, and
began abruptly, and much to Mr. Palmer's astonish-
ment:

'I beg pardon, sir ; I ain't agoin' to say any harm
of miss, sir——'

'I hope not, John.'

'No, sir, it ain't likely. Nor agen' the young gent
neither, for the matter o' that; for he's a good young
gen'leman, an' a well-behaved—that I will say for
'im. But I like things to go straight for'ard, and
the right thing to go on; an' this I will say—as I
don't believe he's no sort o' fittin' mate for some
folk. That I will say, though I respect un, as I did
his pore father, as is gone—an' a better gen'leman
there wa'n't nowhere in his place, I don't care who
he is, than old Muster Gryffen. But like to like—
that's my maxim; an' there ain't no good comes o'
goin' out o' your place.'

Here John stopped. His master had seen he was excited, and had listened with patience. He now said :

'Well, John, what is all this about? Though I cannot guess what you are driving at, I am sure you mean to say what you think right, and to do your duty. What is it you have to tell me? Better say it here than elsewhere, and let me judge for myself if it concerns me.'

Mr. Palmer's long experience on the county bench had taught him that it is best to let people tell their stories in their own way, and he had acquired a habit of patient attention which, strange to say, is seldom displayed by magistrates who happen to be barristers also; perhaps the browbeating habit of the bar clings to them still. However, John, left to himself, resumed his story with digressions.

'Well, sir,' he began, 'to-day—young folk will be young folk, only the old uns must hold 'em wi' good brildes an' light 'ands, as you know, sir—an' so to-day, sir, as I was a-ridin' after Miss Barbara—Miss Palmer, as is—when the 'ounds was a-hangin' in cover, as they will in them 'bominable woods, a-wastin' of all the time, an' a-doin' o' nothink—why, you know, sir, people get tired o' gallopin' about an' no sport like—leastways, young gen'lemen an' young ladies do, as is nat'ral, an' I ha'n't got nothin' to say agin' that; only this here Mr. Gryffen he keeps a-follerin' our young lady like a dog. He have done it a deal sin' his pore father died, and sin' he have come more here, out o' your and miss's great kindness to him in his trouble, as I know, sir——'

'Never mind that, John; go on with your story. What is it?'

'Well, this here Mr. Gryffen he's a keen young gent, and can ride too; an' I thought he'd ha' been a-pressin' to the front, as he mostly is, for I've seed 'im a many a time. But to-day, when the 'ounds, as had been a-doin' o' nothink all the mornin', had got the scent a bit, an' was a-runnin' like smoke, this young gent, Mr. Gryffen, he kep' on a-follerin' of my young missus about, an' she didn't want 'im, I could see that; an' I kept a-tellin' on him where the 'ounds was, but he wouldn't leave our company nohow. An' then, when we was right away from the rest—for miss she never likes bein' near a crowd—why, he come as close as could be up alongside her, an' begun a-whisperin' an' a-talkin' low like; an' I don't know what he said, an' I don't want to, for I ain't no listener. But miss she shook her head like; only she is so uncommon good-natured is miss, an' wouldn't hurt no one's feelin's if it was ever so, I could see that. An', to be sure, he's an uncommon nice young gent, an' a gret favourite wi' most folk. An' I tho't it my duty to tell you what I see, in my place, 'bout his 'tentions, an' I've told you; an' I've had hard work to get it out, for, if you'll believe me, sir, I'd rayther ha' cut my tongue out. But I tho't it my duty to you, an' to our missus as is gone, as I foller'd many a day, an' to our young miss, as has allus been so kind an' good to me an' mine. An' I 'ope, sir, you'll excuse me for bein' so bold. I ha'n't said not a word to no-body but you, sir, as is my master, an' I won't.'

'Quite right, John; there is no occasion. Thank you, John. You have done what you considered your duty; quite right. I am much obliged to you. Good-night, John.'

'Miss Palmer, sir,' said John, now with his breast cleared and his usual manner, 'Miss Palmer, sir, has hordered the 'osses again for to-morrow; they didn't do nothink to-day.'

'Very well, John. Order my horse to be ready too; I have not been out for some time, and I dare say she finds it dull going by herself.'

'In course, sir, in course she does.'

'Well, good-night, John,' again said the master; and as the door closed on the man, 'I don't understand what Barbara is at; but she is so shrewd, and so true to whatever is right, that I shall trust her to take her own way, as I have always done—though,' he added, 'perhaps hers is not always just the way I should choose for her. But she loves managing; it is her nature, and, I suppose, her vocation. However, I must keep an eye upon that young fellow. He means no harm, I dare say; but he is young and raw, and may misunderstand Barbara altogether. And no wonder; to be sure, Barbara is a great temptation to a youngster to forget himself. That must be looked to—must be looked to,' said the rector to himself, as he went to rejoin his daughter in the drawing-room.

CHAPTER XV.

'Till thirty years of age I never received a farthing from the Church : then £50 per annum for two years, then nothing for ten years ; then £500 per annum, increased for two or three years to £800 ; till, in my grand climacteric, I was made Canon of St. Paul's ; and before that period I had built a parsonage-house, with farm-offices for a large farm, which cost me £4000, and had reclaimed another from ruin at an expense of £2000 ; and I am considered a perfect monster of ecclesiastical prosperity.'—Rev. Sydney Smith—*First Letter to Archdeacon Singleton.*

On the morning of the day following that of which the events have just been told, Martel, having met Mr. Finch Adams in the street of Mudleigh, received soon after, from the justice-room, the following note :

' If you will excuse short notice, my ladies will be passing Garton toll-bar about four o'clock to-day, and will have an outside place for you in the carriage, should you be there with your traps. Our dinner-hour is seven, and we shall be glad to see you. I can send you back on Saturday.

'Yours sincerely,

'Thomas Finch Adams.'

Granthorpe Rectory was famed for good cheer and good company. Of course Martel, being happily disengaged, found his way there. There was no house, after Finchdale, that he liked so well.

Small and wiry, dark in complexion and dry in manner, is Mr. Finch-Adams, an influential clergyman and an active magistrate. His father had been a man of fashion, and, as such, had wasted three-fourths of a very large fortune. The son manages to live creditably and handsomely as a squire-parson upon what was left. His parish finds him occupation and a house, with £250 a year, to meet incidental expenses, and he has pretty much his own way in it. Indeed, he has a will and a way of his own in most things. It had showed itself at college to his tailor.

'But, sir,' quoth Snip, 'that is not the fashion.'

'I make the fashion,' quoth the sporting undergraduate.

As it was with the undergraduate, so is it with the smart squire-rector, whose dandyism is of the most severe and neat description. He still sets the fashion, or, at least, enjoys the satisfaction of having a fashion of his own, which extends from his clothes to his horses, and to everything about his place that does not come within the jurisdiction of his wife.

Mrs. Finch Adams is a veritable virtuous woman, and a crown to her eccentric husband, who is as fond of her as he ought to be. In her own house she shows her better, when abroad her more brilliant, side. She is the stay of society in her neighbourhood, the animating spirit and boast of her husband's parishioners, and of her own well-conducted household. Whether she dispenses to old women blankets, or discusses with them their manifold complaints, born and bred and living in refinement, with them she is homely, comfortable, and outspoken. The curate, to whom goes the half of Mr. Finch Adams' clerical income, and who often accompanies his rectoress as aide-de-camp in parochial visitations, has often to be dismissed from her side, by reason of the very unvarnished terms in which the old dames make known their ailments.

How little the people outside her intimate circle know Mrs. Finch Adams. They see her riding, once in a way, very seldom indeed of late years, to meet the hounds, or driving in state to make visits, as 'her custom is of an afternoon.' They mark her handsome dresses, her horses and carriages, and well-appointed, well-drilled servants; and in their wisdom and charity they infer that she is a vain, frivolous woman, very unfit to be the wife of a clergyman, and he, too, 'with such a good living!' The living was worth exactly what has been said, plus £3 4s. 5¾d.; and she, as the wife of a clergyman of fortune, is just as perfect as she can be, thinks Martel, who is a favourite of hers, and not only admires her immensely, but, as a social anatomist, has great delight in watching her in her own home. He joins her Scripture readings, and likes to see her gird up her loins, and tuck up her petticoats, and trudge off after luncheon with her basket full of good things, far better than he ever tastes at home, to make her tour of the old and sick; or when, got up in splendour for the evening, she presides at her table, handsome, agreeable, and gay. And the lord of the manse or mansion amuses as much as the lady charms him.

Martel had a very decided taste for originals—some said he was a bit of one himself—and everything about his host bore a stamp of quaintness. His library was curiously fitted up, and all for use. Here were curious books, old and worm-eaten, though there was plenty of costly binding too; here was the painter's pallet, and there a half-finished caricature, sketched on the canvas. His saddle-room, wherein it was his whim or convenience to dispense justice at home, as a J.P., was deftly decorated with whips and curb-chains, stirrup-irons, and bits of every new mechanical contrivance, arranged in order due, and shining like burnished silver upon the walls. Thus the paraphernalia of modern horsemanship did for this cosy justice-room what rusty armour and rusty bits and spurs of three centuries old do for more pretentious baronial halls. The rector would, it is to be hoped, have delighted Mr. Ruskin by his skill in combining decoration with utility. No one more carefully eschewed ornament that was useless or unmeaning.

'I have a horror of restorations,' he would say. 'Give me an unadulterated old church; modern jig tunes and meretricious ornamentation go fitly together. Old architecture, with Bach and Beethoven, Corelli and Handel, will do for me. And for sermons let me hear John Wesley, though he only half belonged to us, and lived to suspect his error; but there was nothing effeminate or sham about him.'

Such was the parson, as sketched by himself. His church was large and old, and retained its venerable look, because, though put into thorough repair, there was no innovation. The old open oak seats were kept when sound, and, where of necessity renewed, were replaced by exact imitations. Everything was made the most of, by care and neatness, with a good deal of unostentatious expense. The only modern addition was a richly carved and coloured octagonal pulpit, painted and gilded by his own hand, after the pattern of one he had seen in South Devon, that was said to be a relic of the Spanish Armada. To this he applied an invention of his own, and set it upon wheels, so as to be punted about by mechanism, when he wished to bring himself and his discourse within the reach of any old people that were dull of hearing. The chancel he had rebuilt. Towards the fund for the restoration of the nave he gave a thousand pounds, and carried a church-rate for the rest, with but one dissentient voice.

'I am surprised, sir,' said the wealthiest and most purse-proud of the farmers—'I am surprised, sir, that a gentleman of "proputty" like you should think of burdening the parish.'

'Do you speak of me, sir, as a man of property or a man of probity? What I value myself on is the carrying out of what I think right,' was the parson's rejoinder, often quoted afterwards in the parish against the pompous 'man of proputty.'

To the poor, it was little that he was liberal in giving; he was also always punctiliously polite. He entered a cottage hat in hand, with, 'Well, John and Mary,' if they were old friends, or 'Mr. and Mrs.,' if they were not.

There are, or were before curates were scarce, rectors and vicars, of all schools, who were apt to forget that a curate in full orders is a priest and a gentleman. The rector of Granthorpe always presented his curate to his guests, who were not unfrequently of high rank, not as 'my curate,' after the ecclesiastical pattern, but, after the worldly fashion, as 'my friend Mr. So-and-so.'

He had been showing Martel some improvements in his church, and met in the churchyard a lady, who bowed to him, and was passing on, when he turned to her, and said:

'I have been wanting to have a word with you.'

'About my faith?' asked the lady demurely.

'Your faith! no. I doubt if you have any,' replied the parson. 'About John Noakes, of your parish, whose family they have sent to the workhouse.'

Martel, having heard the opening of their conversation, asked afterwards who the lady might be.

'She is a Unitarian, who now and then comes to my church from another parish, which is farther from her house than mine is. Like all that fraternity, she is intelligent and inquiring, and we have little amicable controversies by times. I suppose she expected one now. I fancy she, like most Unitarians of the third generation, is inclining to Trini-

tarianism and the old, broad-bottomed, liberal, reformed Church of England. It won't do to press or
hurry her; the more haste the worse speed, in that
above all matters. My present talk was on a very
mundane subject, in which I am concerned as an
ex-officio guardian of the poor. She is, like most of
her tribe, a generous, kind-hearted woman, a great
deal more charitable every way than many of more
orthodox profession.

Mr. Finch Adams never hurried business of any
sort. On the following morning, in the course of
a coloquy which he had started with Martel about
hunting, the. end of the season, woodlands, and so
forth, he at last came close up to his guest, and
taking him by the arm, and lowering his voice,
said :

'By-the-way, Martel, how is it that Palmer lets
that lovely girl of his, with so fine a fortune too,
ride about the hunting-field with that neat-looking,
gentleman-like son of old Gryffyn ? I saw him at
Beauleigh, and others saw him too—and I dare
say you were one of them, you sly dog!—riding
among the woods with her quite alone, very intimate, quite close, you know. People will talk, you
see ; and the lad will get, if he has not got it now, a
notion of marrying her ! Eh ? It will never do,
never do at all,' said he in an energetic whisper,
raising his eyebrows, and shaking his head, and
touching Martel with his elbow; 'it will never do,'
he repeated. 'I have known Palmer ever since we
were boys together at Eton: he is the most gentle
and most good-natured fellow in the world; but he is

quietly determined—quietly *determined*—and has plenty of cool tact, and knows how to stop a thing he does not like as well as any man of my acquaintance. What I cannot understand is, how, with his knowledge of the world, he has missed seeing what all the rest of us see so plainly. I suppose it is that he has never conceived such a thing possible. You know he has, with all his unobtrusive, modest manners, very strong and very proper ideas about duty to one's family, and all that sort of thing—no one more so. He has been blind; but he will stop it—you'll see he will. It will be hard on the poor boy, for she is a girl to be fond of.' And, turning short round, and again drawing close to Martel, 'How about her? Eh? You see more of her than I do now.'

'Oh, I don't imagine that she has any notion of anything serious,' replied Martel; 'from several little matters I have noticed I am pretty sure she has not. But I can't quite make her out; only she is uncommonly sharp. To be sure, she is very kind to him, has taken him up, and patronises him (though I should not like to tell him so), and no doubt she does not dislike his unsophisticated and genuine admiration. But that says nothing. She is, as you know, good-nature itself; but she is rather ingenious too, and has mostly a plan or two of her own on hand—has, in fact a great turn for managing, and likes making experiments on people, and all that. As to admiration, she is so used to it that it comes natural to her to receive it graciously; but it is little she thinks of it. Why, I am her accepted admirer ever since her infancy,' added Martel, laughing, and looking down on his legs. 'It strikes me she looks on Gryffyn as a nice boy, who has been by accident thrown in her way, and whom she would like to form and bring forward, and perhaps (mind, I am guessing between ourselves) — perhaps marry to some one else, some pet friend whom she considers suitable.'

'But, Martel, he is nearly as old as she is.'

'She does not think so. Nor is he, in fact; though there is little difference in years, he is a boy and she is a woman, and a very clever one.'

'That's true,' said Finch Adams.

'Yes,' said the other, 'and she knows it. I doubt if she thinks her own marriage with him more within the range of reason than her father does. You see, ladies are much older than men of their own age. And Miss Palmer is as keen as mustard —quite a woman of the world; she has seen a good deal of it, and he next to nothing.' He suddenly stopped. 'Oh, the whole thing is absurd,' he added, perhaps rather wishing than assured of it.

'I say, Martel,' said his host, again poking him in the ribs with his elbow, 'fancy Barbara Palmer at the head of a farm, drawing out bills and making cheese, and churning butter, and carrying her eggs to market! Eh? No, no; I agree with you it is too absurd. She never thinks about young Gryffyn, I am sure; but her good-natured encouragement, or patronage, or whatever we may call it, may mislead and injure the poor lad sadly. And by-the-way,

Martel, it has just occurred to me, is she not *affiancée* already, or something of the sort ?'

'Well, indeed, I have a kind of a fancy she is, now you speak of it; but, if so, it is kept in the dark somehow, and never alluded to by any of them. I don't understand that either; but I am sure I have heard there is something "*toward*" in that line.'

'It is all very foolish,' said the elder; 'and, between ourselves,' said he, sinking his voice and using his elbow once more, 'if you, who know the world so well, and are intimate with all the parties to this folly, could in the gentlest way give some delicate hint, and without making mischief, you know, open their eyes a little all round, you might save them a great deal of unpleasantness and pain, and do a world of good—more, probably, than we shall either of us do by our next Sunday's sermons. I am sorry for the lad, who will be the chief sufferer, and of whom I hear nothing but good—a true chip of the old block, with a very much more polished outside, though. But it will be bad for *all* to have it talked about, as it will be, if what I saw at Beauleigh goes on; and I do not know the man who would feel it more than Palmer, though he would never show it. So, in short, if you, as a friend of all, can do anything, pray do it, like a good Christian. It is not just a pleasant office, I know, to meddle in such a matter, but it is a charitable and a Christian act.'

'And so,' said Martel to himself afterwards, 'that was the motive for my being asked here on short notice at this special time; and a very good motive too. I only hope it may come to something; but I doubt it. However, I do always like to see these people at home; and the more I see them the better I like them, and that is more than I can say of all good people. Ah! good manners—what a blessing are they in this rough life !'

CHAPTER XVI.

'Welcome, quod he, and every good fellaw,
Whider ridest thou under this grene shaw !'
CHAUCER—*Frere's Tale.*

ON the day of Martel's departure, while they were
at breakfast, a servant entered the room with a card,
saying :

'If you please, sir, a gentleman wishes to see you
very particularly.'

'Do you know who he is, Thomas ?'

'Seems like a clergyman, sir.'

'Very well,' said Finch Adams; 'show him into
the library ; and as the servant went out, his master
read from the card that had been put into his
hand—

'THE REV. ADOLPHUS JOHN WILLIAMS.

'I do not know the gentleman. Do you know him,
Fanny ?' asked he, addressing his wife.

'Never heard of him.'

'Does anybody know him ? Do you know him,
Martel ?'

'Not I.'

'Well, I suppose I must go and see him,' said the rector, rising from the table, where the eating was already over, and leaving the card with his wife, who eyed it with active curiosity, being quite a woman, and a very energetic one.

As Finch Adams entered his library, the visitor, who rose up to meet him, showed a person apparently about thirty years of age, respectably dressed in grey tweed, such as a clergyman might wear on the tramp, with the knapsack, which now lay on the floor beside him.

'Pray be seated, sir,' said the clerical magistrate. 'What may I have the pleasure of doing for you ?'

'Necessity, sir, which knows no law, has compelled me to intrude myself upon you, a brother clergy- man,' said the visitor. 'I am, sir, on a pedestrian tour, as you might guess,' he added, looking down upon his stout, dusty walking shoes and knapsack. 'I am the curate of Snewkesville. Do you happen to know Snewkesville, sir, in Smutshire ?'

Mr. Finch Adams shook his head in the negative.

'It is a place that I am afraid few people visit for pleasure,' went on the pedestrian. 'I am also chap- lain to the workhouse there, and I have pupils—in short, I am hard-worked, and find myself obliged to take air and exercise now and then in walking ex- cursions, to recruit my health. I have just spent three weeks, chiefly on the Devonshire moors and South-Western Downs, and my intention was to go back to the North by train; but I have been tempted to loiter on my road by the *greenery,* if I may so say, of these grass counties, which is quite new to me, and is very refreshing to my sight after seeing, from year's end to year's end, little beside boys, and books, bricks and mortar, and stone veiled in dirt and smoke. I found the green the greatest relief to my overworked eyes; and I begin to think I made a mistake in going forward to the moors. There is nothing like greenness for a townsman, such as I am, I do believe. Do you know, sir, the Northern Downs, or the Western Downs?'

'I know Salisbury Plain,' said Finch Adams; 'and though it is a proverb of desolation, I think its scenery, on the north side at any rate, very picturesque, and in its way beautiful.'

'Its scenes,' struck in the clerical pedestrian, 'are very unlike those which are commonly quoted as patterns of the rural beauty of England. The land is not enclosed—there are no hedges, fences, walls, or trees, save here and there, fringing the sheltered hollows—no noticeable boundary-marks of any sort to break the extent of surface, which rolls with grand undulations, softly swelling like the female figure, and is, in short, anything but a plane. This vast tract of undulating ground, which spreads in every direction, diversely tinted by plots of all sizes and shapes marking the varieties of cultivation, resembles, in colouring, a huge carpet of an irregular pattern, that runs through all the shades of brown and grey and green, though not so much green as I could wish.'

'I see you have a painter's eye,' remarked Mr. Finch Adams to his visitor. 'Did you happen to remark the amazingly beautiful effects of light and shade upon Salisbury Plain? No spot that I know

in Great Britain shows such glorious effects of light.
It is, of course, reflected from the chalk, which peeps
through the scanty herbage in every direction.   I
wish Turner had made some studies of light there
which I believe he has not.'

'You paint, sir, I am sure ?'

'I daub a little,' said Finch Adams.

'I have no art—I may say I am perfectly artless,'
said this sturdy pedestrian; 'but I love to study
Nature in all her varieties as they come across my
path.   And, by-the-way, the sweetness of the air
upon the chalk downs is unequalled elsewhere.   But,
when all is said, your viridity, your verdancy, your
extreme greenness in these grassy districts delights
me most; and so I am sorry to say I have lingered
too long among your green lanes and green grazing-
grounds—the happy "hunting counties," as I believe
they are called, which I, as of course no sportsman,
have never visited before.   But I have not met with
any scenery so much to my mind—which, you see,
is simple—and so beneficial to my nerves, as your
fields and lanes and hedgerows, all "in verdure clad;"
it is greenness wherever I go—" Everything I look
on seemeth green," as Shakespeare's "Tamed Shrew"
says.   I did not think there was anything so delightfully fresh and green in this weary world,' said he,
with enthusiasm; and then, with depression, added
slowly, 'and so I have outstayed my plan, and—
e-r-r-h—my—pocket.'

Mr. Finch Adams, who had been listening in a
patient, puzzled state of mind, not knowing what to
expect, now began to understand.

And the pedestrian proceeded :

' My plan was to have walked all my way home. But how little a thing will upset all our best calculations, poor blind worms that we are ! As Voltaire says, every event produces another that was not expected ; our politicians should note that. Perhaps, sir, you remember old Fuller says of Cæsar Borgia : " He once bragged to Machiavel that he had so cunningly contrived his plots as to warrant himself against all events. But he never expected that at the same time wherein his father should die, which was his time for striking, he himself should also lie desperately sick, disenabled to prosecute his designs." Well, sir, to compare smallest things with greatest (not but that I think any poor, honest fellow more than a match for Cæsar Borgia), a like misfortune has been sent to upset all my plans, in the form of a chafed foot, which renders me as unable to prosecute my projected walk as Cæsar Borgia was to prosecute his schemes of conquest. It was with the greatest difficulty I made my way here, hopping, I may say ; and, sir, my errand is to open my case to the kindness of you, as a brother clergyman. I have not left myself quite enough to pay my fare home by train—I fall short by about a sovereign. You see, sir, on the tramp I put myself on short commons, soldier's allowance—a small loaf of bread a day, a bit of bacon, a bit of cheese, and a glass of beer : one eats and drinks too much at home ; so the funds that I calculated to be equal to supply my commissariat on the march will not, I grieve to tell you, suffice to pay all my railway fare. Hence, to cut a long story short, I am driven to throw myself upon your mercy, as a brother clergyman, for the loan of a sovereign, which I will repay, with a thousand thanks, the instant I reach home. I might have written, you will think; but it is a two days' post each way, and I should have to get through the four days at an inn very unpleasantly, and at considerable cost. And what is worse, my pupils will be waiting for me, this lameness has so delayed me; and I should, what is worst of all, be absent on a Sunday that is not provided for. And so, sir, if you will generously help me with a loan to the amount of a guinea, I cannot, and I need not, say how much I should be obliged. I am ashamed to ask, but I have no choice—at least, all that is left me is a choice of evils; and so I have taken the liberty of doing to you what I would have had a brother clergyman do to me in like perplexity.'

Just at this crisis Mrs. Finch Adams came into the room, perhaps liking to see what her husband was doing, or whom he was entertaining; and the visitor turned to her politely, and rapidly ran over his story again, adding a number of references.

The lady retired for a few minutes, and, returning, gave her husband a look that he understood, and hoped the gentleman would take some breakfast. It was on the table. Even if he had breakfasted before he came out he must be ready for another.

No; the reverend gentleman had not breakfasted, and he was ready to do so.

This he did in a very hearty manner, conversing the while in a strain so lively and agreeable about the black countries, and the green countries, and the clergy in his neighbourhood, and the state of the Church in general, that both his host and hostess were greatly taken with him, and thought him a very entertaining and worthy man; and Mr. Finch Adams, who had been already won by the quotation from his favourite Fuller, pressed upon the quoter three guineas instead of the one, which they were sure would never take him home; and they further insisted upon sending him to the station in their carriage.

'Good-bye, sir, good-bye. A thousand thanks. You will be sure to hear from me next week. Let me see, what day will be most convenient ? Shall we say Wednesday ? No; Thursday will be surer. We'll say Thursday, then—Thursday.'

'A very pleasant fellow, and really not ungentle-manlike,' remarked Finch Adams to Martel, who, strolling out, had met the carriage taking the pedestrian away. 'It is quite a pleasure to have an opportunity of doing a good turn to an overworked clergyman, and of helping him to enjoy his holiday.'

'He is not an impostor, is he ?' asked Martel. 'I had a pretty good look at him, and had the advantage of seeing him kick up his legs, and throw them on the cushions of your carriage, and cock his hat in a very unclerical, and seemingly triumphant, style.'

'Ah, you suspicious fellow ! a'n't you ashamed of yourself ? Of course the poor fellow was triumphant at getting out of his difficulty so easily. He might well throw up his poor feet, which are saved from hobbling to the station.'

'I hope, for your humanity's sake, you will find him a true man,' said Martel; 'but if he is, I am deceived by him.'

A month or six weeks later Finch Adams met Martel.

'Well, I have a letter at last from our friend in the black country, our clerical tourist. He apologised for not sending the money sooner, said how very delighted he had been with his visit, and kindly added that he should feel himself "*for ever indebted*" to me for that pleasure; said a great deal more about the "*green* countries, so delightfully and absurdly *green.*" Green had always been his favourite colour; it was most reviving. In fact he could live upon it. He had seen many *green* spots, but "of all the green places that e'er he did see, ours was the greenest in its degree." Of all the villages in that verdant district, none so green as Granthorpe, and nothing in it so green as its elderly parson, who might be called an evergreen. He was sorry he had no "green-backs," because he would have liked to discharge in them the little obligation to which he would not further allude, lest he might wound my delicacy. He trusted the lady had found the references, (which she left the room to verify in the Clergy List), all right and satisfactory, for "by her smiling she seemed to say so." She was benevolent and delightful, and, for all her years, as green as Venus's myrtle. He would have been grieved to have made any mistake, and had therefore been particularly careful to look over the Clergy List himself just before he did himself the pleasure of visiting us. He hoped I had not forgotten Cæsar Borgia and his historic illustration of the fallacy of human calculations. He begged I would always remember the Reverend Adolphus John Williams, or, if that were too long, Mr. Green, though, indeed, that appellation belonged more properly to myself. That was his letter. My wife and I have read and laughed over it so often, that I can give it, I believe, word for word. Mr. Green, though he is right about me, and you were right about him, is a very clever and amusing fellow, and, in a way, cultivated —about the best specimen you will get of education without religion. The man is predatory, but not ferocious. He thoroughly enjoys the fun of taking one in. Well, my money is gone to a bad end; but I would not miss a chance of helping a poor brother clergyman to enjoy his hard-earned holiday, to secure myself for ever from the depredations of the whole tribe of clever scamps. And who knows his history, poor fellow! I wonder whether we shall ever meet him again. I should not be surprised at it. This is a green country, and he is adventurous, and is evidently very proud of his dexterity, and no doubt is great at disguises. I fully expect to hear of him again. His humour and vanity are pretty sure to lead him into scrapes: *nous verrons*. Mind you recognise him if he turns up to you.'

'I feel safe,' said Martel, 'of knowing Mr. Green again, should I have the pleasure of seeing him, and I cannot help fancying I have seen him before.'

CHAPTER XVII.

" We scarce thought us bless'd
That God had sent us but this only child.
* * * * Day, night, late, early,
At home, abroad, alone, in company,
Waking, or sleeping, still my care hath been
To have her *matched.*"—*Romeo and Juliet.*

In easy postures, in easy chairs, in a comfortable dining-room, warm with a glowing fire that sparkled on the glass and lit up the red and amber wines upon the table, sat two men, cracking walnuts after dinner, and scarcely could two present a greater contrast. The elder is over six feet high, big-boned and lengthy, with large but not un-shapely hands and feet, blue-eyed, with whole-some, ruddy face, clean-shaved and longish. His hair, nearly white, is cropped close, and brushed upward above the blunt outline of straight-cut features; and his whole man betokens a sound mind in a sound body, all serene, and Anglo-Saxon. His opposite is shorter by the head; and, though he is younger by many years, his face shows more of wear and tear, nor was it ever so comely and regular of feature. His figure is square-built,

with body-joints thick and strong, and extremities
fine and sinewy; the face and make of the man
palpably Celtic.

Those whose minds change with every turn of
fortune hold cheap and talk lightly of the Celt just
now, since the Saxon got him down. But let their
memories go back some sixty or seventy years, and
they will find the Celts of France marching victorious from the one end of the continent of Europe
to the other, and levying tribute from every nation.
When he conquered, the revolutionary Frenchman
was, like most great conquerors, poor and hardy; but
conquest, and peace, and half-a-century of commercial prosperity, corrupted his manhood. The dis-
sipations and effeminacy of luxury, and the reign
of the money-making spirit, did for the Celt of
Gaul what Capua did for the Celt of Carthage.
His 'roaring trade' laid him prostrate at the feet
of a people who, not long since, thought it much
to look him in the face. It is the case of a horse in
racing condition beating one equally good that is
fat from grass. The Celt and the Saxon have very
different merits; but there is perhaps very little to
choose between them, only it is well to speak a
word for the one that is down. It is something to be able to say of a nation that its offi-
cers may be best drawn from the RANKS of its
army, for that every Frenchman has in him the
making of ' an officer and a gentleman,' such is the
breeding of the whole people.

However, to return to the dining-room of Finchdale Rectory, nobody who knew the two races

would be surprised to be told that the lesser man was of recent French extraction, and the bigger a genuine Englishman. The one is, in fact, a fine specimen of the black variety of the English squire; the other is the grandson of a refugee French marquis of the *ancien régime,* proscribed, exiled, and turned into a dancing-master in 1792. 'Birds of a feather flock together,' is the old proverb, and that like should seek like is a law of nature. Our Celt's father found a fitting, though rather young, mate in a grand-daughter of the head of a Highland clan, who was beheaded and attainted in the rebellion of 'Forty-five.'

The pair are alike clad in those consecrated and superfine vestments of black cloth, wherein men at the vesper hour sacrifice solemnly to Bacchus and Ceres; but the elder is a squire-parson, with a small living of three hundred and fifty and a private fortune of four thousand pounds a year, and his guest and junior, though no longer young, is a curate, with a capital of six hundred pounds of his own, and from the Church an annual stipend of one hundred pounds, for all the purposes of life, so long as he had strength to serve a cure; and when that is gone, a claim on the workhouse for his pension, that is, so soon as he shall have spent his six hundred pounds. That he should ever be beneficed beyond the value of a curacy is a piece of good fortune which neither his present prospects nor his family antecedents seem at all to promise. The one is the Reverend Launcelot Palmer, rector of Finchdale; the other, the Reverend Charles Martel, late curate of Fulmere.

'Well, Don Carlos,' said the host, as he stretched
out his feet on the fender, after seeing the ladies out
of the room; 'we had Kitty's cousin Franklin,
here last week; very unlike her, though. He has
that sort of manner which, I suppose, men get in
chambers and clubs in London, and in the society of
sporting bachelors in the country: I can't say I
admire it. He seemed inclined to make up to
Barbara offhand; but I wish you had seen how she
kept him at arms' length with the greatest ease and
good nature, too. But he did not seem to like it.
We wanted you to have met him, but he would not
stay for you; cut his visit short, and was off. He
is used to have his own way, I fancy, and to be
made much of. By the way, has Barbara told you
that Brandon Palmer has offered me Row'nshaw.
You know it's vacant; poor Ellersley is gone
home.

'I did not know that it is vacant; but in the
event of its being so, I had looked on your appointment as a matter of course.'

'Why, yes; though he is my nephew (and he is
nearly as old as I am too), I must say that Brandon
is always the man to do the right thing. He offered
it; and I hope I have not done the wrong thing in
declining it.'

'That,' said the other, 'I could not guess. The living
of Row'nshaw is worth £700 a year, I suppose; and
I am deceived if Finchdale gives you much more
than £300.'

'Very true, very true, Don Carlos; but what then?
I have all I want—"All I want"—as your friend

with the red nose said to you; and then, I am too old for transplanting.'

'Row'nshaw is the head - quarters of your family ?'

'Exactly, Don; and the head of my family lives there : and there can't be two kings of Brentford, you see. Here, I am at home; half the village belongs to my family. I was brought up here very much with my uncle, who was rector before me, and left me most of what I have. The people know me, and I know them and theirs for two or three generations. Brandon is an excellent fellow ; but where he must be head, I must be tail; and after living here so long, I am too old to begin that now : so here I stay, thanking Brandon very much for the offer all the same.'

'To be sure, I don't see what you could get by the exchange, except a new place that you would not like, and money you do not want.'

'There is nothing to gain, nothing whatever, except the pleasure of being near Brandon; and we are probably better friends at a distance. I am as happy as a prince, or rather as happy as any man at my time of life can hope to be, or wish to be, here below ; I am so happy, that I sometimes think it cannot last. But I have had my troubles ; some years ago, how gladly would I have left this place— when I lost my darling wife,' went on the rector, now risen, and walking about, and talking to himself, with tears in his eyes and his arms outstretched. He continued :

'She had not a fault, unless that her fine-strung

constitution required excitement and company; she lived in it, and was the delight of every one. She was very partial to you, Martel!'

'And I shall ever remember her exceeding kindness.'

'You know how happy we were; but I always felt it could not last. Dreams! dreams! Dreams all! He that gave, took her—to Himself; blessed be His name! He, and He alone, knows what I passed through. I never thought I could have out-lived it; but, you see, I have; and, if I could, I would not call her back again, so assured am I of her happiness, and that it is all of love, and ordered all for the best. It brought Barbara, dear girl, nearer to me, for one thing. My own dearest love could not live out of company, it was her element; and poor dear Barbara, for her own good, had to be kept in the schoolroom. I did not like it at all; and I never cared much for "*society*," as it is called. My parish, and the bench, and a few friends, like your-self, to look in on us now and then, is enough for me, and better than more, to my thinking. And it is well for us it is so, just now; for I, like many more, have not received a farthing of rent from my Irish property these two years; and when I shall receive any, my agent knows not. Poor fellows, they are in a bad way over there, it is "semper eadem," "worse and worse," as they say. And I have not the power, if I had the will, to spend my English property upon the Irish, as so many are driven to do. Knowing the state of things, Brandon rather urged me to take Row'nshaw; but I have plenty

for my present way of living, and I never wish to
live better. Why should I ? As for Barbara, she
will have enough to expose her to the risk of being
married for her money; and she is quite good enough
to be married without it. Though I say it, that
shouldn't say it, she would make a man of the right
sort a good companion for life; and I should not be
sorry to see her safely settled, though I should have
to say of her what was said of the decapitated
Scotchman's head—she would be " a sair loss " to
me. And when her time comes, what I shall do
without her I know not; but, for all that, I would
be well content to see her married, suitably to her
bringings-up and belongings. Rely upon it, Martel,
not a little of the happiness of marriage depends
upon our adopting the wisdom of the Shunamite
woman, and marrying so as to live *among our own
people*, and neither drop, nor be lifted, out of the
sphere of our birth ; though that seems but a dull
doctrine in these high-flying days. To have a chart
of the channel and know by instinct, or intuition,
as it were, all the ins and outs and prepossessions
and prejudices of those you live with, is half the
voyage. How many of the jars and upsets of life
come of our having been rubbed the wrong way!
To be sure, you are never safe in this world; but
you are much safer among your own people than
with any others.'

' I have no people,' said Martel.

'Well, you lose some pleasure, and escape some
pain. You are the more free, you know; and freedom,
Don, is your idol, or vanity, just as pine-apple rum

was the vanity of our old friend Stiggins, the
shepherd. Eh, Don Carlos—is not that it ?'

'I only know,' replied the Don, going off at a
tangent, ' that I ought not to grumble. I was as well
aware fifteen years ago, as I am now, that the
Church is not " a mercenary calling," but, as the
Great Duke said of the army, " a profession of
honour," to be entered only by those who either
have as much money as they want, or who have no
wants and do not care for money. *That* I have
known ever since I have thought at all ; and if ever
I murmur at my lot, it is the weakness of the flesh.
I am aware that no man does any thing for a single
motive ; but, so far as I know myself, I did not seek
gain when I took holy orders in the Church ; and,
certainly, gain has not sought me.'

'Why, Don, you are as magnanimous as the great
Hal—"By Jove ! you are not covetous of gold."
We know, Carlos, that gold and silver are, like ourselves, of the earth, earthy ; but while on earth we
can hardly do without them—at least, in a civilised
state, and in a cold, ungenial climate like ours. I
do not understand how bishops look at these things ;
their utterances seem to me rather contradictory. I
suppose *they are* indifferent to such dross; but two-
and-twenty thousand men—which, by-the-way, is
quite a little army for England—will hardly be
found so utterly careless of sublunary things as to
come and put their necks in a noose, and subject
themselves to all sorts of complicated, arbitrary, and
very pinching legal penalties, without any prospect
—I will not say of *gain*, but of the means of living

and paying their way. "More bishops" will not make me believe that the ox which treads out the corn should be muzzled, Don.'

' But what could you do ?' asked the curate.

' I would redistribute the Church property. I would not pay one man £2,000, or £1,000 either, and another £100, for doing the same thing.'

' If the Church funds were equally distributed, they would give to each but £250 or £300 a year.'

' Well, Don, would not that be a great improvement ?'

' But bishops and dignitaries tell us we should get " *no more fine scholars and first-class men.*" '

' I don't believe a word of it, Don. It is that sort of blowing hot and cold that makes Free-thinkers say the standard of the Gospel is too high, and unpractical *when tested by the practice of those who preach it.* The best men do not turn clergymen for what they can get—no, nor common men either. I know I did not, and I know you did not, nor any of our friends, Don. We did not look to the money ; we liked the life.'

' Yes,' repeated the curate, ' we liked the life ; but how much longer shall we like it ? Is there not stealthily growing upon us an intolerable des-potism ?'

' As how, Don ?'

' In the name of " *organisation*," I see the Church rulers assuming brand-new powers, not to be exer-cised directly by themselves—oh no !—but through their nominee, the revived and undefined rural dean. We are told we gain " increased activity." But bishops are of flesh, and lust for power; and we, their subordinates, are forced through a prolonged and very costly education, that makes our clergy the most liberal and cultured in Europe. I am sure that of such a clergy it will never be said—"We order them to march, and they march." "*Organisation*" or education, which you will, but not both.'

'Between ourselves, Don, I am strongly of opinion that simple-minded, unambitious men, like our own bishop, in the prominent places of the Church, are of far more importance than is commonly supposed. The heroes of the platform and of convocation, of congresses and missions, whose theoretical declamation exhibits a bold contrast to their social practice, touching luxury, titular honours, and substantial advancement, do, I verily believe, make, among shrewd, reflective men, more Dissenters and more unbelievers than anything or any one else in our good Church. Men hear them and see them, and complain that, joined with a vast deal of fervid activity and blazing rhetoric, there is a want of serious consistency in these clerical great-guns, that lowers them beneath the standard of "honour," and amazes and repels men of the world.'

'That is not a new complaint,' quoth the curate. 'One very like it was made by that first and best of Reformers, Dean Colet, who had a charitable opinion of those criminous clerks the priests and friars, whose faults were fleshy and scandalous. "For," said he, "these, out of the consciousness of their imperfection, are, for the most part, humble, modest, and tractable; whereas the devil himself, were he not what he is, could hardly abide the pride, the avarice, and the hypocrisy of the other." '

' That is from Colet, is it ? I should have guessed it from Latimer. You have a very good memory, Don, and you don't dislike hard hitting. But, to change the subject a little,' said the rector, taking a letter from the chimney-piece, ' I am reminded of this. It is from a friend of mine, whom I think you do not know ; but since it concerns you in a way, I will read you what he says.'

What was read shall be told in another chapter.

CHAPTER XVIII.

'The chancellor will never hear of him, and his bishop, if a very competent man, tells him that *vegetating* is no claim, and that experience is no claim; and that, before he can hope for promotion, he must show his efficiency. Who is to know what effect Mr. Crawley is producing on the brick-burners of Hoggle-End? And yet what one of the many forms of " efficiency " can be more thorough than the conversion of a horde of blaspheming pagans into decent members of English society? No doubt such work is its own reward; but still poverty and neglect are not inducements to do it; and it is hardly possible, even for Mr. Crawley, to put out the full measure of his powers after the receipt of a very contemptuous dunning note from his butcher or his bookseller.' —*Spectator Newspaper.*

'I can't think how you clergy live.'—*Great lady with contemptuous curiosity.*

'A FRIEND,' said Mr. Palmer, reading the letter, 'tells me that " he wishes to appoint an earnest man, of moderate views and some experience, to a living. The income being small, £105 a year, PRIVATE MEANS ARE ESSENTIAL." (You observe?) "There is *no house*, but an *excellent one* near the church could be rented. An active middle-aged or elderly gentleman would be preferred." Ahem! no doubt. Do you know, Don, I was so foolish as for an instant to think of you for it; but it would simply be your ruin. Why, man, the bishop might take it into his head to make you build a house. They have a good deal of power, those bishops, though they are always, like Oliver Twist, "asking for more." Bad as a curacy is, with your means and acquirements, at your time of life, it is better a thousand times than such a living as that. Why, even if the bishop let you alone—as our good man probably would—who can say, in these law-making, law-breaking days, but that some bustling ministry with a lust for legislation might force you to build the house, or to rebuild the chancel ? What burden may they not lay upon incumbents ? I should not be surprised if, before long, many clergymen will be glad to exchange a poor living for a curacy. Don't have anything to do with one—take my advice, Don; though I do not doubt this is at your service, notwithstanding the hint about *private means*, if you are foolish enough to say yes. But don't; we must wait and see what we can do better. Perhaps I ought not to tell you that, when I declined Row'nshaw, I thought of asking for it for you ; and you may wonder why I did not. In the first place, I learnt that Brandon was pledged to another relative in case of my refusal; and, in the next place, I more than doubt whether it would have suited you. To be sure, the income is over £600 a year—that is, £540 net ; but the house is ruinously large for a single man, even if he had a fair fortune—it is out of all proportion to the living, of course. You know, members of my family—all of them, as it has happened, men of good fortune—have held that living for many generations, and the house has been built up to their convenience. We must try to find a better fit for you, Don; the house at Row'nshaw is as much too large as the income of the other place is too small.'

'By-the-bye, that reminds me,' said the other, 'I have to thank you, I hear, for kind intentions to me in the matter of Hazelwell, though you never told me of that.'

'Where was the good of telling you? I did not succeed, and there was an end of it.'

'I owe you thanks all the same.'

'Ay, Don, it is thank you for nothing; but I confess I did ask and wish for it. It would just have suited you—a pretty little place to gratify your love of country views, and within reach of us and all your old friends. The income is no great thing; but the house is very small, too small for a family man—the very berth for you. And, to say the truth, I made sure of getting it. I heard Stanwell was looking out for some one: his father and I were dear friends, and so, though he is not just my sort of man, I thought I could make free to put in a word for you. I wrote, and, since you have heard of it, you may see his answer. This is what the fellow, says:

'"I regret that I cannot, as patron of Hazelwell, oblige you by appointing to it Mr. Martel. I would have written to you before, but it was a subject that required a great deal of consideration: I felt I must take time to weigh so important a matter, and I thought it well over before I came to a decision."

'Great consideration!' repeated the rector. 'I happen

to know that just as he got my letter, blown by some ill-wind, Donkiesterne dropped in to breakfast with him. You know Alberic Donkiesterne ?'

' I know there is such a man.'

' Well, he thinks he·knows you, bad luck to him, as they say in poor Ireland. Stanwell was digesting his breakfast and my letter, which did not say any harm of you. So, as he has no idea beyond dogs and horses, and is about as fit as they are to represent £16,000 a year, what does he, but put my recommendation of you into Donkiesterne's hand ? How Donkiesterne knows you, or what he knows about you, is out of my ken.'

' " More know Tom-fool than Tom-fool knows," ' grunted the curate. ' I know him but by sight, and should not have supposed that I was honoured by his grand reverence's notice at all.'

' However that may be,' went on the other, ' he said at once :

' " Mr. Martel may have been a long time a curate, and may be a very good sort of man, and a learned and an active man, but does he preach *the truth*, Stanwell ? My impression of him, since you ask me, is that he is a worldly man, and would not do at all for Hazelwell. That he is a downright Radical, I happen to know."

' " That's enough, that's enough," said Stanwell. " He won't do for me."

' He might as well have written at once, for he had made up what he calls his mind. I offered him some explanation, having heard what had passed from one who knew all about it ; but he wrote back

18—2

very bluntly, not to say rudely, "I decline to give
my reasons. The objections are insuperable, and I
consider the matter is at an end." And so it is.
But with that blockhead Donkiesterne I have no
patience. There he is, half-educated, for he betook
himself late in life to holy orders; and, having great
friends in high places, there he is now, with his
living of fifteen hundred a year! And because that
is too little for his merits, they have given him,
moreover, a canonry of some hundreds, one of the
few special rewards of learning left to the Church!
And so he receives as much pay in twelve months
as you receive in twenty years, for doing worse precisely the same work. Not that Donkiesterne is
a bad lad at all; he is only thick, and narrow, and
an egotist, and that is not much out of the way, as
the world goes. But, barring great connections, he
brings nothing special into the service of the Church,
neither learning nor private fortune. I doubt if he
has two thousand pounds of his own; and this is
the fellow that steps in to stop the promotion of a
man like yourself to a living of two hundred a year
after sixteen years' service as a curate, and because
you are not of *his school!* Too bad! too bad! I
cannot tell you how much it has vexed me. People
say that the first "object to be looked to is not the
provision for, or promotion of, clergymen, but the
good of the Church." But it is not for the good of
the Church to discourage those that have undertaken, or to discourage others from undertaking, its
service. One way of promoting the interest of the
Church is to see that its labourers get worthy hire.

But is it so? Do they? The graduate of a university, of Oxford or Cambridge, ever since he took
holy orders at three-and-twenty years of age, has
served his Church with loyalty, and done its work
constantly, according to his abilities, has done his
share in leavening society by living among gentlemen as a gentleman and a Christian should live;
but all his years and all his experience go for
nothing. His bishop says he " vegetates " (that is
a fine word, whatever it may mean), and puts over
him some terribly ardent favourite of his own school,
many years younger. Well, well, it can't be helped.
I did not mean to have told you; but, since you
heard something, it was better you should hear all.
You are a Christian philosopher; and, to be sure,
you have need to be. But how did you come to
hear of it ?'

' " A bird of the air carried the matter." '

' Aye, the same bird that carries many matters to
your cautious ears, Don. Ah, yes, we have had
many changes, some of which I little like; but I
am glad to think that the rich families can no longer
make their greatest geese canons and prebendaries,
and heads of the Church. I hope never to see the
high aristocracy, any more than the small folk,
shut out from the highest offices of the Church ; but
they must offer the Church of their best, and not
of their worst, their most helpful, and not their
most helpless sons. Dull men in high places are
sure to shut the door on talent and learning. They
don't mean it, but they can't help it. The Church's
ministry opens a career for which none of us are

good enough, let alone " the torn, the maimed, the lame, the blind." '

' A young graduate told me t'other day,' said the curate, ' that none now but the worst style of men from the universities take holy orders—needy men, who know not what else to do ; men who have got into debt, and difficulties, and destitution, and have no other refuge.'

' I hope,' returned the rector, ' I shall not live to see the day when the recruits of the Church of England can be described as our old friend the Baron of Bradwarden described those of the Pretender's army in '45. I beg your grandsire's pardon, Don ; but you remember how the baron " could not but have an excellent opinion of them, since they resembled precisely the followers who attached themselves to the good king David at the cave of Adullam ; viz., every one that was in distress, and every one that was in debt, and every one that was discontented, which the Vulgate renders bitter of soul." '

' I, for my part, hope,' said the Don, ' that the clergy will never take up with a religion of formal and rigid conventionalism ; and, therefore, I wish to see them well-to-do, well-educated, and independent men, who will think for themselves, and I must so far qualify my young friend's report. For there were never more gentlemen of independent means taking holy orders in our Church. But what are they among so many ? Twenty-two thousand ! We pauper gentry, who used to make up the rank and file, cannot now afford it.'

'Well, Don Carlos, we must try your matter again. Try again; never say die. Take another glass of wine, Don. "Wet t'other eye," man. By the way, have you never met Stanwell?'

'Never; but I was entertained at his cost t'other day.'

'Indeed! how?'

'One of my many parishioners, a farmer, a cleverish fellow, whose reading I swayed a little when I was his pastor, asked me:

'"Had I read a novel called 'Melton Mowbray'?"

'"Yes, I had."

'"Is it a *very* good one?"

'"In its way, very good indeed. Why do you ask?"

'"Because when I was last out a-hunting I was among some men whom Mr. Stanwell was talking to, and I heard him say that 'Melton Mowbray' was 'the very best book that ever was written.' I did not think much of his opinion; so I thought I would ask you whether it is worth my reading."'

'Bravo! capital!' laughed the rector. 'Very good! Stanwell's opinions on literature! Excellent! Ho! ho! ho!'

'Did you ever hear the story of him and Joe Hobson?' asked the curate, whose bile seemed to have been roused. 'No? Well, I know it is true. Mr. Stanwell went to buy a hunter one fine summer's day, when the ground was as hard as a brick. He got upon a horse, and galloped him about.

'"Can he jump, Hobson?" asks he.

' " Well, sir," says sly Joe, who is chary of giving opinions to his customers, " I should suppose he could jump; I bought him as a perfect hunter. I have never tried him myself."

' " May I try him, Joe ?" asks the squire.

' " Certainly, sir, by all means," says Joe.

' " Here goes, then," says the squire.

' You know that, whatever skill he may have in letters, Mr. Stanwell has plenty of nerve on horseback; so he swung his nag over the hard ground at a newly-cut and strongly-bound fence. The horse caught binder with his knees, toppled over, and landed Mr. Stanwell on his head in the next field. There he lay stunned; how long he never knew. The first thing he was conscious of was old Hobson standing over him rubbing his hands and saying to himself, " Well, it will do the horse good, any way." '

' Bravo, bravo, bravo !' cried the rector, laughing till the tears ran down. ' Poor Stanwell ! lucky he fell on his head ! If he had lit on any other part he would have been killed ! Lucky he fell on his head ! Poor Stanwell !—oh, ho !'

After this story and the laughter that followed it there was a pause, at last broken by Martel saying :

' I have been thinking over what you said about Donkiesterne and Hazelwell. I have an idea that he has got appointed to the living a man of his own, who believes in the black gown, and was his curate.'

' Very likely,' replied Palmer. ' If all the reasons for the distribution of Church preferment were collected in a book and published, it would be one of the most curious books in the world. He might, however, have forborne to speak evil of you.'

'After all,' returned Martel, 'there is no possible system of appointment that would not have its evils and corruptions. We in this old country work, and work well, by a complicated and anomalous system of checks and counter-checks, that have grown up by experience, use, and necessity. Variety of interests gives variety of men and talents, and saves the clergy of the Church of England from hardening into a priestly caste.'

'Yes,' said Palmer; 'and the uncertainty, little as we should expect it, works well too: it reduces intrigue to a minimum. What other profession has anything to show like the contented settling down of nineteen out of every twenty University clergymen upon livings that hardly pay interest on the sum spent in their education—livings of one hundred and fifty or two hundred pounds a year—accepting them as of God's disposal; whilst by the unbeneficed the text which says, " Promotion cometh neither from the east nor from the west, nor yet from the south," is commonly received as a divine declaration that is to quiet all care and anxiety about preferment and their own future ? Yes, yes, our system is anomalous and complicated; but it has bred content and it bars priestly caste, and secures also, as you remark, that variety of representation which is most needful in the ministry of a *National* Church. And then, as things are, you know we have among us more of real "*equality and fraternity*" than is to be seen anywhere else in the world. We are all parish

priests and pastors alike, and each man makes for
himself the place for which his gifts and acquirements and habits fit him. There is no colonel-ing
or major-ing or captain-ing, no precedences and
supremacies, no "junkerism" to sit upon us, so to
speak. We are all on a level, priests and gentlemen;
whatever difference there may be is personal and
social, and is not magnified into the authoritative,
official, or titular. As for archdeacons and bishops,
we see them now and then, and that is a great thing
for us. I think the archdeacon is always the most
gentleman-like man, lay or clerical, in the diocese,
be the diocese which it may.'

'For pure dignity I like rural deans,' quoth the
curate.

'Aye, I forgot rural deans—to be sure, rural deans,'
repeated the rector; 'rural deans and American
colonels, and Welsh judges and Welsh rabbits, and
honorary canons, and Mrs. General Jones and Mrs.
Major Robinson.'

'H'm!' said Martel, 'I think you are the very
man that should be made a rural dean; they are
often, or mostly, excellent fellows.'

'Much obliged to you for your good opinion, Don
Carlos; but I have no fancy for being the eyes and
ears, or nose and great-toe, of anybody—not even of
a bishop, Don. I am a low-minded man, and have
no ambition for anything beyond equality, clerical
and social; and I do not think the clergy are
like ticket-of-leave men, to be put under sur-
veillance of police. I will not turn "detective," any
way. There seems to be just now a strong dis-

position to call out petty ambitions, and to create
trumpery, worldly distinctions and inequalities.'

'But you lay great stress upon the clergy being
" *gentlemen.*" '

' I do, Don, because I think that gentility tends
to equality, and is the best leveller; and further,
because I think that a man who might be a gentleman and is not, can hardly be a very good Christian.'

' I am not sure I take you.'

' Why, Don, you see, " *gentle* " breeding, what is
it but the cultivation of the finer and more sensitive
fibres of the character—quicker sympathies and
nicer perceptions of charity, and a larger generosity ?
What will effect that like the study of the New
Testament ? You remember, Don, Heywood's divine
summary :

> ' " A soft, meek, patient, humble, tranquil spirit ;
>   The first true gentleman that ever breathed." '

' The old Elizabethan tells the truth, and tells it
sweetly. But, you see, we come to the study of the
New Testament perfection half-formed already, full
of prejudices and prepossessions, which dull our
sense of its gentle teaching, and put us on miscon-
ceptions of it. Old wealth, as things are now, gives
one the best chance—it gives leisure and good tutors
—for the preoccupation of our minds by good seed,
and for the cultivation of our gentlest feelings ; only
you know how many there are who throw away
their opportunities.'

' I,' said the curate, ' have found a great deal of
gentle spirit here and there among the agricultural

poor—the peasantry, that is. They, next to the gentry, have, to my thinking, the best manners, and speak the best English.'

'Eh, Don? How is that?' quoth the rector.

'I mean they have Bible—that is, Hebrew— morals and Bible English. What they fail in is not true feeling, but nice perception. So also their vocabulary, if scanty, is pure Saxon; but they want the niceties of grammar, which require early drill.'

'And mind you, Don, the agricultural labourers, who have, as you say, much of the gentle spirit themselves, expect to find it in their clergyman, and detect the absence of it as soon as any. That is another reason why I lay stress on the clergy, as a body, being gentlemen; and on the whole, our Establishment, though complicated and far from faultless, works as well as any institution so large can ever be expected to do.'

'Have you ever observed,' quoth the curate, 'how well the "*gentle*" character of the Establishment works in another way? The trading classes are, we all know, very jealous of the clergy, and, unless in a partisan spirit, are not ready to contribute of their gains to the maintenance of the Church. But the social standing of the clergy being what it is, when traders grow rich they are pleased to make a son a clergyman, and he brings into the Church's service the father's gains and savings; and so circular justice is done, and the clerical world goes round. The lord chancellor's patronage completes the system: through him old college friends, the chief lawyers, and chief physicians, the prime of professional Lon-

don, find each of them a living for his son, who
takes with him to his parsonage a part of his father's
profits. Thus again the Church takes tithe of the
prosperous. And when these are all provided for,
there still remain the small and ill-conditioned
livings, ranging from £120 to £250 a year. These
crumbs which fall from the rich man's table are
good enough for poor dogs like me—if we can find
any one to step in and speak a word for us.'

'Very philosophic of you, Don Carlos, and, barring
what touches yourself, there is a great deal in what
you say, though it does not make much for our plan
just now—eh ?'

'The constitution of the clerisy,' prosed on Martel,
who liked talking far better than any living, 'the
anomalous and mixed constitution of the clerisy, and
the objections made to it, are met exactly by a speech
Lord Palmerston made a while ago. Do you remember it ? He was replying to an ex-minister's
strictures on the composition of Cabinets. "The
right honourable gentleman," said he, "speaking, no
doubt, from his own experience, asks what can be
so absurd as the present constitution of a British
Cabinet ?—what can be so ridiculous as putting one
man into a Cabinet because he has extensive knowledge of commerce, another because he understands
agriculture ? And the climax of absurdity, according
to the right honourable gentleman, is putting a man
into a Cabinet because he can make a good speech.
I do not follow him through his *theoretical declamation*," said Lord Palmerston. "I am content with
the British Constitution, and so far as my experi-

ence of Cabinets goes, I am content with them. A knowledge of commerce, an acquaintance with agriculture, and powers of oratory may be absurd qualifications for a public career and an official existence, but nevertheless are they the elements of our political life."

'That,' said the curate, 'with very little alteration, might stand for a defence of our custom-made, illogical, rule-of-thumb mode of appointing to their posts the twenty-two thousand clergymen of the Established Church—a mode by which, as you know, I am—personally—no great gainer; but truth is truth, and policy is policy for all that.'

'Talking of policy, and Palmerston,' said the beneficed senior, 'the last time I went to hear a debate I was better entertained outside the House than ever I was in it. An altercation arose about entrance between a dignified gentleman, who condescended for a handsome consideration of some thousands a year to keep the door,' and an Irishman, with an elegant brogue, who was forcing his way in.'

'"I'll till ye what, sorrh," said Paddy, "I'm to take my seat as mimber for Killmany next week; and the virry furrst motion I make in the House will be to put you into *yellow plush*, me foine fellow."

'My memory of the fun was refreshed not long after by hearing "me foine fellow — in yellow plush," that was to be, playing Sir Oracle, and hectoring the clergy at a county meeting. What do you think was the enlightenment that Mr. Yellow

Plush was good enough to give us, and give us in a very dogmatic tone, too? Just that " We must not ask our poor to go to Church as a favour to us, or as a merit in itself. We must visit them as pastors, and so awaken in them an interest in spiritual things, and create a desire for further instruction. And we should remember that many of them were deaf; and so we should read very distinctly; and should never be afraid to preach the elementary truths of Christianity," and so forth. Such were the droppings of Bumble's tongue, which we poor clergy were to take for pearls. I felt sorely tempted to get up and enliven the dull meeting with the story of the "yellow plush.' However, that was, and is likely to remain, my last experience of the House of Commons. I think parliamentary oratory is, and always was, a very dull thing; and the platform is, if possible, still duller. I am not speaking, of course, of the two or three great-guns which, perhaps, every age produces, and of whom we sometimes get a great deal too much.

" But hark ! there is Lady Worlaby's carriage bringing home the ladies; they are back in capital time. What a colloquy we have had, Don! Let us go and hear from Kitty and Barbara how the concert went off, and then off to bed. By the way, Don, while I think of it, will you come to us the week after next on Tuesday, and stay as long as you can ? We have some people coming, and I want to ask little Dicky Gryffyn, your friend, to stay a night or two. Eh, Don ?'

' All right for me, thanks; very happy—always.'

But to the prospect held out of meeting his friend at Finchdale, it might have been observed—though his **host** did not observe it—that Martel made no response, and his brow indicated rather anxiety than pleasure.

END OF VOL. I.

BILLING AND SONS, PRINTERS, GUILDFORD, SURREY.